Praise for t

For Dark A

"[Dark Age_____ _____ _____ _____ ___ ____ _n its reader. This
and it exp_____
is the sort of good, solid tone that can make a reader a
better writer. Fleming takes pains to demonstrate that
this is not just another vampire novel, this is a *Dark
Ages* novel, and does so without lecturing us. There are
few who can do something like that."
—Michael G. William, *RPG.net*

For Dark Ages: Assamite by Stefan Petrucha

"There are quite a few twists and turns and a level of
thoughtfulness that take this above the average
vampire adventure. Dark Ages: Assamite is an imagina-
tive and gripping winner."
—Jim Brock, *Baryon Magazine*

For Dark Ages: Cappadocian by Andrew Bates

"Dark Ages: Cappadocian is, more than anything else,
that wonderful combination of fascinating and fun.
You'll be amazed at how well the seemingly disparate
ends tie together, you'll meet beautifully created
characters who all make sense (considering their
individual positions and needs), and you'll love the story
Andrew Bates has brought alive with his talent and
humor. Cappadocian is topflight vampire literature and
[…] I can't wait for the next installment to come out."
—Laurie Edwards, *Culture Dose*

For Dark Ages: Setite by Kathleen Ryan

"Here is a grand idea—warring vampire clans during
the period of the Dark Ages—that has been brought to
life (or should I say "undeath") by a group of exception-
ally talented writers. Bravo, White Wolf!
TombKeeper's highest recommendation."
—J.L. Comeau, *Creature Feature*

Dark Ages and Vampire Fiction from White Wolf

The Dark Ages Clan Novel Series

Dark Ages: Nosferatu by Gherbod Fleming
Dark Ages: Assamite by Stefan Petrucha
Dark Ages: Cappadocian by Andrew Bates
Dark Ages: Setite by Kathleen Ryan
Dark Ages: Lasombra by David Niall Wilson
Dark Ages: Ravnos by Sarah Roark

Other Dark Ages Fiction

Dark Tyrants by Justin Achilli & Robert Hatch (editors)
The Erciyes Fragments by C. S. Friedman
To Sift Through Bitter Ashes by David Niall Wilson
To Speak in Lifeless Tongues by David Niall Wilson
To Dream of Dreamers Lost by David Niall Wilson

The Clan Novel Series

Clan Novel: Toreador by Stewart Wieck
Clan Novel: Tzimisce by Eric Griffin
Clan Novel: Gangrel by Gherbod Fleming
Clan Novel: Setite by Kathleen Ryan
Clan Novel: Ventrue by Gherbod Fleming
Clan Novel: Lasombra by Richard E. Dansky
Clan Novel: Assamite by Gherbod Fleming
Clan Novel: Ravnos by Kathleen Ryan
Clan Novel: Malkavian by Stewart Wieck
Clan Novel: Giovanni by Justin Achilli
Clan Novel: Brujah by Gherbod Fleming
Clan Novel: Tremere by Eric Griffin
Clan Novel: Nosferatu by Gherbod Fleming

Also by Sarah Roark

"What Shelters Them" in **Demon: Lucifer's Shadow**

For all these titles and more, visit **www.white-wolf.com/fiction**

Dark ages RAVNOS™

Sarah Roark

AD 1208-1220
Sixth of the Dark Ages Clan Novels

Cover art by John Bolton. Map by Eric Hotz. Graphic design by Mike Chaney. Art direction by Richard Thomas. Copyediting by Diane Piron-Gelman.

ISBN 1-58846-823-2
First Edition: June 2003
Printed in Canada

White Wolf Publishing
1554 Litton Drive
Stone Mountain, GA 30083
www.white-wolf.com/fiction

For my parents, Donna and Vic, with love, and with gratitude for more than every page of this novel could cover

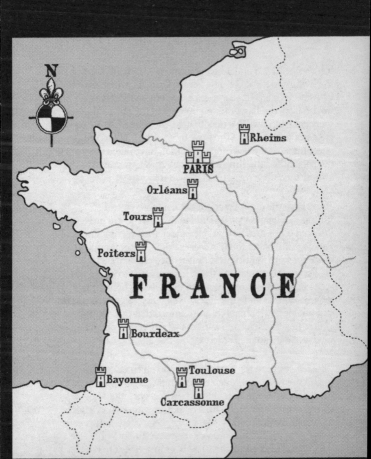

What Has Come Before

It is the year 1208 and religious ferment is in the air among the living and the dead. The Fourth Crusade, which sacked Constantinople four years hence, has resulted in a flow of wealth from the East entering Europe. In the Languedoc, the southern part of what is now France, the independence of great noble houses and the preaching of the Cathars (who reject many of the teachings of Rome), have raised the ire of the papacy and the Kingdom of France. A new crusade against the Albigensian heretics is in the offing.

Away from the eyes of men, in the benighted world of vampires, religious violence and ferment are just as present. Ushered on by dreams that Alexander, the unliving Prince of Paris, would shelter them, refugees from Constantinople have made the hard journey west only to face challenge after challenge. Alexander and the other princes are not happy to see undead Greeks seeking refuge and feeding rights. The refugees do find some measure of welcome, however, from the Cainite Heresy, a church of the damned that teaches that Caine, first murderer and father of all vampires, was blessed by God and reincarnated as Jesus Christ.

One refugee from the East who has had an especially hard road is the young vampire Zoë. A childe of the mistrusted Ravnos line, she saw her beloved sire Gregory murdered by mortal churchmen and is fired by nothing more than a desire to avenge his destruction. She is only beginning to suspect that Brother Isidro, the monk in russet vestments who slaughtered Gregory, is part of a larger movement to take back the night....

Prologue
Chambery, 1208

Chambery, Savoy
Eve of the Feast of St. Nicholas, 1208

They must be very inexperienced, thought Zoë, or very exhausted. Otherwise they would have waited till they'd crossed the plain to make camp. Granted, in the dark it was a bit difficult even for her to see how wide the plain was or whether they were going in the right direction. For mortal eyes it must be harder yet. She could no longer remember what a night like this would have looked like a few years ago, but she could imagine—the vagueness of shapes, the way the moonlight leached color out of everything. Within the circle of firelight was certainty, safety, humanity. Without, in the blackness, anything at all might lurk. She moved closer. They finished gulping down their meager supper and began to talk.

She liked to talk also, when the company was right. Gregory had joked that one night he would find the key that wound her up and throw it away. In the caravan, she and Meribah had chattered the hours away as their horses ambled beside each other in patient tandem. But in this country, she was reduced to the pantomimes of a very small child. "*Perdonança, sénher, èu vase Grenoble?*" together with a wave off southward had to do for "Excuse me, sir, but I'm walking to Grenoble; could you be so kind as to tell me whether that road is the best way?"

And so all she could hope for was to fish the odd phrase here and there out of the river of soft Occitan syllables. The woman spoke especially quickly. Once in a while the monk broke in, repeating a phrase in Latin or Lombardic to see if he had the right idea. "*Papa*" was one of the words he said—the Pope of Rome, that meant. Another she kept hearing was "*cathares*." She didn't know what the Franks meant by this word, but it sounded like the Greek for "pure," and so it made her uneasy. Then a final phrase she knew all too well: "*prenon la crós*."

Take the cross. Crusade.

It was not possible that these people really cared, or even understood, about the ashes of Constantinople. They saw the knights riding home, horses' backs bent with sacks of stolen gold. They heard the troubadour lies. Yet here they were, muttering "*prenon la crós*" to each other, and their faces were not shining with reflected victory, but closed and dark. Something was happening. They huddled together, monk and merchant and rich lady pilgrim with her chaperone. Their fire was small.

Zoë shifted from one haunch to the other. Her legs never hurt or went numb anymore; but sometimes she suddenly realized just how long she'd gone without moving.

At last the monk stood and left the circle of light, peering his way out, and made for the privacy of the tree near her. He pissed a considerable volume. Then he crouched, experimentally. He gathered up his habit with care, just high enough and no more. A monk's modesty should be as a maiden's, Gregory had told her once. The eyes should be lowered, the elbows kept close; neither his gestures or his garments should float abroad. Well, this one's eyes were low all right—drooping in fact. He was sleepy. He wouldn't even see her. His pale, spidery hands were full of russet cloth.

His hands. He settled back against the tree and moved the gathered folds into his lap. There was a glint of gold and blue there at the middle knuckle of his right hand. With a fingernail of his left he worked a miniscule catch. The little jeweled dome rose from the ring itself, sprouting tiny whirring wings and bobbing about on a mechanism of wire and spring so thin it was all but invisible. Amid its buzzing flight soft piping notes both high and low sounded. The monk's lips relaxed into a smile as he watched it. A thing of exquisite craft and occult knowledge, all bent to serve a moment's harmless enchantment; its sole purpose to lift the heart and nothing more.

A thing *she* had built, for Gregory. It was her very first simulacrum—for five months she'd worked on it only in the daytime so as to surprise him. He'd been so proud. He'd laughed and clapped, then put it on his finger and never taken it off again. She'd done better since, of course. But because it was the first it was always dear to him. How much more pain had it earned him? How many hours of torture did it take to satisfy his captors that he told the truth when he said it was a plaything?

And now here was this bald-shaven scuttler, its new master, setting it to dance for him while he shat.

She could not stifle the noise that rose in her throat and warned him as she sprang forward, closing the distance between them in three impossibly long strides. He started and fell sideways, spent the last moment he had catching himself instead of shouting or reaching for the knife at his girdle, and then she was on him. She seized his face, which had fallen into a stupid blank rictus of terror, and wrenched up and sideways. There was a savage, gratifying crack. She sank her teeth into the taut skin of his throat. It was so easy. If Andreas had not made her leave, if he had not held her back, she might have had this man in Bergamo, might have had them all. She saw it now as the hot sweetness of his blood coursed down her throat, multiplied the deaths in her mind. Throat after throat, a scattering of rust-robed corpses painted redder still, lying like trash wherever she dropped them. Her father's agony avenged. And the one who'd defied her, Fra' Isidro, the one who'd stood by the table still dusted white with Gregory's ashes and had the gall to raise a crucifix to her...

Isidro!

The man's body fell through fingers that suddenly turned clumsy. She stared down at him, even more furious with him now that he was dead. This was not what she'd meant. She'd been going to drag him away and question him. She might have gotten the name of a city at least.

She'd waited a good several months for Isidro and his companion to emerge from the fastness of their monastery; then when they'd finally come out they'd ridden damnably fast for monks, and quickly left her behind. She'd since learned they'd headed west. But that meant only that the Susa Pass best served their needs. Now that they were out of the mountains they might go anywhere. Her own mount looked rather woebegone lately, lamed by a stray stone two nights ago. Perhaps she would take this one's horse. There seemed little else to gain from him.

Then she noticed the leather case lying at his side—a messenger's pouch. Bending, she carefully undid its catch and took out the parchments and books nestled within. She broke open the seals on the parchments. Latin, of course. She had a bit of Latin, but not enough to read it, especially not this cramped, hurried hand littered with mysterious abbreviations. Still, she spotted the word *Ysidro* in one of them, buried in a middle paragraph.

Perhaps it was a clue. It had to be.

Moving quickly (surely the others would come to look for him soon), she took the pouch and also unfastened the knife from his girdle, even though she already had one of her own. It was good metal and could be sold, or melted down to make something. His breviary with its illuminations of angels and priests she let him keep. She pulled the ring from his finger and coaxed the little jewel-scarab back to roost on it. It would not fit even on her thumb, so she tucked it away. She could hang it on a chain later.

His eyes were open partway. He was not looking at her, but still there was a dumb reproach in his skewed limbs and bent back. He'd fancied himself a man of God, no doubt. He would have wished to pray. He would have wished to lie down in dignity, to have the rites of his church, to be mourned by his brothers since there was likely no wife or child to do so.

She leaned over him and dropped a carefully aimed gobbet of red spit onto his face. Then she made for the horses.

Chapter One

Grenoble, the Lands of the Dauphins
Feast of St. Damasus, 1208

> *"Cant eu la vei, be m'es parven*
> *als olhs, al vis, a la color*
> *car aissi tremble de paor*
> *com fa la folha contra'l ven.*
> *Non ai de sen per un efan*
> *aissi sui d'amor entrepres;*
> *e d'ome qu'es aissi conques*
> *pot domn'aver almorna gran."*

He finished his verse with a sprawling grin and leaned over the table. "You see? A little wine doesn't wash away my refinements."

Zoë thought all the Occitans sounded slightly drunk even when they weren't. She caught his chin between her thumb and forefinger. "Yes, but it no proves that you go to university. You maybe heard that anywhere. What about Latin?"

"Latin! Latin, is it? I have found myself a lady-love indeed."

"Do you read Latin?" she repeated.

"Yes, of course I read Latin, I argue in it, I gamble in it, I dream in it for pity's sake. It's all I do all day. Are you honestly going to make me sing to you in Latin? Charity, fair maid!"

"I have some letters I no can read," she said to him. "And a book. I want to know what is this book."

"Of course, my dove."

"It must be in private. We go to a room."

He brightened considerably at that. "Of course."

The inn's resident girl gave Zoë an ill-tempered stare as she pushed by with her new companion. She'd gathered many interested looks from the men here. She supposed she was a novelty: olive skin not quite tempered to white by the cold vampire blood, dark Byzantine eyes and a flood of dark brown hair that caught amber glints in the firelight. To her, the Languedocienne women looked washed-out, like a drawing left out on a sunny windowsill. To them, she suspected, she simply looked dirty. Her clothes *were* dirty, spattered with road-mud. She hadn't stopped yet to wash them and had no idea what she would wear while she did so, unless she stole something. Her other clothes had all been in Gregory's wagon.

The scholar didn't seem to mind her grime. He stumbled—on purpose?—and allowed her to catch his elbow. He gave her a smile. She felt her spine stiffen.

The little room was quite bare: the less kept there, the less for guests to make off with. A lumpy bed of mildewed straw sat at one end, and a heavy unfinished trunk crouched at the foot of it, mainly providing a place to rest one's shoes while unlacing them. In the corner were a chipped washbowl and a pitcher of water. The scholar turned down the coverlets, peered at the mattress and groped it dubiously, and finally hoisted himself up to sit on it.

"The letter." She handed it to him.

He looked at it blankly a moment, then smiled at her again. "Yes, the letter." He reached for her hand.

She stepped back. "Well?"

"Well—what?"

"What does it say?"

He glanced at the parchment again. "What do you mean, what does it say? Ah. Half a moment. It is a letter, isn't it. In Latin."

"Yes. Is what I told you." She fought down her rising voice.

"But who would be writing a little dove like you?"

"What matters it? You say you will help me, you read me this letter."

"Well, I didn't think you meant me to read it in the pitch dark," he snapped.

She started to take it back from him. "Very well—"

"No, wait—wait, wait, wait, my dove. Don't be cross. Don't be hasty. Come… your hair is so lovely in the moonlight. Why don't you just go and get us a little candle, and we'll have a look at your letter, I promise."

As she left he was already struggling out of his gown. *Didn't think I meant him to read in the dark? Didn't think I meant him to read at all.* The innkeeper charged her what she thought was an awful lot even for a candle. Then she got him to slow down and repeat himself and realized it was for the rent on the room as well. She also bought a pitcher of beer and brought it up. Considerable expense… the letter had better be worth it.

"This isn't addressed to you, I can make out that much," he said when she came back. He was down to his chemise and *braies*, and he shivered a little. Let him shiver.

"I know." She poured him some beer and came to sit beside him, holding up the candle. He rested the hand holding the letter on her thigh.

"Well, all right. It says something here about a shipment of oranges…"

"Oranges?"

"Yes, oranges from Chambery. That doesn't make any sense. Anyway, the shipment made it to Bergamo all right, but there was some trouble from the sellers, who followed them to Bergamo and demanded the oranges back, and there was a fight. Two crates of oranges were ruined, two crates of apples ruined also and three more crates of apples were damaged… this is nonsense, I don't see where the apples came into it."

"No mind the oranges. Go on. The letter say something about a man named Isidro, right here." She tapped her finger on the word.

"I'm getting to that, my dove. There's a very long bit here on everyone's health, everyone's coughs and rheumatism. Two monks are dead, the Lord took them very suddenly. Here's your Isidro. Let's see; it says he's going back to Toulouse by the speediest route. He would have done better to stay in Lombardy, I'm sure…"

"What is the speediest route?"

"It doesn't say. The only way I know is through Valence, Avignon, St. Gilles, and then—what would it be—Béziers, Montpellier, Carcassonne, Narbonne, is that right? Maybe. Anyway—Castelnaudary, and then you're more or less there."

"And what else?"

"Er… nothing else, really. The rest is all verbose blessing."

"Then here." She handed him the little book. "Tell me what this is."

"My… my. This is a nice binding. Awful, crabby hand though. First thing in the morning I'll look at it, in the good light."

"No, now."

"The things I do for a pretty face. Ehhh." He thumbed through it. "These look like strange little dice with too many spots. The world abounds with cheats! *Geomantia*… ah, I see. It's a handbook on geomancy, casting the dots. Been picking sorcerers pockets, have you? Orange-eating devil-monks. Tch-tch-tch." She gave him a sharp glance, but his voice was light, and though his eyebrows buckled in a slight frown he didn't really seem to be connecting the chain of facts. He looked more befuddled than suspicious. It was doubtless too much to hope that he'd out-and-out forget their meeting, but at least he probably wouldn't make as much of it as he might have sober.

"Casting the dots?" she echoed.

"Yes, my dove." He put his arms around her waist. "You see, you take a long stick and you poke it into the ground, over and over…"

"I think I understand." She squirmed.

"Do you now?" His lips sought out the hollow of her neck.

"No. Leave me."

"Come, come. Shh… it's all right. Haven't I been good?—Uff!"

She put her hands on his chest and shoved, forcing a puff of air out of his chest and causing his hands to fly loose. He sat back up and stared at her a moment, his expression piteously slack. Then all at once his young face hardened. He reached for her again, and this time no soothing words tumbled from his lips; they were pressed tight together.

She got up. He wavered to his feet and pitched himself at her. He was bigger than she was, and should have bowled her over. But she caught him easily and took hold of his hair, bending his head back until he was looking into her face, into her eyes glittering like the sharp edge of a cut obsidian. At that moment he decided to start taking her seriously. He balled up his fist and shot it upward, landing a cracking blow on her jaw. She roared—the voice hardly sounded her own, it was so deep and raw—and threw him into bed, which slid a good foot sideways from the force of it. He landed slantwise against the frame, then gracelessly collapsed.

For a moment he didn't stir. Then he half-lifted himself and began to edge away. His fearful gaze never left her.

"I see it now," he said hoarsely. "You were sent by the devil. You are a nightmare in dark woman's shape, sent to tempt me to drink and lechery. But you can't hurt me. We're in the church's very shadow, and I'll go there, where you can't follow. *Pater Noster, qui es in caelis*—"

"*You* are an idiot," she fired back. Her vampire teeth filled the front of her mouth now, making it hard to talk. "Your lechery is all your own, and you can keep it. Crawl to your church." She gathered up her letters and her book and fled.

"I should have known you weren't a woman!" he shouted after her. "You have none of a woman's natural desire, and I thank God I never entered your cold cleft to my damnation!" Coming down the stairs she could still hear him. She half-expected the other patrons to turn to her and fall on her as one, but they only gave her curious glances, as they had all evening. She shoved through them, tumbling queasily among the slabs of living, heaving flesh until she fell out the door into the bitter winter gusts. The inn's heat

Sarah Roark   17

remained in her cheeks as she made her way through the narrow streets.

Her cold cleft. How dare he! How dare he grasp for her with his skinny fingers one moment and accuse *her* of inciting his lust in the next. He'd been watching her as the wolf watched the lamb before she'd even crossed the common room. Who was he to tell her about a woman's desire? Had he ever so much as consulted a woman for her desire? At least the Cainite thirst was a thirst for sustenance, it was a necessity. These mortal men lusted for flesh no less greedily, whether any necessary purpose could be served or not. It was their delight, this plundering of innocence, and then of the tatters of whatever remained once innocence was gone. Before Gregory took her in, she'd seen it. She'd learned from the other urchins how not to be found, where to sleep and where never to sleep. She'd learned from the example of those who fell victim as well as from the wilier, older children. And she'd been lucky.

Her cold cleft. Natural! So being a vulture, a carrion-crow was natural.

He was simply upset because he'd run into a stronger beast of prey than himself. She clutched her bundle to her chest. She hadn't even gotten to the second of the two letters. But Isidro, that other vulture, thief and hypocrite, he was on his way to Toulouse. So be it. She would not waste further moonlight in this town.

She turned her face to the sky, seeking out Polaris where her foster father had taught her to find it, drawing an imaginary line from the edge of Ursa Major. Her path lay westward still.

Chapter Two

Through all her journeys, she was always on the pilgrim road. She never escaped it. If she kept on westward past Toulouse, eventually she'd reach Compostela—the Holy Land of the West. Or if she wished, she could go down to the harbor where the occasional lantern still winked and stow herself aboard a Hospitaler ship bound for the real Holy Land. Either way, God ruled her every step. Lately that didn't seem the comfort it should. Supposing she did go on to Compostela, would the apostle receive her? Could she stand in the fierce corona of the Holy Sepulcher in Jerusalem? If even the little cross of Isidro terrified her, what was left of pilgrimage?

Andreas had his answer. He put his trust in Set, Lord of Storms, and no matter where the winds blew him he went forward calmly, secure in the protection of one little god among a thronging pantheon of little gods. The snake-priest had once said that he couldn't credit the idea of a Lord of All—or if there was such a Lord, He was clearly fickle, inattentive, even cruel. Unworthy of worship, in any case. The God of the Hebrews and Christians Andreas counted simply another little god, perhaps pettier than most.

Meribah—Meribah had always kept rather close about her own beliefs, now that Zoë thought back to it. The little redhead seemed to regard herself as the gatekeeper on Zoë's path to truth-in-Set, and so said what she felt Zoë was ready to hear rather than what she really thought. Meribah's comfort never lay in words, in any case. It was in a sprightly glance, a wry remark, a sudden appearance at one's shoulder just when she was wished for…

Zoë looked over her shoulder, feeling more than a bit foolish for it. No luck.

She herself hoped for nothing from Set anymore. If his priest and priestess had both abandoned her, it was useless to look to the little god himself.

She clambered barefoot down the wall on the knotted rope she had left over from the raid at Bergamo and spent what seemed like far too long snapping and working the rope to get the hook free again. If she could only find a proper hammer she was sure she could bend it into a better shape. Then she laced her shoes back on and headed for the abbey. Its bells tolled, calling the beginning of some night-service. Isidro had to be there, or had to have been there very recently. Where else would he stay?

But as she drew nearer, she heard another sort of music, and a light blossomed at the far end of the courtyard, a campfire. A lone tinker sat by it, cooking what smelled like salt pork and singing in a tongue she didn't recognize. As she walked by, she caught the gleam of his tools, laid out with great care on a square of sheepskin. He took a bite of his meal, picked up a tool and began to polish and oil it. The song sounded like a work-song, lively but just a bit monotonous.

Gregory's face had been spare and sad, not round and affable, and he'd never chewed pork-fat or anything else while he worked. But he had sung quiet songs like that at his bench as he fitted tiny cogs together or drew up plans in lead point. All at once she felt a compulsion, enormously seductive, to join this man and follow him back to wherever home might be. Or maybe he traveled the fairs year round. She could give him the blood and teach him how to make planetariums and mirrored spinning tops and puzzle-boxes for lovers to keep their tokens in. Mortals would cheer when they unfurled their banner, and mighty Cainite princes would be cross at first until she and her new friend delighted them with enchanting presents.

Unconscionable. Tonight she would pray her foster-father's indulgence for such thoughts, whether he could hear them or not. She skirted around the front of the abbey. The best she could hope for would be to catch a glimpse of red habit in between the arches of an outer walkway, or perhaps to overhear a snatch of conversation. Or—a new thought—there might be servants still up at this hour, squaring away the last horses that had made it in before sundown. She followed the smell of horses to the heavy stable yard gate. She banged at it, and then banged at it harder with the soft side of her fist when no one answered at first.

A little panel set in it opened. "What? If you're seeking lodging, you should go around."

"Not lodging—I only want to give a letter." She moved her hands up toward the panel; to his mortal eyes, there seemed to be a parchment there, bearing the unbroken seal of the Bergamo monastery.

"Oh? Can't quite make the name on it out." She could tell he was fibbing. He couldn't read—that part of her illusion went entirely to waste.

"It's for Brother Isidro. I was told for finding him here. Is he inside?"

"How would I know?" The man's voice turned irritated.

"Is a tall monk, in a red robe—" she began.

"Oh yes! The odd red habits. There's a pair of them here, yes. Here, give me the letter and I'll see it gets to the right one." He reached out through the panel.

She drew back. "No, wait. I have news for him too, is not in the letter."

A sigh. "Well, if you'll give me a moment, I can show you to the guesthouse. All the brothers are saying the office, so you'll have to wait."

"No. Tell him I wait here."

"Little girl, he's not going to come out here to meet you. Or even if he is, I'm not about to be party to it. This is St. Gilles."

"I come back later, then."

"That's fine, you do that. Good night to you—" The panel closed.

She hissed a Greek curse to herself. Then again, perhaps curiosity was among Isidro's flaws, and perhaps the stable hand would say something to him about the girl with the mysterious missive from Bergamo. She could return tomorrow and see if she'd piqued any interest, and if it might be possible to arrange a meeting after all. Even if he wouldn't take that bait, at least he had to leave again before too long. Perhaps she should go now before the night got any older, spy out the road ahead and try to determine where a pair of monks would most likely take lodging the first night out. The trouble with only being up after sundown was that by then even the most adventurous mortals were ensconced somewhere, and rarely alone. She still had no idea how to separate Isidro and his companion. Or how she could possibly fight the two of them together. If anyone had come with her, anyone at all—!

But that still hurt too much to think about. No one had come for either her sake or Gregory's. That was that.

The sound of pounding hoofbeats echoed in the square. She threw herself into a recess in the wall. A great black warhorse clattered up to the stable-yard gate. The helmeted knight riding it called out "Open up!" and then took off his helmet and shouted it again. The gate was hurriedly thrown open.

"Sénher Gauthier," the stable hand puffed. "Back so soon!"

"He's all done for the night now," said the knight, evidently meaning his horse. The stable hand helped him swing down and then took the reins. The knight's dark mantle moved aside as he dismounted, revealing a white tunic with a red cross at the left breast.

"The brothers are all at prayer."

"Good. I should pray also—" The knight tucked his bucket-shaped helm under his arm and looked around with a frown, as though he'd forgotten something. His face was hard, built in almost crystalline planes, and he had a long dark mustache.

Then his gaze went right toward Zoë. She shrank back further into the wall and didn't move. She thought she'd hidden in time—their eyes didn't connect—but she couldn't be sure.

"Sénher? Is everything all right?"

"Yes, I should pray. Take care of him, he's done well. Yes you have, old lad, there's a good lad..."

"Of course, sénher. I'll give him a good rubdown and a nice thick blanket."

She dared another peek as horse and man were led inside. He did not turn in her direction again—not with his body. But his shoulders were squared in an odd, vigilant way.

***

The following evening she woke, climbed the stable yard wall and discovered the two monks' horses were already gone, as well as the knight's.

It didn't mean they had left together. Not necessarily.

Chapter Three

Zoë no longer feared a candle flame when it was a little way away, or when she held it herself. But with what looked like near a thousand mortals passing by, each knot bearing its tiny fire, they might as well have been torches. The constellations seemed to have fallen to earth and continued unawares their track across the sky, setting the world ablaze as they went. Everyone from several miles around was headed for midnight Mass at the church.

She gathered her ragged cloak about her and followed as near as she dared. They were singing, mostly in the *langue d'oc* with the occasional phrase in Latin. Was it Christmas already? Most families let the youngest capable child carry the candle. Some had a lantern instead—not much brighter, but easier to guard against a sudden gust. There were many small earnest faces glowing with pride and the reflected flame, bent in concentration on their high duty, many thick workmen's and mothers' hands set fondly on the little shoulders to guide them. Occasionally a candle would go out, and a relighting was requested with an easy smile from a neighbor. It made a fine opportunity for a lot of "God save you!" and "God keep you and your family in health, my friend!"

She saw no monks among them. The only knights were a few men walking at the head of the procession along with their families, and none of them was Sénher Gauthier. Still, if the church was the place to be right now, it was probably the place to seek Isidro.

"Look, Sicard. Who is that pretty little girl?"

"I don't know. I've never seen her before."

"Well, she looks half-frozen. That cloak! Little one…"

Zoë was dazed by the brilliance of the lights, by the mass of people; it took her a moment to realize she was being addressed. A family of mother, father and six children had stopped in their tracks to turn toward her. The children regarded her solemnly out of blue wide-pupiled eyes. But the mother reached for her with a kind expression.

"Little one, are you cold? I have an extra blanket here. Come, don't be afraid. Where is your family?"

Zoë blinked at her. It was such a simple question and so impossible to answer. The whole story rose unbidden almost to her lips.

"I—I don't know," she said instead. "My parents are dead and my—I look for my uncle. He said he will come here."

The woman clucked and wrapped her blanket around Zoë's shoulders. "Well, I'm sure he didn't mean to miss you. So easy to lose people in the dark. He was going to Mass, wasn't he?"

"I think so."

"Well, then, we'll find him there I'm sure. My Sicard is tall, as you see—just tell him what your uncle looks like, and he'll keep lookout." She gathered Zoë to her right side and her own eldest daughter to her left. All at once Zoë was in the midst of the lights. Thankfully the nearest one was in front of her, in a child's hands. "Jacme, don't tip the candle— Poor thing, your hands are like ice!"

"We're almost there," said Sicard. "It should be plenty warm inside."

The woman gave Zoë a reassuring nod. She nodded back and tried to think of the elaboration for her story. She was orphaned recently. Yes, just three months ago, and she was being taken to meet her uncle by a family friend, but— but what? The friend fell ill and died in Avignon, and no one would do anything, no one would come with her. And she only had a vague idea of the way. Yes, that was close enough to true.

Sicard *was* tall—she could imagine him towering a head and a half over most of the congregation. A shame she couldn't just make Isidro her "uncle." They were of a complexion, at least. But if he actually did turn out to be there after all, it would be hard to explain why her beloved relative wasn't happier to see her.

She hummed along with the songs as best she could. It seemed to make the mother happy, and the daughter didn't give her such apprehensive looks after a little while. The next-to-youngest boy bounced along next to her.

"What's your name?"

"Zoë."

Why do you talk so funny? Where do you come from? Are you Catalan?"

"Hush, Durant. Don't pelt her. There'll be time to talk after Mass. You should be singing. Don't you like to sing?"

It was, indeed, quite warm in the church, almost too warm, though an occasional draft caught at their legs. Immense candelabras were lit from end to end, and the smells of incense and garland greenery hung heavy in the air. One Latin chant after another wound past them. Zoë had no pleasant associations to make with that tongue. And as the priest and his deacons censed the altar and the choir sang the processional, her feeling of unease only grew. They were consecrating this space, by most ancient methods, to the use of God and of His Christian lambs. The powerful implication was that nothing not dear to that God should be here. The impulse from it pushed at her, pushed her in the direction of the door, pressed into her body full of blood stolen the previous night, as though to make her vomit it up and betray herself in front of all. She hugged herself and tried in vain to remember what Gregory had said. That most churches held no terror for Cainites. That even the prayers of the fallen were heard. That she had every right to come here. When the crowd sighed in pleasure at the spectacle and at the comfort of the first blessing, her legs flexed instinctively in the desire to flee.

Then the woman rested her hand on Zoë's shoulder and just as the incense had silently cast her out, this gesture silently brought her back in. She could still see the spangled and robed men in tonsures working their holy witchery, but her talisman gave her a measure of shelter from it. Enough for her to keep her mind about her and look for her quarry, who didn't seem to be here.

***

"Father doesn't usually mention the Good Men and Women in his sermon," the woman (whose name was Aycelina) remarked as she set out a hearty soup and a plate of cold roast.

Sicard snorted. "Father doesn't usually worry about convincing anyone of his zeal for the faith. But there's a different smell in the air now."

"Here, Zoë. This will put some warmth back into your bones."

"What smells different, Father?" Durant piped up. He and Jacme rubbed their eyes every few minutes, but seemed determined to stay up for the *reveillon* meal along with everyone else.

"He's talking about the march against the Cathars, silly." This was from Durant's older brother Peire, who was not so very much older that he could resist poking fun at Durant's naïveté. Zoë's dark eyes flashed up at that and caught him; he went on, less steadily. "Haven't you been paying attention? There's going to be a war."

"Is Father going to fight in the war?"

Uneasy chuckles. "Little man, your papa isn't a knight. He's going to stay right here and keep his family and his business safe, that's all. Besides, Montpellier is Christian. We'll be fine."

"I have heard people speak of this march," Zoë said carefully, "but I do not know what it means."

"There isn't a march *yet*." Aycelina brushed off her hands on her apron. "It's only been preached. The Holy Father in Rome is angry, and anyone could understand why. His man was murdered in St. Gilles almost a year ago and no recompense made for it. If the Count would just make restitution, I'm sure everything would be all right."

"That depends on what kind of restitution you mean," said Sicard. "I think he'd pretty well have to burn every *bonhomme* in Languedoc, including the ones that aren't even his vassals, knock every Jew out of public office *and* give the Church all his tax revenue for the next ten years to satisfy the Holy Father now."

"Well, I suppose if the Church really wants a war, then there'll be a war." Aycelina passed Zoë a trencher full of roast. Zoë set it down before her, pondering what to do with it. The soup she could dump out on the floor-rushes, once she got a moment unwatched; the adults were immersed in politics and the children drowsy. She supposed she could take the strips of roast and squirrel them into her lap, and from there under the table. If she managed to empty most of the trencher, then she might create an illusion of food and eat that. She peeked at the dog and tried to motion him over, but he was having nothing of her and cowered away.

"Excuse me," said the eldest daughter abruptly. She got up and went in the other room. Aycelina made an exasperated noise but didn't call her back.

"Did you say your uncle lives in these parts, Zoë?"

"No, mostly he live in Toulouse. But he is traveling on coast for the past few months." Since there now seemed little likelihood of Isidro actually appearing, he'd become her uncle after all. It was always possible these people knew something about the Red Brothers that they might let slip.

"Oh. Is he preaching the war?"

"No," said Zoë. "It is monastery business, I think."

"Well, I admit if I were from Toulouse I'd be anywhere but home now," Sicard half-joked.

"Why?"

"Why, because Toulouse is under interdict." Aycelina looked at her closely. "Excommunicate."

Zoë very deliberately lifted her hand and crossed herself in the way she had seen the Latins do it. "God save them," she said. The words felt dirty in her mouth. The mortals echoed the gesture. She wondered if Isidro knew that he was coming home to find his own city condemned by the very Church he served.

"I daresay they won't starve, at least."

The conversation went on in this vein for some time. At last Aycelina stood up in irritation. "Maura," she called, "come back and finish your supper, for heaven's sake! We all want to get in bed."

No reply. "She didn't look sick, did she?" asked Sicard with a frown.

"I'll go see," said Zoë. She was eager now to get away from all this talk of holy war, useful as the information was.

She quickly found her way to the bedrooms, but no one was there. After a moment's earnest cogitation she hit upon something she hadn't personally had to think about in a long time—the privy. She ran up to it and tapped on the door.

"Maura?" she called softly. She could hear mumbling within, like a prayer. "Maura, your mother sent me…"

"It is," the voice came back. "It is."

"What is what?" Zoë prodded. The door opened. There stood the girl, kirtle bunched up to her waist and the cloth at the back of her shift pulled and twisted around front. Zoë's Cainite gaze fell immediately to the little patch of red blooming there.

"It is," Maura repeated, eyes large. "Please—get mama."

***

"I'll tell your father later, after we've all slept a bit," said Aycelina. She had what looked like a bundle of rags in her hand. "My clout will be large on you. We'll sew one to your size after third Mass, but for now we'll just tie this one up tight as we can."

"It doesn't hurt, mama." Maura was still staring at the little spatter of blood on her shift, fascinated.

"Well, that's fine."

"Isn't it supposed to hurt?"

"It might tomorrow. Eventually it will, in any case. Don't worry." Aycelina unfolded the clout, a large square of scrap cloth gathered up into a rectangle along a drawstring sewn into each end. She had Maura lift up her skirts and slide it on.

"Tie there and there, you see, and then you can move the clout as you need to."

"Mama, you're crying."

"A little." Aycelina gathered Maura's head to her chest and kissed her.

"Are you crying because of the curse?"

"The curse…" Aycelina looked surprised for a moment. "Why, no, *nina*. I'm crying because it won't be many more winters before my little girl has her own home with her own husband and I'll have to beg her to visit her poor old mother. Zoë, dear, have you had your first courses yet?"

"No," said Zoë. She'd been slightly overdue for her first courses when Gregory took her. An appalling question suddenly presented itself: Where *was* all that dark menstrual blood now? Dammed up within her still, clotting up her viscera? A never-ending accumulation of sin, forever vainly awaiting its time to flow out?

"La, well, I doubt your uncle the monk will enjoy talking to you about this. I have something to tell you both about this curse, so you listen to me. Eve was cursed, yes. Adam was cursed also. We're all cursed, my children; anyone living today with a pair of open eyes can see that. The priests say it as much as the *bonshommes*." She sat down with Maura upon the straw mattress. "This little pain… my daughter, I fear you've only begun to know life's sufferings. But if you bleed, you can be sure that the world bleeds with you. And if you are cursed, well, you're hardly alone." Aycelina looked up and frowned at Zoë, who had fallen into a glazing stare. "Zoë, are you all right?"

"I'm all right," Zoë blurted. Then she looked away. "I— I think of my mother."

"Of course." Aycelina went over to Zoë and embraced her for a moment—there was a heady rush of sweat-and-lavender scent, underlaid with the somewhat less appetizing smell of mortal cooking. "Poor little lamb. But you must try to catch a few winks while you can now. It's a long holiday and I'm sure you won't want to nod off for any of it!"

Aycelina left and a few minutes later the other two girls trooped into the bedroom and piled into the straw.

"Where will Bone go if Zoë sleeps with us?" the littlest wanted to know.

"He'll squeeze in at the bottom somehow, like he always does," Maura said reassuringly, but the dog was nowhere in evidence. She reached beside the bed and brought up several loops of twine, passing them around, then sat cross-legged across from Zoë.

"Which ones do you know?" she asked, whispering conspiratorially.

"Which ones do *you* know?" returned Zoë, because it was a better answer than *none*. She hoped it wouldn't take long for everyone to fall asleep, or else she'd have to make a distinctly graceless exit. It had all been very pleasant, if eerie, but there was no question of staying with these people till dawn.

"Well, this one's called the tower." Maura worked her fingers deftly, creating an entwined figure of a long vertical steeple. "And these are the cat's eyes. This one is called the pilgrim's palm."

"Do that one again."

"It's tricky. Look." Maura showed them again. The younger girls tried unsuccessfully to imitate her. One's palm was all stem and no leaves. The other one's would only have been passable as 'the cobweb,' or something like that; she threw down her loop in frustration, snuggled into the bed to mope and was soon sound asleep. Zoë's palm, however, came out rather better.

"Exactly! Now this one is called the filet band. And the fish…"

After several more figures only Maura and Zoë were still awake, and Maura at last insisted on learning one of Zoë's. Zoë took two loops and refastened them together to make a double length. Then on the pretext of "trying to remember how it went" she experimented for a little while and soon produced, to her great satisfaction, a pattern of diamond-shapes. "There. That one is called the stained glass."

"Stained glass! Wonderful! I must learn that." Trying to, however, occupied what little remained of Maura's concentration.

"I'll get it for certain in the morning," she said at last, yawning. "Ohhhh… sweet sleep to you, Zoë." She started to pull back the covers to get underneath. Zoë's hand shot out and caught her wrist.

Maura turned back to look at her. "What?" Then concern grew in her eyes. "What?"

Yes, what?

"Nothing," Zoë said. "Good night."

She settled down between Maura and the littlest girl. It shouldn't be long to wait before she could make her escape. She didn't feel that hungry yet. If they felt the coldness of her skin, it didn't bother them, and the proximity of their flesh to hers soon warmed her almost to their temperature.

It wasn't so different, she told herself, from other nights years ago, when she and other little children whose names seemed to change from week to week had bundled together for warmth under a tattered cloak. Sometimes a shopkeeper was kind and let them sleep in the downstairs under the counter. Sometimes a baker would let them huddle in the oven, still warm from the day's cooking, and they'd go about the next day with ashes on their backs. On other occasions they slept in the church, although that had its own humiliations: well-meaning lectures trying to persuade them to become public wards, usually.

In any case, this was like that, the tangle of limbs and breath. Then Maura moved, and the scent of blood rose from under the cloth. She turned and the buds of her breasts dawned into view. Her hand came to rest on her belly in what seemed to Zoë almost a protective gesture, as though to say behold, here is the seat of life…

Zoë's teeth had pushed out so far they ached. A little sob escaped her. The other child at her back planted her feet against her. Zoë saw the pulse that flashed under Maura's jaw and curled toward it. Everyone had gotten to eat except for her.

Leave. Leave now.

Cursed. All of us cursed, she thought thickly as she struggled up out of their midst. Me with them and they with me. Whose sins are being punished?

She stumbled out through the room where Aycelina's and Sicard's snores mingled, down the stairs and through the gate into the streets outside. Rage like a fever chill swept through her again and again, shaking her bones and even making her teeth chatter. She had no idea who she was angriest at—herself for nearly slipping, the family for tempting her, Gregory for leaving her to the mercy of this vile thirst, God for allowing it to happen. The fury came from nowhere and went nowhere.

From a side alley near the town church she heard a racking, wheezing cough. She stalked down it. There lay a man in rags with a leprous-looking sore running down his face and another on his neck, tears tracking through the crevices of his cheeks.

"Oh, God, yes," he said when he saw her. "Yes, thank you."

"Quiet," she snarled, and fell on him.

All cursed.

Chapter Four

One thing she'd learned during her travels on her own: The *first* order of business for any given night was to figure out where she would spend the following day. In Valence she'd waited far too long and ended up squirreling desperately under a haystack as the first fingers of dawn appeared at the horizon; in Bourg Saint André she'd resorted to breaking into a church crypt and spending the night among the pious departed, where ill dreams had plagued her daytime sleep. Tonight she'd succeeded in finding a house whose upper floor had collapsed. A family of squatters slept there now among the fallen beams, but she thought she could sneak past them into the cellar easily enough. So that was settled.

The second order of business was to find someplace to put up her horse. She usually couldn't afford to stable it, even in a peasant's barn. Right now it was tied up in a stand of trees outside the city walls. If the horse were stolen, she'd simply take another. Everything of real importance was in the satchel that she carried with her. So that was settled.

The next order of business was hunting. It had been three nights since her last meal and she was supposed to hunt.

She skulked outside an inn in a dilapidated neighborhood just outside the Jewish quarter. A roil of jabber and the clatter of drink-ware filtered out through its greased-parchment windows. Many Cainites claimed inns and taverns as prized prowling grounds; a visitor couldn't always hunt in them safely. However, once a customer came *out*, they were usually fair game. Or so Meribah had said once.

She walked around the building. Here was the kitchen side—she might catch a servant emerging to toss out dirty dishwater or something, but the servant would probably scream. There were the guest chambers, with a few upper-story windows allowing inlet. Likely none of the guests were sleeping alone. No one was coming out. This was a waste of time; she wasn't feeding and she wasn't getting any closer to Isidro. Perhaps she should just let it go for one more night and try again tomorrow.

"Charity, miss, charity!" piped a voice at her side. A child of about ten years approached her from his spot beside the front door. He clinked his bowl at her.

She appraised him. "What makes you think I have any coin for you?"

"Any gift, however so small, helps me through another day, miss, and God and his angels in paradise will remember it to you." He had his patter well down; he knew not to smile during such a recitation. It was a shame the priests didn't recruit their numbers from among the beggars. "And this inn's beds are all full, miss, but I know where there's a room and a nice family who'll rent it at a reasonable price. Come and I'll show you!"

She allowed herself to be led away. Hopefully the city watch wouldn't happen upon them—but it was probably well paid to enter this neighborhood only when called for. The child looked healthy, despite the sorry state of his clothes. She laid a hand on his head.

Gregory would have said *no, absolutely not*. His instinct had always been to protect innocence. Almost always. He'd been a patient and selective hunter. Usually he waited for evidence that someone deserved to be fed upon, some crime, some misdeed; even a hurtful word to another mortal might do in a pinch. And then, despite having passed judgment, he would generally be merciful. Even a panderer who'd just beaten his whores Gregory would simply knock out with a blow of his powerful hand, then feed shallowly upon the unconscious body. Never take more than needed, never take from those who might not survive. He wouldn't risk a child for that reason alone.

Meribah, however, had still *been* a child when the serpent-vampires took her. A child weaned at Ma'arat on the flesh of other children, who'd learned to address any man who went in to her mother as father. Like Zoë, she had few illusions about the care with which the world handled the fragile. She would have said *certainly; just don't kill unless you must*.

Meribah understood. Gregory never had. He'd loved Zoë unreservedly, but somewhere in his tinker's soul he'd always cherished the notion that he was going to fix her somehow, rescue her, nurse away every wound she'd ever been dealt—even, at the last, those wounds he himself had inadvertently dealt her. He was centuries old and yet he'd died still not understanding. He was too good for it all, that was the problem.

Zoë's hand moved down to the child's neck, slipping under the edge of his tunic. It slid aside, revealing an angry little boil that marred his otherwise flawless skin.

"Where you say this house is?" she murmured.

"Not far." He pointed. "Look, miss, it's just over there, at the row's end."

"*That* house?" It looked scarcely better than the one with the collapsed floor, covered over with vandals' scribblings, its façade chipped and defaced. If it wasn't abandoned, it should be.

"Yes. This way."

"Just a moment." She stopped him, going down on one knee before him.

"Why?"

"I have something for you."

"Oh. Thank you, miss."

She reached in her purse and took out a couple of coins, laying them in his outstretched hand. They were clearly of higher denomination than he expected. His eyes widened. While his attention was elsewhere, she opened her lips.

"I wouldn't do that."

36   Ravnos

The new voice wasn't much further away than the boy. Zoë stumbled violently to her feet.

For several seconds she looked around, seeing no one. "Who are you?"

"I'm the one with the right to ask that, I fear." A figure came toward her from the direction of the house. She first noticed the clothes: a once-fine *bliaut* of good blue perse, stained and moth-eaten, a chemise with embroidered edges showing through the gaps, and over them both an odd wide sash made out of damask. But when she raised her eyes, she saw very little she could identify. That is, the face had every feature a face should have, but whenever she focused on any particular part it somehow became less distinct. The first time she looked at the nose it seemed long and thin, the next time it was blunt.

"Good eye, Pedro. Thank you for bringing her." The voice was undistinguishable as well, a well-modulated Occitan in a cool middle register. The figure slit open its wrist with a long fingernail and then let it fall. The boy was there to catch the first drop. His suckling looked almost like gnawing. After a brief while the figure put its other hand on the child's head and gently forced it away.

The formless countenance seemed to study her.

"Now then. What to do with you…"

"I gladly leave," she volunteered.

"I daresay. But what's done is done. When you passed the fountain you entered my domain. I suppose you thought mine would be safer. That I wouldn't defend my own because it's so meager."

"I—I thought nothing like that, sénher. I just look for people up after dark…"

"Don't." It stepped closer and seized her shoulder just as she began to back up. Its fingers dug immovably into her flesh. Something damp and foul-smelling began to soak through her clothes. She couldn't outpull it; she'd simply have to startle it into releasing her somehow. "At this very moment the viscount is up late with his mistress and several others, and probably will be until the dawn. But somehow I doubt you considered trying their courtyard. No, everyone, every gobbet of scum in Christendom who passes through Béziers comes *here* to slake his thirst. It doesn't seem to matter how many examples I make of them. Do you see my position?"

"Yes, sénher." Give it nothing to argue with, play the straw dummy and it might talk itself out.

It thrust its hand into her hair and dragged her up by it. "*Do* you?"

"Yes!" she shouted. She meant it to be a pathetic cry, but it rose and sharpened at the end.

It threw her down again.

"If I thought it'd do any good to kill you…" it growled, then shook its blurry head.

"I am sorry," she said. "Perhaps I can give you something?"

"Give me something?" It glanced down at her in surprise. "If you had anything I didn't, what would you be doing here?—None of that, now, if that's what you mean. We Lepers aren't all sinks of lust."

Well, that was the end of one mystery. She'd met other Cainites of this kind, whom the others called Lepers and even less flattering names. She knew they could disguise their hideousness with their blood-arts. But she'd only seen those arts used to replace a terrible face with an ordinary one, never to create this protean effect of many faces and no face all at once; after all, the object was usually to attract *less* notice. The colorful, almost garish clothes were no less odd.

Zoë drew the front of her dalmatic up tighter. "That is not what I meant."

"Then what did you mean?"

Her mind raced. Actually, the only things she had worth giving she desperately wanted to keep. "I… I could carry message for you, if you wish to send word to someone."

"Which way are you headed?"

"Toulouse."

"Hmmph. Toulouse." It pulled her up by her elbow. "Come along in."

She followed it into the house's depths. The place had the smell of a sickroom. It also somehow felt as though its inhabitants had left in a hurry to get somewhere just that morning, and would return by sunup. Perhaps that was because of the various things still littering it. A platter sat on the table, with the picked-over bones of some roast bird upon it, and a molding soup tureen and bowls and a knife. A child's doll slumped at the foot of the table. A trunk full of good fabrics lay overturned on the floor, the cloth snowed over with a layer of dust.

Then she heard a creak above her and looked up with a gasp. A man's corpse hung from the beam on a decaying rope. It too was picked partway clean, though the clothes remained, helping to hold it together.

The creature gazed up along with her, then drew her out from underneath.

"I don't advise standing just there," it said, in an odd admiring tone. "Old Nicholas might fall on you for pure spite."

"What happened here?" she whispered.

"A family dinner." It guided her over to the corner where a writing-desk stood, nearly the only thing in the house not covered with dust. A small candle burned atop it.

"How can you talk so?"

"I'm telling the perfect truth. Nicholas there was a carver. A good one, too—look at the decoration on the back of this desk here. He had a wife who quarreled a lot, but no more than most wives; two little children who clamored, but no more than most children; and an old father-in-law who complained a lot, but no more than most fathers-in-law. I'm told they were happy. All seemed well but for the fact that Nicholas missed Easter confession for the first time this year. Then one fine day this winter, he came home from the joiner's shop as they all sat down to eat. He killed them one by one with that knife there, wiped it very carefully on his wife's trencher, ate his dinner, and hanged himself."

Sarah Roark   39

Zoë stared up at the corpse again. It refused to give up its secrets.

"The neighbors arrived only too late—perhaps they thought it was nothing more than patriarchal discipline going on, perhaps not. In any case, they came and took the bodies out at last, but not Nicholas. He is to hang until he falls, and then to be dragged through the streets and buried in unconsecrated ground, which is the most they can do to him now. And I'm not sure it'll get that far. As you see, no one's cared to come in, not even to plunder the place. I admit I've taken a few steps of my own to discourage them."

"You make your home here?" she asked, and she couldn't quite keep the loathing out of her voice.

"I don't invite strangers into my home," it said imperturbably. "But the place is mine, yes. I find it useful to have many places to duck into. Quantity over quality, that's our way. This place… I'm no Graverobber, but do you feel it? It has the feel of a beautiful dream interrupted. I know how that goes," it finished in a softer voice, "oh yes indeed. He hoped to wipe it all out in a stroke, you see. Wipe out his whole life as though it had never existed, but he couldn't. Only time can accomplish that. We can try, but the ugly traces linger, like they do here. I suspect Nicholas and I would have a lot to talk about, if he could only talk back."

"For myself, I do not want to erase things… just… to do them again, different."

"Wouldn't we all like that." It had a sheet of parchment out and was readying writing accoutrements at the desk. It looked at her with what seemed like curiosity. "I am remiss. I am not gathering the news. You haven't said what brings you to Béziers… I think as host I can demand that much."

"Nothing bring me to Béziers. I am only looking for the Red Brothers."

"Red Brothers?"

"Their robes are red. Like dried blood."

"Yes, there are monks like that in Toulouse, a fine house with a big library. The Order of St. Theodosius, I believe. But why are you looking for them?"

"They kill vampires," she said simply.

"Hm." The phantasmal mouth bent visibly into a frown for a moment. "I would hope my brethren there would have mentioned such a thing by now."

"Have you seen them? I look for two of them. One is named Isidro, is tall and thin and dark, and the other one is shorter and thicker. Or there is a knight also, a hard knight with a cross on his tunic, and his name is Gauthier."

"No." A flat, certain *no*. "And I'm fairly sure that if anyone like that had passed through Béziers, I would have heard of it."

She looked down. Their footprints marred the coating of dust on the floor. She toed a small arc in it.

"I find nothing of them in Montpellier either."

The creature set down the quill it was sharpening and looked at her closely.

"Perhaps they didn't come this way," it said, not unsympathetically.

She nodded. It was time to admit it. She had lost them again. She'd been forced to start this alone and so she'd sworn to finish it alone. But perhaps she should take a mortal at least, give him the blood. Set him to spy for her in the daytime, to get into places she dared not enter…no. No, not yet. She was not so helpless. In any case, she had to figure out where the paths had diverged first, or a bevy of spies would do her no good.

"I have a—cousin of sorts in Provence," the creature began at last. "He tells me that Arles and Avignon have each had a Cainite disappear in the last two months."

That piqued her interest. "Do they know why?"

"No. Much is happening there. Everyone knows that if an army marches in from the north, it'll probably come down the Rhone. Even now, would-be camp followers make their way there, *ribauz* and whores and kitchen boys. Wild-eyed preachers. Others too, of theoretically more elevated spirits… from what I hear, the pope and his legates are calling the Templars and Hospitalers to war. And of course, Cainites follow the movements of the kine, so if mortals descend on

Provence, so do we. In such circumstances, disappearances aren't unusual. But if vampire-hunters have come to Provence—and especially if they are Red Brothers of Toulouse…" It looked up. "Well? Which way are you going? West or east?"

"A moment."

She walked away from the creature, avoiding Nicholas, out to the doorway where the air was clean. There she reached her hand under her dalmatic and drew out the little scarab ring on its chain.

"You must help me now. Which way must I fly?" she asked it in Greek. "Which way to the one that killed your master?"

She released it from its fixture. She had no idea what god or fate she was appealing to—any that could look down on her with sympathy would do for now, she supposed. The little simulacrum lifted its scintillating wings and flew as far as its spring would let it, fluttering off witlessly in the direction fortune chose.

"I go east," she announced as she came back inside.

The Cainite nodded. It was already writing.

"It seems you can carry a letter for me after all. Do you read the Latin?"

"No." In truth she'd begun to decipher the letters from Bergamo just a bit, going by what the scholar had told her, but that hardly counted.

"Good. What is your name?"

"Zoë."

"Zoë." It evidently wrote that down. "When you get back into Provence, go to Arles and give this to the elder of my people there. His name is Salomon. Just walk into the Alyscamps and they will find you easily enough, I promise."

It finished up the note, folded the parchment, dripped candle wax onto the seam, and then handed it to Zoë.

"Tell them that Blanche in Béziers sent you."

Chapter Five

A mortal would have been too cold, but Zoë found it pleasant strolling the moonlit lane of the dead. It had been built to Roman aesthetics, and insofar as Constantinople was the eastern Rome, it reminded her of home. No rattling of bones here, no smell of sulfur, no promises sweet or dire. Only a sensible recognition of the need for some pleasant place where the living could store their departed. The decay here was not the horrid putrefaction of Nicholas either, but the gentler crumbling of weeds and stone. The tombs almost seemed part of the vegetation, as though they'd been planted as pebbles in neat furrow upon furrow, then sprung out of the soil and swelled like gourds to full size.

She held the letter in her hand. She hoped it would inspire curiosity. Curious vampires would ask before they started biting.

She drew herself up on one of the sarcophagi to sit and wait, just as though she had an appointment. A wind had picked up—a breeze now, but it could easily turn into a pounding mistral later in the night. She lay down and faced the sky, head toward the wind so her skirts wouldn't fly up. The clouds streamed past. She almost felt she could fall asleep here. She closed her eyes.

"If you sleep with the dead, you dream of the dead." The voice was at her side. She felt so much in a dream already that she didn't even start.

"I know," she said.

She looked. It was a young woman, a mortal, although her skin was so pale that only the warmth of her hand as she laid it over Zoë's gave her away.

"You have something for us?"

"For Salomon."

"Give it to me."

"I only give it to Salomon. It's from Blanche in Béziers."

"They can't be disturbed now. None of them can."

"I give it only to Salomon."

"She can come, Beatriz." Another woman, an older woman, came up beside the young one. She too was pale as veined marble, and her hand was cold. She wore a diaphanous gown of fine-woven linen, pleated and belted with gold and brass. Strange designs in ochre traversed her arms and forehead. "As long as she's willing to pay respects."

"Respects?"

"The Elysian field welcomes a very special newcomer," the older woman said.

***

Weeping. Lamentation. Only one mourner made the sound, but it echoed in the tiny chapel, multiplying a dozenfold.

Others murmured, inarticulate utterances of attempted comfort. They put their arms around the gnarled old Cainite who bent nearly double in his grief.

"The well-beloved son has lain down and will not rise again," the old woman recited. She walked into the chamber with a stained and folded tunic and placed it respectfully on the floor before them. Nestled in the center was a vial filled with what looked like fine white ash.

"The well-beloved brother has lain down and will not rise again. The one whose cunning confounded his enemies has lain down and will not rise again. The one who faithfully performed his duties at tomb-side and in town has lain down and will not rise again. The one whose heart was valiant has lain down and will not rise again. The one who gave his father joy has lain down and will not rise again.

"The death-wail sounds over the plain. Let the cry come from his kin in Avignon. Let the cry come from his kin in Valence. Let the cry come from the assembled hosts of dead and the angels of heaven. Let the horse bow his head and let the bull bend his knee. Let the wind fall silent and the rain be dammed, let the stars hide their faces and the moon turn dark. For he who was our light is no more."

She picked the tunic and vial up again and addressed them. The ritual tone of her lamentation was edged with a decidedly unstudied pain.

"O Beloved! You must have been told that just as your umbilical cord was cut, so your time on this earth would someday be cut off. You must have been told that this is the lot of all who are born mortal. Now the unstoppable wave is upon you. Now the darkest night of Adam's get is upon you. Now the loneliest desolation of Eve's children is upon you. Now the unwinnable battle awaits, and even the blood of Caine will not avail you."

As she spoke the assembled, undead and mortal alike, began to sniffle and sob. Finally some of them wailed aloud, rocking on their knees on the cold stone floor. From all around Zoë the clamor and the smell of vampire blood rose, filling the vault of the chapel until she half-expected it to fall apart, stone from stone.

A mother whose milk wouldn't come anymore. Someone had found some stale bread that she'd mashed to a pap in water. Now she tried to get the squalling infant to take it by brushing it across the roof of his mouth with her finger, but he only screamed louder.

A pair of vampires who claimed to be Michaelites (which evidently at one time had meant something), crouched on their haunches like beasts under a tattered lean-to, staring sullenly out through the rain at the mortals stronger undead had claimed.

A grimacing official from Adrianople's Cainite court standing over a table where a dead mortal lay, squeezing the blood from the body into outstretched bowls. Gregory, Wonder-Maker of Byzantium, pressed forward with his own bowl, but the others shoved him back. He stumbled on his malformed legs and fell into the mud. When he stood, for just a moment the fury of Hell itself reared in his eyes, but then he came back to Zoë and patted her knee affably. "Tomorrow, then."

A quarter-acre of flesh striped red by bits of rope twisted into makeshift lashes. Wild prayers to a derelict god, an ancient murderer and a dead archangel. Temporary "marriages" constantly dissolving and reforming between the bereaved. And always weeping, weeping, weeping, especially just before dawn.

She tried to stand up amid the convulsing mass, but it dragged her back under. There was nothing noble to grief, no, not even to her grief for Gregory. There was only the dumb animal pain, the rawness. There was all the dignity of a bleeding arm-stump. When she could think of revenge, when she could forge it into fury, that seemed finer somehow; and every ghost including Gregory himself could rise from the grave to tell her it was a deadly sin—she didn't care.

And now the unstoppable wave was upon them all. She wailed without thought of restraint for this childe she'd never met, for her foster father, for her mortal parents, for her city, for herself. The priestess allowed the tide of sorrow to swell and crest, as though space for it were specially reserved in the rite. Perhaps it was. Then she turned to the votive statue.

"Mother of Grace, Queen of Heaven, Most Perfect," she beseeched it. "Let his heart not go knotted into the hereafter. Spread it like palm fibers and peel it like garlic. Calm its fury, open it serenely to the gaze of our Lord, that he might be judged by the worthiness with which he met his many tests. I beg you also, Gentlest One, to rain cool tears of pity down upon this father who has seen his childe go to death before him. Send your angels to minister; do not turn your face from him. I pray that you comfort his brothers and sisters in blood who have lost part of themselves forever on this night, and the children of Lazarus who loved him also, and the children of Seth who grieve for him."

She gave the tunic and the vial to the old Cainite, who gathered the tunic to his breast and took the vial in his hand. She then took up a little strongbox that stood along the side wall of the chapel and opened it before them. It contained a

Ravnos

heart—a cow's heart, Zoë guessed, with the veins emerging from it tied off in knots. The old woman held the heart aloft.

"As for the ones who killed our beloved," she said, her face luminous with rage now, "let their eyes be dimmed and their ears be stopped. Let their limbs wither and their teeth rot. Let them be assailed by disease and stricken by sorrow. Let them be parted from all loved ones. Let them suffer as they have made others suffer. As I do unto this flesh, so may it be with the flesh and spirit of our enemy." She cut the heart open and drained several drops into the old Cainite's mouth, then into that of every other mourner in turn. Zoë accepted her share dutifully, though it was cold and already rancid.

The priestess cut the heart into several pieces, letting each one drop to the floor. With a cry she stamped on them, grinding them down savagely under her feet. She spat upon them and cursed them in some tongue that was not Greek or Latin or Saracen. None of the other vampires or mortals moved, but Zoë could see them staring at the filthy gobbets of tissue as though their eyes alone could set them afire. Finally the priestess kicked the pieces over before Mary.

"Renounce them, we beg you! Turn your face away! Withdraw your favor from them! Hear the prayers of those who have shepherded souls to your arms for age upon age! In the name of the Father who keeps the secret of spirit, in the name of the Mother who keeps the secret of life and in the name of the Son who keeps the secret of death and the blood of all sacrifice, we pray. Amen."

Each of them crawled forward on their knees and kissed the feet of Mary, and then proceeded out of the chapel. Wordlessly they went to one of the stone sarcophagi that lined the paths of the Alyscamps. Its lid had already been pried off and set aside; the inside was empty. The old Cainite—one of the Lepers, Zoë knew, for while the boils that covered his flesh could have existed in mortal nights, the uneven size of his limbs and features spoke to a heavier malediction—laid the garments and the ashes of his childe inside. The others returned the lid.

"For an age I've tended this plantation of the dead," he said over the tomb. All sign of tears had fled. His malformed face was as empty as the sarcophagus had been a moment ago, as though his spirit had been entombed along with the rest. "I know their names and the names of their families, and how old they were when they died. I've planted flowers and fragrant trees at their sides. I remember them in prayer. I visit the ones who would otherwise stand desolate. For an age I have done this work for the Lord's sake, and my son with me, and this... this is how I am repaid."

The priestess laid a hand on his arm.

"Don't, Proserpine," he rebuffed her. "I fear your cry for justice is no more in His ears than the sound of the wind. Somehow we've failed. I have failed. That is all."

His gaze lifted to Zoë, not for the first time, but it was the first time he seemed actually to register her presence.

"Who is this?"

"This is Zoë. She bears a letter, Salomon," Proserpine said. "From Blanche."

Zoë handed it to him.

"Your son, sénher." She hesitated, then went on. "How... how did it happen?"

He merely turned away, opening the letter as he began to walk back down the path.

Proserpine answered for him. "Forgive him. Bertolomieu was killed in the name of the God he served. That's all we know right now."

Beatriz joined them as the group moved to follow Salomon. "Mother," the mortal woman asked quietly, "would it not be possible to find out?"

The priestess shook her head. "No, we mustn't, daughter. Even as we speak Bertolomieu chooses his path to the throne of judgment. It's too soon to call him back for questions that, however urgently we might wish them answered, can do him no good now."

"Maybe I can tell you something about it," Zoë said. "If you tell me what you know."

The two women looked at each other doubtfully.

"Show her the thing," the bitter voice of Salomon floated back. Zoë heard a crackling sound; Salomon was crumbling up the letter, half-tearing it. "Her warning comes a night too late, but it proves true enough."

"Come," said Proserpine. She led Zoë and part of the company into another, larger church in the necropolis and took them down into the crypt.

"Whoever it was doesn't seem to have connected us to the Alyscamps yet," she said as they descended the stairs. "Thank the Holy Family. But the hospital is no longer safe for us."

One of those who had followed spoke softly. "His magpie Martin saw the whole thing. Of course it's useless trying to get too many details even from talkative birds. Martin says all men look alike…" A sad, wry chuckle. "We know there were at least two of them. Somehow they learned that he fed at the hospital. Somehow they pierced his disguise as he came out. Then they pierced his flesh as well and burned it, and finally cut off his head."

Proserpine reached onto a niche shelf and brought out a length of what looked like shroud-winding, which she folded away to reveal a crucifix. "This flew from the hand of one in the struggle. It might have fallen into the dark where he couldn't see it, or else he simply didn't bother recovering it. They fled like cowards just after the fatal blow was struck, to escape the alarm their noise raised." She handed it to Zoë.

Zoë turned it over in her hands, looking at it back and front. How could she not know it? She'd seen it so many times since in her mind's eye, blazing forth from his hand as he thrust it arrogantly upward. It had traveled with him. Where her exploring fingers touched it now, it had just last night known the touch of his hand. She hadn't been so close since Bergamo. Her hand tightened of its own volition, as though to splinter the wood, but it withstood her grip.

"Isidro has lost his cross," she said. "Perhaps that is not all he has lost." Her heart filled with hope. The others looked at her in confusion.

"You will avenge him, will you not?" she asked them, more sharply than she meant to. "Or were they only hard words in the chapel?"

It was a long moment before anyone spoke.

Chapter Six

"Now you said there was a cross on his tunic. Did it look like that?"

"Like what?"

"There, look just there at the mantle of the man coming out."

"That isn't him."

"Not surprised. But is it the same sort of cross?"

Zoë peered at it. She didn't have Gregory's sharp eyesight yet. Luckily the design was large. She nodded to Mascaro, who blew out a sigh.

"He's a Templar, then. If the entire Templar order knows about us now, that can't come to any good. And if they band with the learned monks in Toulouse... even worse."

They sat on a high tiled roof. Blasts of wind assailed them every now and again, blowing dirt into Zoë's eyes and stirring up all sorts of debris in the streets below. She had her shoes off so that her toes could grip against the slope.

"Do you think Isidro is inside?" she asked.

"I have no idea. I don't know what's going on in there, except that Bishop Fulk and the Templars are visiting the archbishop."

"Can you get us closer?"

Mascaro shook his head. "I can't hide us both. Even if I could, Branoc claims all of Saint-Trophime. One of his folk might notice us. On the other hand... there's a thought. Come this way. Wait, first—have you fed recently?"

"Two nights ago," she lied.

"All right. Then come on."

Zoë followed him, clambering down the wall. He loped along in front of her. He was using his Leper blood-art to make himself look like a simple gap-toothed townsman, but he didn't disguise his movements anywhere near as well. The quicker he went, the more he reminded Zoë of one of the brass monkeys from Gregory's menagerie, which used to scamper up and jump on her back whenever she walked in the garden, curling their jointed tails around her collarbone. (Where were they now? Capering for the pleasure of some whey-faced Latin?)

To Zoë's surprise, a mass of mortals waited at the kitchen's back door. "Supper's running very late," Mascaro said with satisfaction. "Had a feeling it might be. Ecclesiastical jibber-jabber."

"War jibber-jabber," Zoë muttered darkly.

"Likely. When the almoner comes out, you try to slip past him. Get inside and hide where you can." The Nosferatu thrust his hands into a filthy puddle, rubbing them together as though to wash them.

"What about you?"

"I'm going to distract him, of course. Then I'll be along. Hide and wait."

They settled themselves on the outer edge of the throng. At least there was no trouble about blending in, Zoë thought, with her stained clothes.

The crowd rumbled discontentedly—the ones who'd already elbowed up to the front complaining the loudest. It was cold. It was late. Surely His Grace and the noble guests had done with eating by now. They could argue on all night if they liked, but was that any reason to delay alms? Some people had children to put to bed. Well, you never know, His Grace might have children too. Such talk when you're waiting to eat the man's bread!

At length a man in deacon's vestments came to the door. "All right, no pushing," were the first words out of his mouth, but before he'd even finished them Mascaro had jostled up and seized his garments in a lusty parody of desperation.

"For God's sake, pity, lord!" he cried out, nearly shaking the poor man off-balance. "Pity on a poor Christian as was drove out of business by heretic merchants! Pity on a father who's already watched two of his little ones starve!"

"Get down, you," the almoner grimaced, trying to pry Mascaro's hands off one by one without dropping his basket. Zoë quickly made her way up near the pair. "I said get down, or I'll call the guard!"

Finally the almoner planted his foot in Mascaro's midsection and shoved him away. He tumbled down the steps and ran off into the night, or appeared to do so at least, sped along by the jeers of his fellow beggars. Zoë ducked around the recovering mortal, who now reached into his basket for the leftover trenchers.

"Yes, let that remind you all *not to push*, I assure you there's plenty…"

Inside the kitchen it was dim but still warm, the great hearth radiating the last of its heat, banked ashes still edged in red. The meal must be down to the marzipan and spiced wine, and the kitchen staff all either in the hall attending or stealing a private moment before bed. Though one at least had decided to skip the latter—the sound of snoring came from an adjacent doorway. She padded through the room and found herself in the covered passageway leading to the hall. Voices wafted down it from the other end.

Hide, Mascaro had said. A fine thing for him to say. Hide where?

She went back into the kitchen again. The angry glow of the broken-down fire made her uneasy, but she crouched in the space under a shelf just by it.

Almost as soon as she'd done so, Mascaro found her and squeezed in beside her. They waited in silence for the almoner to finish. He walked past still trying to brush the mud from Mascaro's hands off his robes, muttering.

"Wait here a moment," Mascaro whispered. Whoever had told her once that all Lepers stank had been misinformed; not even the taint of blood lay on his breath. "I'll look out ahead and come back. All right?"

Zoë nodded. He extracted himself. A little while later he returned.

"Well. I think we can get into a position to watch the goings-on at table, but you'll have to follow my instructions carefully. When you come out of the passage you'll be behind the screen. Now the servants are done fixing platters, so you should be safe to wait there at least a few moments, but if you hear the archbishop call for anything but more wine, duck back into the passage where it's dark. Otherwise, wait for the conversation to get a bit denser, or for someone to raise his voice—trust me, there's a lot of that going on tonight—so that everyone's eyes will be on him. Then you scurry along the edge of the room and get behind the very first wall-hanging. It's only a few yards. I've cut a little hole in it for you to see out of. Oh. And if they see you, run back this way, it's your best escape route. Understand?"

"I understand. Are they there?"

"For heaven's sake, how would I know? I only took a quick look. You can see for yourself. Now go on."

Even though she knew speed was of the essence, she found herself hesitating from step to step as she crept down the passageway into the great hall. She emerged behind a wooden screen, just as promised—fortunately not a half-transparent lacework such as the households of Constantinople had borrowed from the Turks, but long solid sheets of paneling. The voices grew louder, and not just from proximity. It sounded as though several men were talking nearly on top of each other.

"But Your Grace, that isn't what Templars *do*. It's not the purpose for which we were founded."

"What are you talking about?" A banquet of a voice, rich and sweet and musical, even if it sharpened now in annoyance. "You defend the faith, don't you?"

"We defend the Holy Land. We defend the pilgrims. We consider that our part in defending the faith. We don't have the might or the numbers to act as the Holy Father's army in all things, and in this case it would be unwise even to try."

"Since when have the Poor Knights of Christ required superiority of numbers in order to do what's right? You shame your order, Commander! You are under the Holy Father's direct authority. Shall you not be his army when he deems it meet?"

"Simply because he wishes something done, Your Grace, that doesn't mean things will proceed in a manner he can approve of. We've all seen this in the ruin of Constantinople. A miserable mistake whose issue, I fear, will haunt the Church forever." The last was delivered in a heavy, sorrowful tone. Zoë thought bitterly, *All very well to say such things now*. "This campaign, however compelling the cause, is also a mistake. You've already contracted with a number of knights and lords from the north. How many of them honestly know the difference between a Cathar and a Christian? I challenge you to ask them and find five who can answer. You may say that you and the other prelates will make all these distinctions for them, but you can't possibly be everywhere at once. How will you keep these men under control? The short answer is, you can't. There's no way to destroy *only* the Cathar portion of a city with a worldly army and you know it. Is it really your intent to make the true faithful suffer for the sins of their neighbors?"

"Exactly," put in another voice. "I've heard that not a few of these French are lacklands and opportunists, more interested in seizing property than cleansing souls, which is hardly surprising given that plunder and land is exactly what they've been promised for taking part. If that's the sort of pilgrim you're looking for, I don't see why Your Grace bothers to approach the Temple."

"There's also the purely military problem. Most of these men will only sign up for the forty days, and after that they'll get their indulgence and go home. What exactly is Your Grace hoping to accomplish in that short a time?"

"If we cannot crush the heresy altogether in forty days, gentlemen," the rich voice overlapped, rising, "then we will make a dent in it that no one in the Languedoc will be able to ignore. You forget how long I've been preaching myself hoarse! Would you have me go on and on until I drop dead without a thing to show for it? These people are mules in tunics. They do not *listen* to words!"

The thud of a hand on the table, a rattle of platters and goblets. Zoë took her opportunity and pattered across the gap between the end of the screen and the velvet hanging. She deliberately didn't look in the direction of the table, as though they couldn't spot her if she didn't spot them.

The rich voice went on. "If it takes the rattle of swords to get their attention and make them give up their heretics, then so be it. I'd far rather save their souls through such a method than lose them by any other. And if even then they won't give the Cathars up, then how much better than Cathars are they really?"

"It's not a question of how much better they are. We don't condemn Christians as heretics simply because they lack courage."

"Ah, I see. Not everyone can be a Templar. Are you actually lecturing me on theology, Commander?"

"What strength the Templars have God delivers unto them out of His mercy, Your Grace. What I mean is that if this army commits the sort of crimes I suspect they're capable of, for every Cathar you kill you'll plant the poisonous seed of doubt in a Christian heart. You'll make martyrs of the *bonshommes*."

"Then you won't take up this cross, and that's that."

"Not as currently planned, no."

"I see."

Peeping now through the little hole Mascaro had cut for her, she could see who was where. The rich voice belonged to a man in purple robes and a skullcap who sat at his host's right side. The archbishop himself wore much the same attire, but instead of leaning forward and gesticulating, he slumped slightly in his chair, leaning an arm on the armrest and massaging one temple. Several of the other guests were knights bearing the Templar cross.

All at once she felt a presence at her side. For a moment she saw nothing, but then the form of Mascaro's human disguise melted into sight.

"Gauthier!" she mouthed at him excitedly. He nodded, holding his hand up in a faint warning: Yes, yes, be calm.

She turned back to the hole. The steel-eyed knight sat quietly, leaving the argument to those she guessed to be his seniors in the order. He didn't fidget, but his eyes roamed from one face to another. Every so often he took a dutiful sip of wine.

Her eye traveled down the other half of the table. Along that part of the board sat a few priests and a monk, and the monk...

Her heart didn't beat, but it climbed high in her throat.

She knew him at once from the russet habit, but she would have found him in any attire. There could be no mistaking that face. It was elegantly formed, though too spare to be called handsome in the old classical sense. He had a fine nose with nostrils delicate and expressive as a silk veil, faintly olive skin, deep brown eyes and dark hair shaved in a severe tonsure. In another life he could have been Zoë's considerably older brother. He watched the conversation with what seemed to be growing distaste. Of course, thought Zoë; here were all these wretched folk sitting and arguing about the need to kill a mere mortal menace when he spent his nights striving against the very forces of Hell itself. Or perhaps he simply wasn't one for marzipan.

Zoë turned to Mascaro, trying to think how to convey the information without making noise. She held up her fingers all in a row. Luck was with her here, ten fingers for ten men at table. She wiggled the third from the left and the last on the right.

"Gauthier," she mouthed again. "Isidro."

He put his eye up to the hole. Almost immediately he recoiled with a look of shock.

"The lunatic—!" he began to whisper, then thought better of it and shook his head.

"What?" she mouthed.

He waggled a finger of his own: third from the right. She looked. At first she had no idea what she was meant to notice. There was only a priest there, a handsome young priest with rosy cheeks, who conversed amiably with those around him. But then she trained her attention on his hands. Now he had a square of marzipan, held daintily by the fingertips; when she next blinked, he had half a square and was lowering it to the plate again. No telltale crescent ridge from a bite showed on the edge of the sweet. Intrigued, she watched even more carefully as he did it once again, trying to see where the marzipan was going if not into his mouth.

There. It had gone onto the plate of the man next to him, who ate and drank steadily on without seeming to notice anything wrong. A blood-servant, probably. This must be the Cainite of Saint-Trophime, then, posing as a mortal. Perhaps he thought to influence the goings-on, but more likely, given that he hadn't spoken yet, he was simply spying. Plainly he was skilled at such mummeries.

Just as plainly, he hadn't the first inkling about Isidro and Gauthier, and there was no way to warn him.

"Does Your Grace plan actually to travel with the army?" the archbishop asked, seeking a less charged subject to wind the evening down with.

"No, I return to Toulouse," the rich-voiced bishop answered. "Much to do there."

"What about Raymond?"

"What about Raymond? If the count persists in his error, then I fear I won't have any good news for the people of my city. It's in his power to stop this."

"What do you think, Fraire Isidro?" The Templar Commander looked down the length of the table. "It is Isidro, isn't it? And I remember Paire Aribert said you were from Toulouse."

Isidro glanced around at the eyes that had suddenly turned to him, but he didn't seem surprised to be called on.

"I fear His Grace Bishop Fulk may overestimate my lord Raymond's sway over the other lords of the Languedoc," he said evenly. "The closer one gets to the mountains, the flintier the barons become, and I expect that even some of Raymond's own kin will finally choose the *perfecti* over him. But I agree that it's still in the count's power to divert the war from Toulousain lands. Provided he returns to bend the knee to the Church as he should, that is, and I hope he does."

"If that is how you feel, brother, perhaps you'll prevail upon your abbot to so persuade the count," the bishop put in. "Surely all you've heard tonight has convinced you of the necessity. There *will* be a march against the Cathars—whether the Templars join it or not. "

"I do indeed realize that. And I will plead with him, I assure you."

"It would take a war to get the Red Brothers' noses out of their books," the bishop remarked to the other guests, who chuckled uneasily. "As for the Cathars, sometimes I think the Red Brothers would prefer to keep them around just to have something to study, since they'll have to wait for another campaign into the Saracen lands for more reading material in Arabic."

"We already know all about the Cathars that we care to know, Your Grace." Isidro crooked a little smile. "Their philosophy may be of interest to the curious, but they have nothing to teach in that realm that wouldn't be better learned from orthodox sources. In any case, the errors of Catharism must be extinguished. There's no arguing that."

"But do you think a war such as the bishop and the legate propose really best serves the end of extinguishing those errors?" one of the knights broke in, impassioned. The archbishop gave a near-silent groan.

Isidro said something in another tongue, to the murmuring of most of the assembly. The cassocked Cainite stiffened a moment, then seemed to regard Isidro with new eyes.

"Come again?" said the knight. "Not all of us speak Latin day in and day out…"

Bishop Fulk answered for Isidro. "In the vulgar, it runs thus: 'For men have shed the blood of saints and of prophets, and thou hast given them blood to drink; for they are worthy.' The Book of Revelations. Well said, brother," he added with more than a trace of surprise. "The heretics are long overdue for their apocalypse."

"Gentlemen, on that note…" The archbishop stood. "Your pardon, but it's been one very long day to be followed by another." He clapped his hands; attendants scurried to answer. "My servants will see you all to your various beds. A good night's rest to you all."

Zoë watched as the guests rose and split into their component groups. Though Gauthier joined his fellow knights, he sent a frowning gaze across the room to Isidro, who seemed to ignore it. The Cainite went over to Isidro and spoke to him. Zoë couldn't hear what he said, as it was a quiet undercurrent in the general mumble; afterward the two of them moved toward one of the doors with a young page lighting their way.

Mascaro shook his head, but he put a hand on Zoë's wrist, restraining her while the room cleared out.

"We've got to do something," whispered Zoë. "Where have they gone?"

"The garden, I think, or that's what his lips seemed to shape. Come on."

***

The wind had died down, and the walls and hedges cut out most of the remainder. It still wasn't really weather for a garden stroll, Zoë thought to herself. Instead of following their quarry, Mascaro insisted on running ahead to hide in the bushes opposite one of the garden's remoter stone benches. But he'd guessed well. After some while Isidro and his undead companion came along, talking quietly. The page had mysteriously vanished.

Isidro shivered. The Cainite took off the long fur-lined cloak he wore and offered it to the monk, who hesitated and then wrapped it around his shoulders with murmured thanks.

"You're not cold yourself," he said. It was half statement, half question.

"No." The vampire smiled. They came to stand just before the bench.

"*Jubilis,*" he said.

"*Jesu Vincit,*" Isidro replied.

"*Christi Victis.*" The Cainite sat. "I thought so. I thought so the moment I saw you."

"And I thought so when I saw you."

"Did you?"

"You were the only one whose breath didn't steam in the cold."

"Ah." Something flickered in the Cainite's eyes, then passed away again.

"And then I watched at supper. You didn't eat, or it didn't seem that you did." His eyes widened slightly, and he cast them down to the ground. "You are… among the truly perfect, are you not? Whose blood shines like rubies? In Toulouse it has been five years since one actually graced the church at Communion, and so I have never seen with my own eyes…."

"Sh. Peace, brother." The Cainite extended his hand. "I have heard something of the troubles of Toulouse. That doesn't matter tonight; what matters is that now you see."

"Yes. Now I see."

"Shall we take Communion together?"

"I… I am hardly worthy of the honor, lord." Isidro's knee began to buckle.

"No, no. Don't bow before the messenger." The vampire stood, moving Isidro's cowl aside and dipping his head toward the side of the monk's neck. "You *are* worthy, brother. You did very well in there, playing that bishop's game…"

Twang—the sound of a crossbow discharging its bolt. A shaft of wood protruded from the vampire's back. It had missed its probable mark. He wheeled around, rosy cheeks draining to white fury in an instant.

Gauthier leaped over the hedge. "Now, Isidro!"

The monk whispered what sounded like a brief prayer. All at once his form was rimmed with liquid light, which poured a small pool of radiance onto the ground around him. He caught hold of the Cainite's arm. Something under the vampire's sleeve crackled and hissed. The vampire twisted, howling as the chalky glow fell on his skin; a burning crust spread on his cheek. The next instant he broke away in a blur of motion. Gauthier stepped into his path and stopped him dead with a sword-thrust through the stomach.

"No—" Zoë started to spring out. Mascaro wrapped himself around her and brought her down, then dragged her back behind the adjoining hedge. She struggled against him. The faint smell of vitae arose from his pores. He was using his blood-strength to stop her, the rat! A growl escaped her. He plastered a hand over her mouth.

They could hear the vampire still retching horribly on the point of Gauthier's blade. All of a sudden that was cut off by a squelching noise and a thud. Then silence.

"You missed," came Isidro's voice.

"You didn't give me a clear shot. Or much warning, while we're at it."

"Well, I think the heart is pierced now. Unless it's pretending."

"Let's see." *Whack.* "I don't think it's pretending."

"Keep it?"

"If we can get it away without a fuss. You pull it off the path and wait for me, I'll go get my men to come around to the garden wall. Did you hear something, brother?"

"When?"

"Just now."

"I don't think so."

Another pause. "Take this." The sound of something being unsheathed.

"Gauthier…"

"Take it, you stubborn Spaniard. Don't die for the sake of canon law. I'll be back as soon as I can."

Mascaro listened intently to Gauthier's retreat, then yanked Zoë up to her feet and began pulling her through the garden. She tried to hang back. His hand circled her wrist like a raptor's talon.

"No, go back!" she whispered frantically. "He's alone, we're two!" But Mascaro said nothing until they'd made it out of the garden and indeed out of the complex.

Then he rounded on Zoë and thrust his face nearly into hers.

"*Two* is not *enough*! Not for such a man! My God, can't you see that?"

"That was my chance!" Her voice broke and rose toward a wail. Her eyes felt hot; the blood rushed to them and into her temples as well.

"Your chance to what? To die? I just saved your life!"

"You let him go! Now he get away—" She looked down, gulping for control. "Now they will both get away, and the vampire..."

"Branoc was careless. He was careless, and he paid for it." He turned away from her and started walking.

"Was? He's not even dead yet! What about the curse? What about the curse Proserpine laid?" Mascaro's back seemed to bend further with every word she spat at him, but she couldn't stop. "Who will make Isidro's limbs wither and put out his eyes? You think God will? Let me tell you something about God! He does not make us justice! He hates us! Don't you understand this yet? *He hates us!*"

She put her hands on his hunched shoulders and shoved him. He stumbled, then looked up at her. The mist-mask he wore was slipping now. She caught a hint of the rubbery flesh that was underneath, and his real eyes, blue and soft with sudden hurt.

"Do you think He twist your flesh because he love you for a servant?" she hissed. "Do you think He kill my gentle, beautiful father and leave *you* alone?"

He said nothing, just stared at her for several long moments. Then he turned away again.

Last night he lost a brother. It wasn't Gregory's voice in her head, not really, but when her conscience spoke it tended to sound like his voice. *Have you forgotten this?*

It was a terrible alchemy that took her rage, her pure, incandescent rage and transmuted it into something small and sordid and ludicrous.

"I'm sorry," she said. "I did not think."

He still said nothing. At last he darted a sullen glance at her.

"No, I am sorry. I didn't realize till now that you really are the child you appear to be. I'm going now to tell the prince what's happened, but he will probably counsel us just as I counsel you: hide. Or if you must pursue these men, do not do it in Arles. You won't be warned again."

With the next eye-blink he was gone.

Chapter Seven

The Countryside Around Castelnaudary
Third Week of Advent, 1209

Nearly a year later and she still didn't have her quarry, but at least it was getting easier to track them.

Easier to track Sénher Gauthier, anyway. His pattern was now well established. He spent most of his time roaming the Languedocien countryside just ahead of the Church's army, along with a tiny band of knights and men-at-arms; and folk made far greater note nowadays of knights traveling through their villages. Often she could simply listen at a window to hear talk of armed men and country skirmishes. Such talk didn't always turn out to be about Gauthier, especially once the summer campaigning was over and the few knights who stayed past their quarantine had little left to do but engage in random pillage. Still, it helped her keep tabs. Sometimes she stopped by a town gatehouse to ask what route to take to avoid the soldiers, and was treated to an earful of military gossip from bored sentries.

Whenever the army actually laid siege, however, Gauthier rejoined it. Thus Zoë found herself camped out in a stand of trees outside Béziers on the eve the feast of Mary Magdalene, settling in, like the camp-followers below her, for a good long wait. The following evening she awoke to find columns of smoke dotting the city from end to end. Her vitae-battened horse had snapped its ties in panic and fled. The smell of fire and blood was so powerful that she plunged herself into the river to escape it and the red hunger it unleashed. That was the entire span of the thing. One night the city stood in proud defiance and by the next not a single inhabitant out of 20,000 survived.

And Blanche, thought Zoë grimly, had been worried about Red Brothers.

She likewise camped outside Carcassonne when the army arrived there in August. That, unlike Béziers, was a siege of respectable length. Gauthier's band left and returned twice before it was over. Zoë never actually saw Isidro with them, and evidently he didn't ride out with either of their expeditions. (As for the other Red Brother, the monk that had left Bergamo with Isidro, she hadn't had word or sign of him since St. Gilles, and had long since given up asking after him.)

But several times she heard from a kitchen-slut or washerwoman that a tall monk in russet robes had gone into Gauthier's tent, and once she spotted Isidro's horse. Gauthier had pitched his tent, tellingly, next to those of reluctant crusader Count Raymond of Toulouse and the handful of other Languedocien nobles; the Languedocien contingent kept somewhat separate from the main army camp, so they weren't as difficult to get to as the French commanders. Over the fortnight the army lay outside Carcassonne, Zoë dared her way ever deeper within. At last she got close enough to eavesdrop on two of Gauthier's senior knights discussing the possibility of following the Ariège river up to Toulouse, once the army disbanded in the fall.

And now winter had returned with its blessedly long nights. She felt things were coming together at last. Gauthier and his knights planned to push on to Toulouse. Isidro's monastery lay in Toulouse. Since the hapless Raymond had been excommunicated again in September for what the Church deemed insufficient enthusiasm, the standard of the cross would no doubt unfurl toward his city come spring when the army re-formed. One way or another, Isidro would surely be crowded toward the home he seemed so damnably reluctant to return to.

***

"And this is the wine you take to the donjon tomorrow?" Zoë asked, looking over the barrels. There were three of them. "So much… they will get so drunk."

The lad grinned. "Perhaps we'll be lucky and they'll drink until they pass out. Then our sénher can return and kick them out again…" It had started off as a joke, but it trailed off into a muddle of wishfulness. She smiled back but otherwise let it pass.

He changed the subject back again. "What—what about after Compline? Doesn't your uncle ever sleep?"

"Yes," she answered, flicking her gaze downward in an attempt to match his shyness. Normally that would be no trouble, but she'd found that when she was hungry she tended to stare. "He sleeps. He sleeps light, but he sleeps."

"After Compline, then. Please. Come out to the winepress house and meet me. Or I'll meet you instead, anywhere you like…"

"No, no, that will be fine," she assured him. Where indeed would be more appropriate than the winepress? If she returned tomorrow at all. That depended.

He squeezed her hand and hurried out, hastening to pay due court to his family now that he'd successfully arranged to disobey them later.

She surveyed the barrels again. The idea of spending the day in one of them didn't bother her unless she dwelled on it. In Andreas' desperately overpopulated caravan, it had been necessary to convince some of the Cainite passengers to stow themselves away for months on end in just that fashion. Great immortals sloshing around in wine or buried in salt pork… if they could bear it, she could. Nor did she worry about breaking out of the barrel. Vampire blood was good for a number of things, brute strength among them.

It was getting *in* that would be the trick. For one last instant she considered recruiting the boy's help after all. But how on earth could she convince him without explaining her true nature? And to confess all to a local mortal just before placing herself in an horribly vulnerable position, with Gauthier's knights hunkering in their stolen keep just a stone's throw away… no.

She quickly found a few cooper's tools kept by the wagons for last-minute adjustments, but had to go into the actual cooperage for the rest—a blessing as it turned out, since she also found piles of barrel-staves and dowels there. She took one of the barrels bound for the donjon and rolled it outside. She tapped the top hoops gently upward until they were just loose enough to pry out the barrel-head and quickly tapped them back down into place again once it was removed. She dumped out the wine, not without a twinge of guilt. Then she turned the barrel on its side and lay inside it for what seemed like far too long, auguring, from that awkward position, a pair of holes into the other barrel-head. Gregory had been a metalsmith, not a joiner; the only real woodworking he ever did was to create cabinets for simulacra to spring out of, or to quickly shape a tool for maneuvering some oddly shaped part precisely into place within the gearworks. Still, Zoë knew enough to be able to fashion a crude handle from a loose stave and peg it into the holes she'd made, wetting the dowels slightly to make them swell and hold.

Once finished with that, she replaced the head she'd originally removed, then removed the one with the handle, then rolled the barrel back to its place by the other barrels. The next couple of hours were spent in filling the barrel with water from the well. On a shelf in the cooperage she chanced upon a lump of beeswax, quickly divined its purpose and ran it around the rim of the barrel-head to make it slippery.

At last she gathered her courage and jumped into the barrel, holding the barrel-head—she hadn't guessed it absolutely right, there would be a gap of air between the top of the water and the barrel-head. Hopefully it was still full enough to escape notice. Then she pulled the barrel-head into place by its new handle, a thing far easier described than done. At first she thought the handle, or possibly her wrist joint, would give before the barrel-staves did. But she found if she wedged herself against them and pressed outward she could spread them very slightly. The head popped into its groove.

A thrill of pure panic, pure spinal conviction that she was buried, smothered and drowned passed through her. But as the moments passed, as air bubbled out of her lungs and water bubbled quietly in and nothing came of it, the terror gradually relaxed into a kind of exhausted triumph. She'd done it, and she'd done it alone. She had been quite clever.

Now all that remained was to wedge herself in more properly so that she wouldn't jostle when lifted, try to keep ignoring the fact that she wasn't either breathing or drowning, and wait for dawn... which, she suddenly realized, was still a good six hours away.

***

She awoke to find herself still in the barrel and still crumpled in the position she'd fallen asleep in, a good first sign. She wondered whether she'd roused because the sun had gone down, or because she'd just been dropped or man-handled. She gave herself the space of several prayers to Mary Theotokos. She didn't fall back asleep.

It must be night. She hoped it that it was night. She hoped that the mortals had been industrious and actually carried the barrels into the cellar rather than (for instance) leaving the wagon out in the courtyard. She listened carefully, but heard no sound, mortal or otherwise.

The barrel was on its side now, probably stacked with other barrels. That, too, was a good sign. She unfolded, planted her feet against the bottom barrel-head and her hands against the top barrel-head, and pushed. For a long, awful interval nothing happened even as she added the strength of blood to that of bone and muscle. At last the seam between two planks of the front head gave way with a crack. The water gushed forth and almost spilled her out with it, but she caught the edge and found her way down the stack.

It was close to pitch dark. Clearly she was in the cellar after all. She paused to wring out her skirt partway, then began feeling along the wall. Her hands encountered rounds of crusty bread and cheese on the shelves, and she saw the gleam of a beady pair of eyes as a startled rat scurried away.

Father, I'm in Gauthier's cellar! Are you watching?

The knights probably weren't all asleep yet if it was only just past sunset. Perhaps she should have waited a little longer—but six hours the previous night was quite enough. Her fingertips had withered into raisins and she felt water-logged not just in her clothes but in her flesh as well.

In any case, no one seemed to be down here. She crept out and found herself in another room, slightly less black than the first. After a moment of standing perfectly still she could see this was a little kitchen, with a well sunk into the corner and a fireplace to the side. Though it was a little warmer in here—mortals had been within, recently—she still saw no one.

Then an indistinct clamor of voices suddenly rose up from somewhere far off to the right. She leapt into hiding and waited fearfully, but it soon became apparent that they weren't getting any closer, and so she emerged and made her way through the next empty, rush-strewn chamber, finally coming to stand just aside of the doorway leading further on.

"Quiet, demon! I swear if you raise another alarm, I'll come in there and make you go up in blazes like a streak of Greek fire."

"And I proceeded to where things were chaotic. And I saw there something horrible: I saw neither a heaven above nor a firmly founded earth, but a place chaotic and horrible. And there I saw seven stars of the heaven bound together in it, like great mountains and burning with fire. Then I said: 'For what sin are they bound, and on what account have they been cast in hither?'"

Now Zoë could see the voices' source: one came from behind the door at the far end of the next room, the other belonged to the guard banging irately upon it.

"Stop it! Stop that racket now!"

"Ahh! I am visited! I am visited! The hour of my salvation is at hand!"

"Oh, for—the devil has forsaken you, wretch. Haven't you got that through your thick skull yet?"

"It comes like a thief in the night! Our Lord turned water into wine at Cana. Who is this bold apostate who now presumes to reverse the deed? Show me, O angel!"

Those words froze her to the spot.

Reverse it… wine into water?—Thief in the night!

No, that was a ridiculous notion. Impossible.

"With the Lord all things are possible," the voice trumpeted.

The guard loosened his sword in its sheath and took up his lantern. "I'm coming in, blasphemer."

It fell silent immediately.

"All right then." The weary mortal man sat back down on his bench and rubbed his forehead.

She considered for a long time. Either conclusion felt foolish. It was too elliptical to be a definite message but too relevant to be babble. Of course, one thing was quite clear, and that was that Gauthier once again had acquired a "hellspawn" prisoner.

She stared at the guard, who, despite his rubbings and yawnings, showed not a sign of nodding at his post. How best to accomplish the thing?

"Ah! Father, it's watching me!"

Gregory chuckled, though there was a note of guilt in the chuckle, and laid his hand on Zoë's head as she ran to bury her face in the folds of tunic at his hip.

"Now, now, Zoë, it's all right. It's not really watching you, I promise. Go back and look again."

But as she walked back toward it, sure enough, the Roman bust turned once more to stare at her from behind the glass in its wooden case.

"It is watching me! How does it work? Father, please teach me."

"I needn't teach you a thing, dear one. You could make this illusion yourself now." He opened the case and showed her. "You see? It's not a real bust at all, but a hollow face carved into a marble slab and surrounded with black velvet. But since you've seen marble busts before, you assume that's

what this is as well, and thus your mind can only explain the effect by saying that it must have come alive. So you see, your expectations betray you."

She fingered the inside of the hollow, then laughed delightedly, as she did whenever he showed her one of his million and one secrets.

She shook her head, unsure whether to be heartened or despondent at the sudden memory. *Very well, Father, but what are you trying to say?* Well, she could conjure an illusion to lure the guard away, a pillar of blue fire, a screeching owl, even a Cainite with fangs dripping gore. But then he would undoubtedly summon the other knights. These men served under Gauthier's command. She couldn't depend on them to panic or flee like ordinary mortals.

Your expectations betray you. What might the guard be expecting down here?

Ah, of course. She'd been thinking far too dramatically.

An odd skittering sound erupted from the corner to the guard's right, just outside the rim of his lantern-light. He started to his feet, hesitated, then picked up the lantern and went to see. The sound moved as he came toward it, leading him to peer first into the corner and then behind some old rotten sacks. Then just as he was leaning forward, he felt something scrabble partway up his leg. He gave a shout and fell off-balance, dropping the lantern, which clattered to its side and went out, darkening the room completely.

"Damned rats! And damned fool of a Picard…" She heard him gather it up again and stumble toward the stairway. "Hi up there! A light! Look alive up there, sluggards, my light's out! Hello? Anyone awake up there—"

A laugh rumbled out from behind the door.

"And *you* still that tongue if you want to keep it! *Cordieu.*" He felt his way up the stairs and was gone entirely, at least for the moment.

Well, that was even better. She went to the door and found it neither locked nor barred, which surprised her. It

72   Ravnos

opened onto blackness like that which she'd just left. The only sound was an occasional faint squeak of rope and wood. She closed the door behind her. Ah, the bar was on *this* side. She considered setting it in place and then decided against it. Where was the owner of the voice? She edged along the wall for a few feet, then grew impatient and began to step out into the room.

"No closer." It came from above her. She had a sudden awful thought of Nicholas of Béziers, now granted the power of speech, but immediately banished it from her mind.

"Can you hear me?" she murmured. She didn't know how quiet a sound she could get away with. She herself heard no better than a mortal, but many Cainites—if that's what this was—had far keener senses.

"Yes, I hear you." The voice was male. It was absurdly calm now; any calmer and she would have suspected drugs.

"Why no closer?"

"There's a… what they heathenishly call a warding circle around me, traced out in salt and fortified with relics at each compass point. Stretch your hand out a few inches and you'll feel it, like a curtain of cold flame. Stretch your hand out another few inches…"

"I take your word for it." In fact, now that he said it, she felt a stirring of cool air against her face. There were no windows in here. She stepped back.

"How did you get here? How they caught you?"

"I presented myself."

"You present yourself?" she repeated in disbelief. "You just walk up to them?"

"Of course not. I mean that I tested them." He waited, as though expecting her to understand, then seemed to re-alize she hadn't and went on in that same measured tone. "They're here in advance of the army to judge the people of Caine and all Satan's minions, so that the others need only deal with heretics. It's in God's name that they claim this power, and so their spirits must be pure in God. Therefore they had to be tested." Another pause. "They passed."

"So I see." She almost chuckled, but there wasn't a drop of humor in his tone, and certainly none in his situation. "Do you know of these knights and their ways?"

"Yes. I followed them for some time, and many things have been whispered into my ears about them. During the day I can't sleep, because of John and Anne and Gregory and... and what's the other one's name... and so I hear the knights talking through the walls."

"John and Anne and—" She almost choked on the name. "Gregory?"

"That, there, which your toe nearly trod on to its great unhappiness, that is a strip of John Chrysostom's tongue that he's been lashing me with, and St. Anne keeps jabbing me with a bit of her own rib-bone. The pope has left me in peace for the most part, but he still holds the eastern gate fast."

"The pope?"

"The sword that lies on the eastern edge. It has Pope Gregory's relic in the hilt."

"If I get you out, will you tell me more about these knights?"

"How would you get me out?"

An excellent question. She felt around and found a burnt-out stub of torch that had been thrown down on the floor. Experimentally she moved it forward, toward the chill air. Her arm trembled even as she raised it, as though from fear of even contemplating such an act, and as she brought it closer, it turned aside as though dashed against a heavy shield. Coming at it from both above and below gave the same result.

"Will you tell me about them?" she repeated.

"If you wish."

"And the ones who travel with them, the red monks?"

"Red monks..."

"Yes, monks robed in red."

A sigh. "So many churchmen are drenched in red in my sight."

Zoë scowled. "This one is called Isidro. He's tall, and he can force our kind by the cross. There may be another with him. They kill my sire," she added. She had no idea why she'd said that last. There was an intensity to his silence she didn't like. He was *listening* to her—listening so hard it almost made a sound of its own.

"And what will you do when you find them?" he asked simply.

"What do you think I do?"

"How would I know unless I'm told?"

"I *will* destroy them."

"It may be harder than you think." He was grinning now. She couldn't see it, but she knew all the same. "Wrath is not your sin."

"Is not your business," she hissed. "Will you tell me, yes or no?"

"Isidro's gone. He instructed the knights on how to bind me and then he left for home."

"This Isidro has very roundabout way of making for home," said Zoë dryly.

"There was no other monk with him under the rushes."

"What?"

"Get under one of the rush-piles in the corner, someone's coming."

Zoë hastily did so. Through the door she could hear the guardsman speaking with someone else. Then it creaked open and the clink of iron mail announced the entrance of a knight. She peeked through the rushes. It was Sénher Gauthier, hand on the hilt of his sword, carrying a torch.

At least she could see the room now. Unfinished wooden racks that looked as though they were meant to hold weapons sat along one wall. That explained the bar on the inside of the door; this must be the donjon's guardroom, but they'd cleared it out to hold their captive instead and set up the cots elsewhere. In the center of the floor lay the warding circle just as the prisoner had described it: a ten-foot circle of salt, with tiny gem-crusted reliquaries at three of the quarters and a fine, broad sword with a braided-leather pommel at the last. The floor-rushes had been shoved out to the edges of the room to accommodate it.

She could see the prisoner as well. A pair of manacles held his wrists together behind his back; the chain attached to them ran over a pulley at the top of a tall triangular wooden frame in the circle's center and then tied off in such a way that he could be raised or lowered at his captor's whim. Just now he hung a few feet off the ground. He wore a hooded cassock of dark grey sackcloth tied with a bit of rope. His white feet were bare and filthy. Blond hair that clearly hadn't seen the business end of a comb for years fell away from his dangling head in thick ropes. The face underneath was young—not as young as hers, but surprisingly young. It didn't seem to match the voice at all. With every motion or twitch he twirled slightly on the chain, so that as soon as it had appeared his countenance receded out of sight again.

"Last chance, demon," Gauthier informed the vampire curtly. "I know how to kill your kind quickly, but I'll be happy to pretend I don't." He spoke not Occitan but the *langue d'oïl*, and it was hard for Zoë to understand the exact words, but the sentiments were clear enough.

The Cainite said nothing for a moment. Then he spoke, also in the northern tongue. "It's not in Pamiers anymore. The weaver-queen has sent it on ahead."

"On ahead to where?"

"Its course will wind like the serpent's."

Gauthier stepped one foot over the salt border and brushed the torch against the bottom of his prisoner's feet, eliciting a scream. The undead skin lit like oil. It was all Zoë could do to remain frozen. She felt the start of a blood sweat on her forehead and under her shift. Gauthier then grabbed a bucket in the corner and sloshed part of its contents against the fire with a well-aimed motion, putting it out.

"That is the penalty for anything but a straight answer. We'll discover how much of you can burn before the evil spirit flees. I expect quite a lot. Now speak. Where is the she-cat sending it?"

"Out of the path of the holy army. More than that I don't know."

"We'll see about that. You said the course would wind like the serpent's. Why?"

"Because you and I aren't the only ones seeking it. I expect it will have many adventures before it meets its final fate."

"And what final fate would that be? What are the blasted heretics planning to do with it?"

"Who knows? They might lock it in a treasure-vault, or, if it proves useless to them, they might tear it up for rags for the poor or even menstrual clouts. It is nothing to them and everything to you." Such words would have been a taunt in anyone else's mouth. "If you really want it so badly, it would probably be best to approach them and offer to arrange a parley between them and de Montfort."

"Parley with Cathars," snorted Gauthier.

"Yes," replied the other quite seriously. "They're eager to negotiate after Béziers. Eager, indeed, for anyone to stand between them and the rabid hounds who kill Christian children and Cathar *perfecti* in two arcs of the same sword-stroke. Was it the children you dreamed of again last night, captain?"

"Demon!" Gauthier's voice was suddenly hoarse. He thrust the torch into the dangling legs again, nearly igniting the sackcloth. The vampire screamed unreservedly for the entire length of the prayer Zoë muttered for help.

An idea had come to her, but it wasn't near as simple as the rat-noise. As a mortal it would have taken her weeks. First an armature of brass pipes, yes, driven by air-pistons such as Philo of Alexandria had invented. Then cover it with tatters of gray and black gauze, and there should be jet-holes under some of the gauze to make it blow around; grasping wire-drawn talons, and twin fires leaping in the eyes. Then the final ingredient, which set apart Gregory's automata from all others in the Empire—the willingness to *birth* the creation and not just build it, to bestow on it a piece of one's very soul. To care as much about it as though it were a real thing, maybe even more. Her heart burned with the memory and the effort.

"Enough." The knight slumped back. He picked up the bucket and splashed the fire out once more. Then he turned for the door. "You burn for good at dawn."

Sarah Roark   77

"You're disappointing me, messire." The calmness in the vampire's voice had worn thin, but incredibly, it remained, moments after he'd stopped screaming. Only an occasional hiccough of pain disturbed his speech. "You've done so well up to now. But... a man so strong in God as yourself should know that it's God's will that I continue my work."

"It is God's will that all minions of Satan exist, yes." She couldn't see Gauthier's lips under his whiskers, but the mustache bent in what looked like irony. "Just as it is God's will that we be set against them, and this sophistry will no more avail you with me than it did with Frère Isidro."

"You are pious. But you haven't escaped the sin of pride, Gauthier de Dampiere. It blinds you to any holy labors that don't resemble your own."

Gauthier scoffed. "That could well be. But I discuss my sins with my priest and my God, not with *you*—" He froze in mid-sentence. An apparition had formed in the air before him, a ghostly but sprawling vision of a creature with black goat's head and serpent's tail and the talons of a vast raptor bird. In a flash his sword was out. The creature reached towards him. He swung at it, and it swirled away from him.

"You conjure your fellow-demons to fight me? Dismiss it, or you die now—Mathieu!"

The door opened again and the guardsman burst in the room, his sword out as well.

"Mother of God!" the guardsman rasped. After a moment of terror he made a rather clumsy stab at it with his sword. The metal slid right through it as though it were no more than mist. It roared a laugh at them. Gauthier interposed himself, menacing the thing as best he could with sheer force of spirit.

"Hold, damn you. You have no power here. In the name of the Father, the Son and the Holy Spirit, I cast you out." Indeed Zoë *felt* his menace radiating from him like the chill from the surface of a frozen lake. Only the fact that it wasn't turned directly on her saved her from fleeing and giving herself away. As it was, her "demon" fluttered and winked a bit under the assault. She gritted her teeth and willed it life.

"Listen to me, Mathieu," Gauthier said evenly. "Let the blood-drinker down to the ground."

"Why?"

"Because I theorize that cutting off his head will send this one back as well."

"Yes, captain." The guardsman edged over to the chain, stepping dangerously close to Zoë's pile en route, and un-hooked it. No sooner was he supporting the prisoner's weight in his own hands than the floating demon turned away from Gauthier and swooped down on him, enveloping him like a death-shroud. He screeched and bent over double, drop-ping the chain. The Cainite crashed to the ground.

"Mathieu—no!" shouted Gauthier. Then raised his voice yet another notch. "*Aux armes! Aux armes!*"

But it was too late. Mathieu, in a panic, had lunged headlong for the sword that lay at the circle's eastern quar-ter and now seized it, thrusting it upward into the phantasm, which crumbled completely at his assault.

In a flash the vampire was up on his feet, with his hands bound in front rather than behind. He leapt over the edge of the broken circle. Then he swept his chain around in an arc, causing it to wrap around Gauthier, and gave it a sharp yank. Gauthier crashed to the floor in a clamor of mail, but he didn't drop his sword.

"*Enfante!*" the vampire cried. "Come quickly!"

Zoë burst out of her cover. Mathieu snatched his signal horn out of his belt and blew a sharp blast on it; then he bore down on the blond Cainite, who waited for his sword stroke to begin and then edged out of its path with a motion almost too fast to see. He set a foot in the man's side and kicked him aside. Gauthier was already struggling to his feet.

"Hurry, on my back. On my back!" Zoë obeyed instantly, hoisting herself up by her arms around his neck and locking her knees to his sides so her legs would be clear of his. The Cainite then took off at inhuman speed, knocking Gauthier to the floor once again. The quick-thinking knight tried to catch at the edge of the doorway as he slid past, but didn't quite make it.

Several armed men were already in the chamber outside. The blond vampire charged heedlessly through them. Two of them dodged, hacking at him and Zoë as they blurred past—she felt a blow graze her shoulder and draw blood. The last planted his feet apart, blocking the stairway, and had to be barreled into. The shock of the impact nearly unlatched Zoë's arms. The other men followed, but the sight of their leader being dragged on a chain seemed to dismay them, or at least they seemed unwilling to risk trampling him to get to their enemy. Gauthier clutched at the leg of one of his knights.

"Hold me!" he snarled.

And so the next moment found the Cainites pinned halfway up the stairs, as several of the knights rushed to seize Gauthier and hold him fast. The blond vampire struggled against the manacles binding his hands, but to no avail. Gauthier cried out as the chain drew even tighter around his body.

Zoë leapt down, scrabbled around front and grabbed the sword from the knight they'd knocked over, which lay slantwise on the stair above him. It was long and heavy, but her desperate strength rose to match it. First she plunged it into the space between his chin and the edge of his mail coif, driving it deep into his neck. A sheet of blood flew into her face. To her it was like a dash of cool water on a hot day, giving her courage. She caught part of it in her mouth.

"Don't wiggle. Pull!" she called to the other Cainite. "Pull!"

He did so—she couldn't see the effect on Gauthier because of the two knights bearing down on her, but the chain went taut as a harp-string and she heard the mortal man cry out even more horribly.

She swung the sword wildly at her attackers; that and the obstacle of the chain held them off for a few seconds, but then one found an opening and made an expert jab that pierced her gut.

"Get him free!" one of the other knights shouted at his fellows. "His back will break!"

"No! Kill the demons!" Gauthier roared.

"Pull!" Zoë exhorted her companion, her shout tinged with pain now.

"Get him out, Baudioun! *Now!*" The other knight's voice brooked no argument.

Someone stepped on the chain near Gauthier's end. The next moment a frightful clanging rose up from among the men, and Zoë saw an axe-blade at the top of its swing emerge from their midst. The knight facing her kissed the cross-guard of his blade and murmured a prayer, then swung. She tried to raise her own blade to block him, but went about it awkwardly, and her sword was knocked aside by his blow instead, twisting her wrist almost completely around. She growled and lunged at him. He caught her by her garments and raised his sword again. The severed end of the chain went flying by their feet.

"Come on!" A flash of sackcloth; the blond vampire's still-bound hands fell over her head and shoulders, a length of chain gathered up the right fist. He tore her away from the knight and ran. With a shout the men were after them, but he was far swifter. He ran to the donjon's front door, setting Zoë down to throw the bar and pull the door open. She leaped on his back again.

The courtyard without was near-bare except for a couple of wagons. The outer gate, to their relief, had a door with well-oiled hinges set in it, and they were already through even as the watchman cried alarm. Behind them, the men poured out of the donjon, joined now by several more of their fellows; a few split off and headed for the stables, and the rest pursued on foot.

Zoë's companion carried her down into the neighboring village, where they tumbled into an empty granary bin to hide. She examined his manacles. Each was held fast by a sleeve with cross-shaped holes that fitted over the manacle's tabs, which bore matching holes; the chain then threaded through those holes and secured the entire thing. Quietly she pulled the chain out, removed the sleeves and opened the cuffs. He rubbed his wrists, grimacing. They heard horses' hooves a couple of times over the next few hours, but none that came near. At last they looked at each other and, by a nod of agreement, gave each other permission to move. They climbed out of the bin.

"Good thing it *was* empty," remarked the blond vampire, "or the fleeing vermin would have given us away—ohh!"

As each foot touched the ground it crumpled. He fell like a sack of cabbage. Zoë came over and lifted up his soles to look at them. They were singed black over much of their surface, and the rest was blistered.

"How you run on these?" she asked, amazed. He struggled up on one elbow.

"*Enfante*, in that moment I would have run on bone-splinters from severed stumps. Ahh! Don't touch."

"Well, I doubt you go further on them tonight."

"Perhaps, but we can't stay here. The knights may still be looking."

"A moment," she said, and went into the barn. The sounds of distressed livestock arose from within. She emerged with a wheelbarrow and a broken-necked goose.

"Ah, perfect," he nodded. "Like Lancelot in the cart, only humbler yet."

"Get in. I'll push you." She helped him up and over. The fantastic strength that had carried them through their escape was clearly spent, though he still spoke amiably.

"What should we make for?" she asked, thinking that she still had to retrieve her bag from where she'd hidden it at the very least, and then they should both rest or hunt, one of the two.

"Follow the footpath east out of the village," he said. "You can deliver me to my people at the wood's edge."

"What people?"

"I am fortunate enough to have some of Seth's kin that travel with me and heed my words," he explained, then finished dryly, "even when I command them to wait while I go

82   Ravnos

on alone. They'll let you drink from them, I think, so long as it's not too deeply."

As they left she peered back through the darkness toward the keep. The gate was fast shut and most of the lights put out. Her passenger bled the goose dry and then set it in his lap, absently stroking its feathers.

"You're a pitiless little girl, aren't you?" he said after a while. "*Pull! Pull!*"

"*He* was pitiless," was her only answer.

"Yes. He preferred to die rather than let us get away…" A satisfied look came over his face. "In time he could be great indeed. I must test him again some night."

"You nearly get killed testing him this time," she pointed out.

"Exactly."

"You want to be killed?"

"If God had so willed it, I would have counted it a privilege." He looked up at her. His pupils widened and caught the starlight. "But instead, He sent you to free me."

"God does not send me. I follow Isidro to Toulouse."

"Don't bother."

"I tell you it is none of your business," she began, her jaw hardening.

"I mean that you needn't bother with Toulouse. Isidro only thinks he's going home. His cloister lies in smoking ruins, raided by Fulk's disciples who go hooded in white. It happened several days ago. He just hasn't gotten word yet."

Zoë stared at him. "How you know that?"

"Because I came from that direction."

She wheeled him a little while in silence. Isidro's monastery burnt! A gratifying thought. She would have to see for herself.

"But if he cannot go home… then where?"

"Anatole."

"Anatolia?"

"My name is Anatole. What's yours?"

"Oh. Zoë."

"Ah, from the Greek. Let's see, it means…"

She hesitated a long moment, then grudgingly finished his sentence. "It means 'life.'"

"That's all right. Anatole means 'dawn'…"

"I know."

He nodded and sprawled out in the wheelbarrow. "Zoë. What about Zoë now…" For a little while his limbs dangled numbly, as though he'd gone into complete torpor.

"Paris," he mumbled at last.

"What about Paris?"

"Paris rings the changes; the stigmata bleed there. Ah yes, red for the stigmata. And the rose-gardener finds a thorn to crown his heart… and the watchman returns to his post. The children of Israel weep, and those who are consoled will not be saved, and those who are saved shall not be consoled. In a cruel world, pity is what damns a man. The masterpiece is finished at last, and a bright insect flies away, twinkling… most interesting."

She leaned over him, trying to get a look at his face. Where did this strange talk come from? Was he asleep, and talking in his sleep?

"What are you talking about?" she asked, in the clearest Occitan she possessed. He roused.

"There's another monastery of the Red Brothers at St. Denis. I remember now. Near Paris. If their house at Toulouse is destroyed, its monks might well flee there." He turned and grinned at her. "Including your Isidro."

***

It was quite well past Compline when she finally kept her appointment at the winepress, but the lad didn't complain of her lateness.

She sat with him a while afterward, savoring the warmth that spread through her limbs, watching his breathing. It seemed regular and shallow as a sleeping mortal's should. He might get too cold, though. She laid her cloak over him. Then after a little further dithering she got a length of burlap cloth from where it hung on the wall. It smelled strongly of grape must, but it was dry. She tucked it around him as well.

He stirred and looked at her. "Are you one of Herodias' women?" he asked drowsily.

"Herodias' women?"

"The *strigas* that fly at night."

She thought about that. "Yes," she said at last.

He shook his head, then reached out and touched one of her curls. "I should be angry. But maybe you'll work your devilry on the French. If you do, then I don't mind you using part of my strength to do it."

His eyes drooped shut again. She guided his head down to rest. Andreas and Meribah would have approved. For once she hadn't waited too long and gone into the killing madness. She'd taken the blood Anatole's servants offered her without losing control. She hadn't drained this boy too deeply, either, and he'd even forgiven her. She'd preserved her maidenhead from yet another attempt on it. Even by Gregory's standards, she had done well. She'd come as close to deserving her nourishment as she ever would.

She got up and walked out of the winepress house. The sky was a mottling of blue-black and grey-black; hours of darkness remained to her yet. The moon still shone. The weather was fine. She could start out for Toulouse.

She reached the fence and leaned on it with one hand. The blood all came up in a rotten flood, splashing on the defenseless ground below her. She heaved again, and there was more.

Chapter Eight

Orléans, France
Ash Wednesday, 1210

"Sundry petitioners, come to pay homage to his Highness Olderic, Prince of Cainites for Orléans and all its subject demesnes," the herald called. The man sounded a bit hoarse. It had been a long evening.

Zoë didn't deliberately put herself last in line, but somehow she ended up there. She kept her head bowed just a fraction as they walked up the aisle left clear by the other courtiers and stopped, each in turn, before the raised wooden throne. "Come to pay homage" was a rather polite way of wording it. "Caught trying to do a little quiet hunting on the outskirts and threatened into presenting themselves" was more like it, at least in her case.

The mortal man who sat on the dais' edge taking notes cast a professionally distrustful eye over them. "You will give your names."

The others made awkward, overbalanced bows, eager to prove their humility. She bent her knees in a deep curtsey, just touching the back one to the ground, the way Andreas had showed her after their audience in Sofia. It was a difficult pose to hold gracefully, which seemed to be the point.

"Yves de Quimper of Toreador, milord."

"Arnaud du Roche, milord."

"Nicolò of House Corvino, great Highness."

"Zoë of Constantinople, Your Highness."

"Very well. Rise, all of you."

There, hopefully that had been courtly enough. The prince—her very image of a Frankish invader with his long braided flaxen hair—might as well have been an icon, lead-white and staring. There was no telling from his face what he thought of his visitors or if he'd even noticed them. Then he moved and addressed them.

"Constantinople?" he began. "You're a long way from home." The syllables of his northern speech seemed to dissolve on his tongue, blurring and softening, but at least he spoke slowly.

"Yes, Your Highness." She curtseyed again.

"What brings you to us?"

"I go on to Paris, Highness."

"I see. I'm not sure that's the wisest place for a foreigner right now."

She struggled against what she would have liked to say. She didn't have the words to put it respectfully. She simply repeated, "I go to Paris."

"I see," he said again. "You didn't say what your blood was."

"I am the daughter of Gregory Lakeritos."

"Never heard of him," His Highness said flatly.

Barbarians. "Gregory Lakeritos, Wonder-Maker of Constantinople."

"That doesn't help me, *lapinette*. Where is he now? Not Constantinople, I'm sure."

Subdued chuckles erupted elsewhere in the room. The prince held up his hand, but Zoë could still feel their derision bearing down on her. She glanced around; one woman, dressed all in silk and velvet, returned her scrutiny with an uplifted eyebrow.

"No, not Constantinople. He is dead."

"Then that makes it a bit difficult to verify, doesn't it?"

"Many things are difficult since he die," she blurted. Her voice threatened to rise. She tamped it down as best she could.

His eyes narrowed, but he only said, "Calm down. Do you have anything, anything at all that could establish your identity? A letter? A token? Can anyone here speak to this Lakeritos' existence?"

"I have a token. Look, I have this token." She thrust a hand into her bag and drew out a large garnet brooch, such as might fasten a cloak shut. She fiddled with the back of it and the garnet leaped to life. An orange flame seemed to wink and burn within its depths, and once in a while it clouded over grey as if with smoke. She extended it to his Highness, who took it.

"What in Caine's name *is* it?"

"It's a brooch, Highness."

"Yes, I can see that." He poked at it gingerly, as though he expected to be burned. She thought of one of old Magda's cats pawing at something unfamiliar on the floor. "But what does it do? What is its sorcery?"

"No sorcery. Merely great cleverness. Is only beautiful." She couldn't help the pride that swelled in her heart as she said this. "Only the Wonder-Maker could make such a thing."

His Highness handed it to another Cainite that came up to stand beside him, a bearded man in a long robe. The man peered at it.

"I don't know, Highness. I doubt it's Tremere make, or even Saracen. No wizard would bend the very forces of nature to create something so useless. Such things are not to be trifled with."

The prince turned back to Zoë. His eyes were strangely alight. "If you are his childe, perhaps he taught you something of his trade."

"Yes, Your Highness. Some of it."

"Then you can create such things yourself?"

Zoë hesitated, feeling her one chance to get out unscathed vanish. She could still *explain* how the wonders were constructed, as much of it as was explainable anyway. But she had no idea how Gregory had forced his blood-strength to power brass clockwork birds so they could sing and silver rosebushes so they could bloom; and her own days of wonder-making seemed to be over now. There was still Gregory's ring, of course. She could truthfully say she'd made that, leaving out the fact that she'd still been mortal at the time. She could offer it to the prince in goodwill…

No.

"Not as yet, Highness. I was only his student."

"Of course."

"Your Highness, if I may," the bearded man said. "The girl must be lying. I see nothing here but the sign of the times: one more vagabond with a bagful of trinkets. She obviously had the fortune to cut a more exquisite purse than most."

"Cut a purse!" The words escaped her before she could stop them, and were followed by the beginning of a Greek epithet she'd heard the pimps in Constantinople use of those they felt especially unkind toward. A murmur went through the assembled crowd.

"Stop!" the prince roared. There was the force of a blow in his voice. She fell silent immediately. "It's a fair point, *lapinette*. How do we know this actually belongs to you? Can you prove it?"

"How I prove it?" she protested.

A new thought seemed to come to him then. "Well, can you even prove your legitimacy?—Yes, that's the better place to start. Let's have you recite the Traditions."

"The Traditions." Her accent was getting even worse. She looked around again, a bit wildly. No help was forthcoming. Even her fellow supplicants found other places to direct their eyes.

"Yes, the Traditions. Even in the lands of the schismatics they still respect the Traditions, do they not?"

"Of course they do." She tried to gather her thready attention. "Of course."

"The First Tradition," he prompted.

"The First Tradition… is the, the promise between Caine and his children, that binds them together."

"Yes, that's right." The prince nodded. "And the Second?"

"The Second is not to make a childe without the permission."

"I'm afraid that's the Third."

"Yes, the Third. The Second…" She knew the essentials, but she'd never learned the actual recitation. That was

Sarah Roark   89

to have been the rite marking her passage out of Gregory's charge and into her own. From the way Gregory fussed over her, she'd always guessed that night to be a long way off indeed. And Andreas and Meribah, followers of a heathen god, didn't care one jot about Caine or Abel, Jehovah or His curses, to say nothing of the six Traditions.

Nor would this prince likely listen if she tried to explain. No Cainite really *cared* how ignorant younglings came to be on their own. The simple fact of their existence was danger enough. If she wasn't "full-grown" according to the custom, then she couldn't answer for herself, and she had no sire anymore to answer for her.

Therefore her only hope now lay in remembering the Traditions. There was the Tradition against making childer. There was the Tradition against killing older vampires. That was one of the later ones, she was sure of it…

"There's your answer, Highness." The bearded man smiled. His gaze strayed to the brooch still in the prince's hands. "Surely an honest daughter of Michael's great dream-city should be able to say the Traditions both forwards and backwards."

"True enough. Well, that's that then." The prince motioned another Cainite forward, this one an armored guard. He seized hold of her arm. She gritted her teeth to avoid crying out.

"Your Highness," came a new voice.

Zoë didn't recognize it at first. But it was followed by a glimpse of spattered sackcloth and blonde hair in rattails, flashing here and there as Anatole pushed his way through onlookers to the front of the crowd. He came directly to Zoë and laid his hand on her head a moment as though to bless her. Zoë just stared at him. The guard holding her arm was quite a bit taller than herself, and had her tilted at a painful angle.

"Ah," said the prince. His tone was dry, but she also detected a note of something else within it—could it be unease? "Now the holy man is going to preach to me, I suppose, and say that to raise a hand against this girl would be

90   Ravnos

the same as raising a hand to Caine Himself, or something along that line."

"I offer no sermon, most gracious prince," Anatole answered with a low bow. "Indeed I'm sorry to speak out of turn, so soon after Your Highness' kind welcome. But I feel moved by the Spirit to offer myself as this one's sire, in plight and troth if not in blood."

"You will play the sire's part for this girl?" the prince repeated, as though convinced he couldn't have heard properly.

"I will take the sire's part, with Your Highness' kind permission, and will guarantee her good conduct by whatever means Your Highness requires."

The prince nodded slowly. "Yes. And you said you were moving on soon as well, didn't you?"

"To Paris, Highness." Anatole ignored the look Zoë threw him.

His Highness glanced at the woman in velvet and silk. "Well, what do you think, Mademoiselle Veronique? You're there much more than I."

She cleared her throat delicately. "While I do affirm to all here the wisdom of Your Highness's counsel against visiting Paris just now, if this girl insists on going, it's certainly better that someone stand surety for her. And Brother Anatole's name is not entirely unknown to me. Though it may well be so to Prince Alexander."

The prince sat back. "So be it. Then let the girl take a draught of his blood here before us, and I will have my notary make written witness of the proceeding."

"*No.*" Zoë said it under her breath, to Anatole. The guard heard it and gave her a vicious shake.

"His Highness has accepted the terms," Anatole explained, almost apologetically. "Please. I have seen it. This is not the night of your martyrdom."

A goblet was produced from somewhere and handed to Anatole. He pulled back his lips, showing a thick pair of fangs, and tore at his wrist with no more concern than if it were a leg of mutton. Deprived of a heartbeat, the blood that should have leapt out in a fountain trickled down his arm instead in a dark, twisting line. He watched it bleed into the cup, then licked the cut closed and handed her the goblet.

She took it. The metal in her hands was cold to the touch, and the edge of the pooling liquid glittered in the torchlight. She'd never been presented vitae like this, as though it were a sacrament.

She looked up. He smiled at her, not his wide madman's grin but something deeper, quieter, far more frightening. "Drink," he said. "It's for you."

What had the Apostles felt so many years ago, when their Prince of Peace over the supper table ordered them to drink blood and consume flesh? Probably something similar. She tipped the cup. The power of the liquor burned on her tongue at first, but she kept swallowing and swallowing. She felt the parched country of her gullet and innards grow lush and soft again. Mortal blood was water in comparison. In this she could taste the edge of a Templar sword, the braid of a Roman lash, the hot ripeness of Mary's afterbirth all at once. It *was* a sacrament.

And for that little space, as she handed the goblet back to Anatole, none of the rest of it mattered. Isidro and his companions, sneering Cainite lords—all were reduced to secondary figures in the panel, flat gesturers and frozen onlookers. Only she and her new "sire" moved. Only they were painted large across the scene. Anatole took the cup and bowed to her.

"Welcome."

***

"You had me where you want me," she railed at him as they finished loading up their horses. "You said you owe me. That you pay me back for helping you."

"I did the only thing I could do," the blond Frenchman answered. "I don't consider that I've repaid you yet, Zoë of Constantinople. Let's say rather that I've kept you in the semblance of life, so that I may yet have the opportunity to do so."

"Why? What are your plans? Did you follow me?"

He seemed not to hear that question, even though she repeated it twice.

"You just chance to go to Paris then," she went on at last, exasperated. "Were you not tempting the soldiers of the cross?"

"Yes, I was. But that must be put aside for a while. I have new work."

"What new work?"

"I don't know. I only know it waits for me in Paris."

"How can you do this work if you don't know what it is?"

"How can you lead a peaceful existence constantly worrying yourself with trifles?" he returned. "It's enough that I know my next step. When I get to Paris, the Lord will show me what I need. He is kind. He knows the fragility of my soul and frequently hides the rest of the truth from me until I'm ready to face it."

"I suppose the Lord told you… to speak out in court like that."

"No, that was my own idea. But Belifares approves."

"Belifares?"

"Yes, that's the one who helped you pack your saddle-bags."

She blinked. No one had helped her pack her saddle-bags. She looked around regardless, hoping for some hint of what he might be talking about.

He noted her frown and turned to her. "I'm afraid that when you travel with me you also travel with the hosts of the invisible, both good- and ill-willed. Forevermore, you will cross paths again and again with that which can neither be explained nor denied. It's annoying, I agree, but it cannot be helped. You're not the first companion of mine to suffer this fate, if that's any comfort."

The face of a mortal page appeared at the stable door. "Brother Anatole?"

"Yes? Come in, child."

The lad came to Anatole and bowed. "His Highness' seneschal has asked me to see to your supper... yours and your childe's."

Anatole looked him over. "That's very kind of him. But as you can see, we were on our way out."

"I know. His Highness is desirous that you leave on, on a full stomach." He bowed again to cover his awkwardness.

Now Anatole smiled. "I see. I wonder what he's heard. Well, never mind that. I will not insult my host." Anatole took off the lad's cap, then fed from him shallowly. The boy's legs wobbled and he took hold of Anatole's shoulder for support. When it was done, Anatole guided him over to Zoë.

"I feed last night," Zoë said, and swung up on her horse.

"That will do, child," Anatole told the page. "Thank you and your master both." He sent the boy out on unsteady feet.

Anatole got up on his mule and together they rode out through the stable yard and onto the road.

"Last night?" Anatole asked, scrutinizing her. "It can't have been much."

Zoë shrugged.

"If the boy wasn't to your liking, we can find another on the way in."

"We should get to the city first."

After a pause, he spoke again, more quietly. "I know it's easier, but you should think of others."

She stared at him. "Easier..."

"Easier when it comes as an accident. It saves you the planning, the need to acknowledge the thirst and account for it. And afterward you can say it was the Beast, not you, that killed. But you must consider whether that is worth the price you make them pay." A hint of pleading crept into his voice. "You are *thirsty*, child. Do you mean to fight that thirst forever?"

She shook her head. "I." The word broke even as it was born. She reined up so as to fall behind Anatole where he wouldn't see, wiping her eyes on the side of her hand.

94   Ravnos

She started again. "I *try* to hunt. Sometimes I succeed. But I can't—I cannot embrace it. I think it would make them happy. Even *he* would be happier I think, and so I try…"

Anatole sighed. The sigh was such a desolate sound that she came forward again to look at him. He dashed his sleeve across his cheek. Was he actually weeping, weeping for her?

He put his hand on her shoulder.

"You don't have to embrace it," he said. "You only have to do it."

The words were like a benediction. The rest of the way to Paris she felt only an odd, fleeting peace with herself and the world.

Chapter Nine

The Theodosian Abbey at St.-Denis
Candlemas, 1210

"Does it always snow like this in Paris?" Isidro asked as he came into the guesthouse, stamping and brushing his shoes against each other.

"Your wits are frozen, Spaniard," said Gervèse. He helped Isidro shrug off his cloak, then took it and flapped it a few times toward the corner. "The great rhetorician of the Laurendine would never leave me such an opening for ridicule."

Isidro laughed. "Does that mean you won't take it? You disappoint me. Very well—does it *commonly* snow so much *in wintertime*?"

"Not that commonly. This is the city's welcome to you, it seems… I'd hoped she'd muster a little more charity. But you made it in safely, thanks be to God." Gervèse deposited a kiss on each of Isidro's cheeks; Isidro returned them with vigor. "And I have a posset cooking for you on the fire. Come along and warm yourselves, all of you."

"Ah, you remind me of my duty. Pardon me, brothers." Isidro turned to his companions. "Frère Jaufres, Frère Nicholas, Frère Amaldric and Frère Esteve. This is my old friend and stalwart Frère Gervèse, who must have had quite a time convincing his abbot to take in a clutch of—"

Just at that moment he saw the stricken face of the young novice standing behind Gervèse, who shifted uncomfortably. Isidro flicked his friend a worried glance and now spotted what he'd missed before: a ring with a tiny constellation of multicolored stones set in the shape of a cross, sitting on Gervèse's finger.

"*Abba*," he cried, going down on one knee. The other monks followed suit. Gervèse reluctantly offered his ring to each of them in turn.

"One blunder after another! Forgive my clumsiness, my stupidity, *Abba*," Isidro went on. "I hadn't heard."

"Oh, get up, Isidro. I can't bear it. How could you have heard? The word went out just last week, while you were on the road. Each of the past four winters Abbé Peyre swore it would be his last. None of us truly expected him to be right this time. But this last cold snap was so cruel… it's brought death to many houses besides ours. God rest him." Gervèse crossed himself, a gesture they all echoed.

"We'll pray for him with all our hearts, and for the abbey. Still, the brothers have had the wisdom to elect you." Isidro laid a hand on his shoulder. "I don't see how they could have chosen better."

"You're letting your affection speak for your judgment," said Gervèse, "but it's good to have them both here. Come on, before icicles hang from all our noses. I'll have the wagons unloaded. How many are there?"

"Just the one, I'm afraid." Isidro motioned for the others to come along as they made their way to the fireplace.

"Just the one!" Gervèse gave him a horrified glance. "And the rest? The library?"

"I don't know. Possibly burned to the ground, for pure spite. I'm doing my best not to dwell on it."

"Then let's not speak of it till tomorrow. Tears and posset don't mix very well."

All at once Isidro hesitated. For a moment Gervèse wondered what the matter was; then he realized Isidro the count's son was waiting for Gervèse the fuller's son to take the seat of honor by the fire. He shook his head as he sat.

"I'll never get used to it."

"Nonsense. You've gotten used to far stranger." Isidro arranged himself gratefully in another chair.

"I suppose that's true. Was the journey hard?"

"Frightening in the beginning, tedious in the middle, cold at the end. At least we were allowed to leave in peace, once they saw we didn't have any Cathars stuffed into the crypt."

"Yes, they let you leave so they could help themselves to the candlesticks and altar furnishings," Gervèse growled. He waved away the novice and poured out the bowls of posset himself, so as to occupy his hands. "No doubt Abbé Bernard will be vindicated and someone or other sharply punished, but you'll never see a pennyworth of reparations. The price of rooting out heresy."

"They can have the candlesticks," said Isidro morosely. "Drink up, brothers, take off the chill. You're very kind, Gervèse. I hope there's room?"

"Of course. Don't worry. Even if there weren't room, there'd be room, but in this case there really is." He paused. "When you wrote, you said you weren't at the Laurendine when they raided it."

Isidro looked down. "No."

"He reproaches himself for it constantly, *Abba*," said Frère Jaufres.

"Well, he's like that," said Gervèse. "Where were you, Isidro?"

"With Sire Gauthier and his men."

"Still? What on earth happened after I left the two of you in Arles?"

"Well…" Isidro shifted in his chair. "Remember, we'd decided to stay and learn what we could about the war and its likely course."

"Yes, I hear the Templars told Bishop Fulk what he could do with his mandate."

"They did. But then Gauthier asked permission to travel with the army regardless. He was worried what the agents of the Enemy might do to repel the Church's assault."

"Sensible enough."

"And I believe he also had some other purpose. He was close about it, but he spoke darkly of Cathar connivers and thieving Abbé Martin."

"Abbé Martin…"

"The one who plundered the holiest relics of Constantinople," Isidro reminded him.

"Ahh. So you think Gauthier is hunting relics again."

"Yes, but as I said, he wouldn't speak much of it even to me, so this time it must be something very important indeed."

"And yet you came along."

"Well. The army and Gauthier were… already headed west," Isidro said with more irony than really became a monk. "Once we got back into the Toulousain I went home of course, but a few times afterward he asked me back out to help him with this or that. That's why I was away—"

"This or that?" Gervèse lifted an eyebrow.

"He wanted me to bless some oils for him before the army took Carcassonne. Then a few months later he actually caught a Cainite in a gray monk's habit and had a little trouble containing it."

"In a monk's habit! Is there no end to the blasphemy?"

"Evidently not, *Abba*."

"Sounds like he kept you busy. A wonder you bothered going home at all."

"He certainly didn't want me to leave," Isidro remarked. "In fact, on the last occasion he almost begged me not to. The man seems to think some unseen power of hell is shadowing me."

"Is it?" Gervèse brought these relatively light words down to earth with his leaden question.

"*Abba*." Another brother was in the doorway, ducking his head.

"Yes, come in, man. What is it?"

"There are two nuns at the gate asking for you."

"Now? Why? Is someone ill?"

"They're—they're not of our order, *Abba*. They look like Benedictines, but there's something odd in their garb, I don't know quite what to…"

"Did any of them give a name?" Isidro broke in. The monk stared at him, but something in Isidro's smooth, calm voice seemed to settle him out.

"Oh. Yes, they did," he answered. "Soeur Cecilia, companion in Christ to Mère Teresa, abbess of St. John the Divine at Tyre."

"What!" Gervèse stood.

"The abbess is *here*?" Isidro asked.

"No. But Soeur Cecilia bears a letter from her. The other nun is called Soeur Faustina."

"Soeur Cecilia… Gervèse, isn't that the one who wrote you about that creature we found in Brittany several years back?"

"Well, don't just stand there," Gervèse admonished the monk. "We're already in the guesthouse. See them in. Let's find out what they want."

Once the monk was gone, Gervèse resettled himself. He glanced warily at the four who stood nearby, then looked at Isidro again.

"She has written me more than once," he said at last. "Both to ask and to give advice."

"About our work, I presume."

"Yes. But what's she doing here now? She's a contemplative."

"Who knows? I expect she'll be happy to tell us."

Amaldric and Esteve, both less than two years out of their novitiates, shifted nervously and hid their hands in their sleeves; they knew the others tended to scrutinize them most closely for signs of weakness in the face of temptation.

When the nuns were brought in, however, there seemed little to be tempted by at first. They were both swathed, gloved and muffled in heavy hooded cloaks. Gervèse went to greet them, stopping a bit before them and offering a bow as they curtseyed low. They doffed their hoods. They were dark-eyed, and the similarity of their expressions might have made them sisters. But one was a plump, comely young woman with cheeks stung red by the wind; the other in her middle years, her sharper-planed face saved from severity by its fine brows and its lips bent in the faintest hint of a smile.

"Sisters."

"My lord abbot." The older of the two spoke. "We thank you most humbly for your kindness in receiving us. We carry a letter to you from our superior, Teresa of the convent of St. John the Divine in Tyre." She took it out of her pouch and handed it to him. He jounced it in his hand a bit, as though trying to judge its literal or figurative weight.

"And do you know the content of this letter?" he asked.

"Yes, my lord. She speaks of many visions, troubles she believes may face your house in the near future—troubles from the servants of the Pit. She also meekly requests that you permit Soeur Faustina and myself to remain in Paris for a time."

Gervèse frowned and cracked open the seal. "In Paris? Might I ask what about Paris piques her interest, or yours?"

Cecilia's eyebrows lifted slightly. "We come at her bidding, my lord. She tells me we're needed here, that the hour grows dark. And so here I am. I must warn you that the mother abbess' visions are often of such a nature that their purpose cannot be put into so many words. But I trust in them absolutely. I believe that the Lord speaks through her, and so to disobey her in such a thing would be to disobey the Lord Himself."

Faustina nodded in reverent agreement.

"And your own insights?" he asked them.

"I myself have had no visions on these particular subjects, my lord abbot," Cecilia answered, "but I will let you know at once if any come."

"And, regrettably, I have never possessed the gift of visions," said Faustina. "I simply attend Soeur Cecilia. I see to the particulars of this world so that she may concentrate on matters of the spirit."

"Very well." Gervèse skimmed over the letter, then put it away. "I'll give the Reverend Mother's words my full attention. You're more than welcome to stay in the guesthouse tonight if you want to keep out of the snow, or if you'd rather press on I would also be happy to have you escorted to the sisters' house."

"I see." Cecilia nodded. "Then even St.-Denis is no longer a double monastery?"

"No, the Red Sisters have been moved out to their own house within the walls of Paris."

Isidro watched this exchange with interest. When the pope ordered the abbots to dissolve the double houses of the Red Order, it was largely the brothers that got to stay and the sisters that had to move; and while the abbots had made some effort to divide up the libraries among the split houses, they'd done little to insure that the division was an equal one. Isidro hadn't yet seen the sisters' new house in Paris, but he did not need the gift of visions to guess that it was probably smaller and meaner than their former quarters. As a Benedictine nun, Isidro doubted Cecilia would feel as bitter about it as did the Red Sisters themselves. Yet there was a distinct note in her voice that suggested her sympathies.

"We will go there, then. My deepest thanks, my lord abbot." Cecilia curtseyed again, Faustina following suit.

"Think nothing of it, sister. Our colleagues in God's service are always welcome among the Order. Come, brothers, let's retire to the cloister and get you settled in. Frère Guillaume, please assist the sisters."

"Of course, *Abba*."

***

"I wonder what it all means." Isidro opened his book chest and began checking on the condition of his precious tomes. He also unwrapped a ground crystal lens from its packing of straw and wool, studying the little pool of concentrated candlelight it gathered into his hand with satisfaction.

"They'll tell us when they're good and ready to, I expect," said Gervèse.

"You think they'd hold anything back?"

Gervèse shook his head. "I'm sure Soeur Cecilia would gladly walk into the proverbial lion's den if the abbess asked it of her, so it's quite possible she really does know nothing. But it would be unlike her to lack, at the very least, an instinct."

"Perhaps she doesn't always trust her instincts," Isidro murmured. "There are certainly times when it's better not to follow them. That the oracle of Tyre sends her and Soeur Faustina here just when I also arrive on your doorstep, however, that worries me. I hope I haven't brought trouble to you."

"What kind of trouble could you have brought?" The abbot tried to make it sound dismissive. "The White Brotherhood will hardly follow you to Paris."

"Yes, I know, but they wouldn't have to. If it turns out that Abbé Bernard is not vindicated after all…"

Gervèse turned back to Isidro at that.

"Why wouldn't he be vindicated?" he asked slowly. "Brother, surely you don't mean there's an iota of truth to it."

"The Abbé a heretic? Of course not. You've seen him preach against the *bonshommes*. But his object was always to convert, not to destroy. Destruction apparently being the order of the day—"

"You're saying he *did* shelter them. They weren't stuffed in the crypt, but he found some other hiding place on the abbey grounds."

"I've said no such thing." Isidro's eyes, dark as currants, seemed to go even darker. Gervèse had, on occasion, suspected a strain of the Moorish in Isidro. Whenever his face went solemn the idea particularly compelled.

"Or did he robe them as novices? My God, Isidro."

"The Abbé has always acted from the very spirit of Christ." Isidro unintentionally raised his voice for just an instant; he got up and shut the chest as though that would choke off the protest in his own heart.

"Acting from the spirit of Christ can look a lot like softness toward heresy, in the wrong light," Gervèse reminded him.

"My point is, should Abbé Bernard be condemned, or— or should he not live even to gain a hearing before the Holy Father, it may be that your having received us will look ill to the king, and to Rome."

"Well. If the master of the Laurendine is condemned, no brother or sister anywhere is safe anymore." Gervèse went over to him and squeezed his shoulder. "None of this moping, Isidro. Your companions are looking to you for hope and courage. Let me worry about the price of looking after you, should there be any, and you look after them."

"And who will look after you, old friend?" Isidro inquired with a slight, wry smile.

"The Lord, of course."

"Then let us hope His favor will be even more bountiful than usual." The Spaniard hesitated. "When we were in Bergamo, you received a letter you didn't show me. Was it from Soeur Cecilia?"

"It wasn't you I was thinking of. Prior Ugo is a staunch zealot against the Enemy's soldiers on earth, but he also—"

"Leaps to the presumption of evil where there is none," Isidro finished. "And the virtue of forgiveness...if I can be forgiven myself for judging him so... could bloom more abundantly in his nature. I understand."

"If you want to see the letter, I have it in my study. It's all information after the fact, I'm afraid, but you're welcome to it."

Isidro held up a hand. "Brother, I'm quite confident neither of you has written a word that Benedict would have shamed to say to Scholastica or Monica to Augustine. Be at peace." Gervèse subsided, although peace seemed to elude him; he twisted the ring on his finger fitfully. "Besides, how could there be any scandal in it? You'd never even met her before tonight, had you?"

"No. No, I'd never heard of her before she wrote us with that warning back in Brittany. I still have no idea how she knew my name or where to reach me."

"Teresa is the same way, they say. If the sisters of Tyre feel there's work for them here in Paris, no doubt they know their business. And I daresay the Red Sisters in the city will put them up gladly enough."

"I daresay."

"I should let you attend to whatever other business awaits you before the office, my lord abbot. I'm all settled here. My belly is full of warm posset, and my feet are nearly dry."

"All right. I'll have more candlesticks brought to you, and pen and parchment in if you want it."

"Thank you, yes. I have a few letters of my own to write."

"Then God grant you your ease until we speak again."

"And you, my friend." Isidro saw Gervèse the two paces' length to the door of the cell and watched his broad back disappear down the hall.

And God look after you, indeed, and all of us, he thought. *I have a feeling we'll sore need it before long.*

***

"So those are the adventurers of the Red Order," said Faustina as she unpacked Cecilia's breviary and handed it to her.

"I don't know if 'adventurers' is the right word," the older woman demurred. "My impression's always been that they were drawn by fate to their battle, rather than seeking it out."

"The mistress of the novices at my old convent always said the Red Order had one foot on the Christian side of the Bosporus and the other on the heathen side."

"Well, that's true enough. I understand there's a community at Antioch and at Tripoli. What of it? We live in Tyre. If you're casting aspersions on their orthodoxy, Soeur Faustina, you know I can't be party to it."

Faustina only smiled. "Abbé Gervèse is older than I imagined him."

"No doubt he's seen many cares. My—it's cold in here. This must be the windward side of the house."

They both looked around. Convent training had long ago schooled them out of anything like disappointment at meager accommodations. What disturbed them more about the Red Sisters' house was that it was built nothing like a proper convent. It must have been some wealthy burgher's or widow's home once, donated to buy a shorter stay in purgatory. The remnants of a fresco (luckily nothing more worldly than a birds-and-vines theme) could still be discerned on the outer wall of Soeur Cecilia's cell, but it was rudely interrupted halfway through a peacock's tail by one of the new walls that had been added to create enough cells for the twenty sisters. Sleeping in such a room one would feel more like a lady's handmaid currently out of favor than a bride of Christ.

"I'll get something to warm the room, sister."

"No, don't! Don't complain on my behalf, for goodness' sake. There's a pair of spare blankets in that trunk. That should do us well enough. I'm so tired I think I could sleep out there in the snow." She covered her mouth for a yawn, then started to unpin her veil.

"As you wish. Will you be needing anything else, Soeur Cecilia?"

"No, Soeur Faustina, I don't believe so. Thank you."

"Sister…" Faustina paused in the doorway, her round face sobered by concern.

"Yes?" Cecilia looked up.

"Does it not trouble you that we've been sent all this way to help these men?"

"Not at all. I've heard nothing but good of Frère Isidro, and I tell you emphatically that Abbé Gervèse is a man of the most impeccable character and a devoted brother in the service of God. Whatever evil we face now, we have stalwart allies at least."

"Yes, sister, I know."

"Then what is it?"

"Nothing, sister. I've never been so far from home before. If I don't sleep well, you may have to pinch me to keep me awake in services."

Cecilia chuckled. "Not once the singing starts, I won't. You and I both know that. God grant you good rest, sister."

"And you." Soeur Faustina ducked her head in a quick farewell and left.

***

An ancient spider squats before of a row of tall wooden racks outside his cottage. Each rack has several loose skins hung on it to dry, the poles of the rack threaded through the eyeholes and the empty tubes of the limbs draped and wrapped round to splay them out. She walks along the row. Some of the skins are of men and women, some are of beasts, wolves and basilisks; some are like human beings but too long, or oddly colored, or traced all over with spiraling designs.

"Which will it be today?" she asks him.

"Whichever you least expect."

She nods and walks away. She sees something glistening in the dirt of the forest path and bends over to pick it up. It's an openwork pewter pilgrim's badge, a large Roman X set inside a circle. Stamped around the circle's edge is TEMPUS SATIS NUNQUAM EST SATIS. The beginning and end of the phrase touch at the bottom. She longs to turn it over and see what lies on the other side but is too afraid. She begins to cast it aside.

"You'll bitterly regret it if you do," says a voice. "No, you want to hold onto that while you can." Just off the path she spies a gray fox. It stares at her. Its eyes are sky-blue.

She reads the words aloud to it. "Tempus satis nunquam est satis tempus..."

"Yes. Time enough is never enough time."

"But why?"

"You are a woman with a hand with five good fingers," it says. "When you can grasp, you grasp, and when you must let go you let go. To be otherwise you'd have to have grown from a different seed and been nourished in a different water, like this holly that grows along your path."

She stares at the bushes. "And then I would bear poisonous fruit."

"Yes, you would. But you'd also grow alongside the path and watch its traffic for age upon age. Nothing that went on in the world would be unknown to you, for there is no mystery that doesn't pass this way."

"What about you?" But she can see the dark red of berry-juice on its lips.

"You're the one that made me a fox, Cecilia, my Inspiration. You tell me."

"The fox both hunts and is hunted."

"Exactly. When we meet again, may you choose as well."

"I don't wish to meet you again."

"Nonsense. We must both do our duty." It grins at her, jagged red-stained teeth showing, and then turns with a flash of its tufted tail and is gone.

Chapter Ten

Paris, Ile de la Cité
The Night After St. Blaise's Feast, 1210

"How long we have to wait, messire?" asked Zoë in the humblest tone she could call forth.

The scourge, who despite his fearsome title was actually a rather skinny and inoffensive-looking young man in modest clothes, twisted his pale lips thoughtfully.

"However long His Highness pleases. More than a couple of hours, less than a week, I expect."

"I only ask because I wonder, would it be possible to get a bowl of water? I wish to make myself presentable to the great prince."

"Ah. Of course." The scourge nodded, approving now, then cast a doubtful glance at Anatole, who knelt on the floor in an attitude of prayer.

"Thank you, messire.—And some scissors," Zoë added in an undertone.

The scourge nodded again and left. Anatole looked up suddenly.

"Scissors…?"

But Zoë said nothing until the requested things were brought in by a mortal attendant.

"Scissors?" Anatole repeated, following her as she went to the bowl and splashed her face and arms clean.

"Think of it as tonsure," Zoë said.

"John the Baptist never had a tonsure."

"John the Baptist wind up with his head on a plate because he did not impress King Herod. Your lice will become man-eating monsters that scare vampires. Sit down."

"Oh, all right. It'll all grow back tomorrow anyway."

she would some night have it from the Red Brothers whose fault this all was in the first place.

"I… most humbly beg pardon, messire," she said. "I pray you please…though I do not deserve, please forget your anger against me which is just."

The scourge visibly considered. "I forgive you," he said at last, in a far more formal tone than he'd taken yet. "I will bear you no ill will."

"I am in your debt," Anatole said just as gravely, completing the ritual.

The scourge gave a brisk nod then. "In the Bière Forest, a good mile in down by Milly-la-Forêt, there's an abandoned hunting lodge. That's the seedling for the fragrant little flower that is the refugee camp. Leave here at sunset sharp, go directly there, feed once as you need on the way and no more. After that, you may only hunt in the camp's territory, which I trust they'll show you."

"Come, *enfante*." Anatole squared his shoulders and offered Zoë his hand, like a knight about to lead his lady to table. "We go where the Lord calls us. There can be no better destination."

She straightened, brushed off her dingy overtunic where her knees had touched the floor with it, and went to his side.

We are even now for certain, he and I, she thought uneasily.

***

"It's all right, Folcaut. Approach."

Bishop Antoine stood at the window. White moonlight fell on him in a curtain, rendering him in absolute contrasts: pearlescent skin, rich purple robes, sharp black shadows. Folcaut often wondered if the bishop simply enjoyed a God-given gift of elegance, or if his every waking motion was calculated for effect. In either case, there was nothing to condemn in it. It served him well in his calling. The flock usually did not have the wisdom, at first, to see the grace within. Fishers of men must bait their hooks.

Folcaut came to his superior's side and went down on one knee to kiss his ring. The bishop bit his fingertip and swabbed a bit of his vitae across Folcaut's brow.

"May you be replete with the glory of His shining blood, my son."

"Your Grace," Folcaut murmured.

"How do you find your work in Paris of late?" the bishop asked.

"We have gained another half-dozen of Seth's kin and given them their first consolation in blood, my lord. They in turn have offered of themselves freely and with joy."

"Praise be unto God." Antoine glanced down at the gaunt, kneeling figure. "Rise, my son. And of Caine's lost children?"

Folcaut rose. He could feel the ash-dry skin of his forehead gradually absorbing the blood; it left a pleasant warmth behind as it disappeared. "None this month, my lord. I still believe that Gerthrude will come to us in time, but something holds her back yet, most likely her sire. The others... remain even more reluctant."

"That sounds frustrating."

"I can only keep working in patience, and pray Caine softens their hearts to the Word."

Antoine nodded. He went over to his writing desk and toyed with a parchment there.

Folcaut held his tongue, but when Antoine did not speak for some time he cleared his throat. "News from the Languedoc, my lord?"

The bishop put the parchment down again at that. "The time of our testing has come."

"The prophecies?"

"Some of the prophecies worry me, yes. Some are only the vomitus of fools that other fools take for nourishment. Prophecies come cheap in such an age as ours. What I meant is that we French have too long taken the strength of our faith in this world for granted, because of the great success it's had in the Languedoc. We've stood on the shoulders of our southern fellows and called ourselves tall. That must

end now. We must take up the oriflamme that has fallen to the ground and been trampled in martyrs' blood."

"Yes, my lord." Folcaut knew he hadn't been called in to play trial audience to a sermon. He stood in perfect patience, hands demurely folded.

Which, paradoxically, prompted the bishop to come to the point. "I want you to go to the camp."

Folcaut's brow creased slightly. "As you wish, lord, but I... that is, I understood that there already were believers in the camp."

"That is a rumor."

"Yes, lord."

"We can have no idea of the truth of it without seeing for ourselves. Certainly no one of the camp has approached me to enter the obedience of our diocese. And so I send you to them. If there are true believers after all—or even believers of a debased sort who will consent to be corrected—then they can serve as your leaven."

"And if not?"

"And if not, then you shall preach to them. Our Cainites in the city are so comfortable, Folcaut."

"Yes, that is true." Folcaut rolled this around in his mind, considering it from various angles. "They are thoroughly ensnared in the flesh. They have no idea why they should hollow themselves out. The blood they drink gluts their souls rather than cleansing them, and so they cannot conceive of the joy of becoming the empty vessel of the shining blood. But these refugees have suffered."

"They have starved. In body and spirit." Antoine smiled.

"Blessed are they who hunger and thirst..."

"Perhaps they are ready to be filled. Will you agree, then?"

"Even if I didn't I would go where my bishop commands me, of course. But yes. I agree."

Antoine put a firm hand on his shoulder. "Bless you, my son. And may Caine in His grace and mercy look upon your efforts with every favor. Go now to my deacons. They will assist you. Purify yourself and pray. Tomorrow night, we will consecrate you to your new purpose."

"Yes, my lord." Folcaut bowed his way out.

Antoine picked up a little brass bell that lay on his desk and rang it. A few seconds later, an altar boy in acolyte's robes ran in, huffing.

"Your Grace?"

"Call the priests, the deacons and subdeacons, the acolytes and the *capellanus*. Tell them to ready the font and dress the chapel. I officiate tomorrow night."

"At once, my lord." The boy bowed his head, then hesitated. "Which—which font, my lord?"

"The great gilded one," the bishop answered. "And tell them to be sure the congregation is of a size to fill it."

Chapter Eleven

The Bière Forest
Feast of St. Vedast, 1210

When one went to the cities of the Franks and gazed on their great buildings, cathedrals especially, the eye started at the base and was quickly drawn up by lines leaping on high into graceful spires and towers. Which had surprised Zoë at first; her original impression of the Franks had been of armored beasts with no skyward yearnings at all, arsonists and plunderers.

Here the eye started at the ground, tried to rise and kept getting weighted back down again. Some effort had been made to push the rubbish into piles away from the outer ring of twig shacks and wattle-and-daub huts. Nevertheless, sucked-on animal bones, rag scraps, shards of drinking cups badly fired in the reeking pit-kiln on the camp's outskirts, and other listless bits of residue littered the floor of the clearing wherever they'd happened to rain down. The eye was compelled to spend much of its time turned downward simply for the sake of the hapless feet.

Anatole offered her a hand. She gave him a nod but refused to take it. It was just the two of them. Anatole had debated with one of his unseen partners as to the wisdom of bringing his little clutch of mortal followers into the camp; then he'd pronounced something about sowing wheat among the tares, called them all together and commanded them to disperse as they saw fit within the city and its environs— including the villages along the edge of the forest.

She walked on into the camp, breaking stride only to step around some foulness. She could already feel the slurry descend upon her soul again, settle on it like a coating of wet ash.

"You were right. No better."

"I don't wash my hair because I forget to," he said. "I become preoccupied."

She looked at him, wondering why the sudden reproach. His hair had all re-grown to its former length with a single day's sleep, and truth be told, it was beautiful. Fine strands of gold fell in a wind-ruffled curtain around his shoulders. "Yes, and?"

"That's because I'm a distracted fool. But I don't think these people are preoccupied, though some may tell themselves they are." He frowned, surveying the garbage as though it were some kind of tally that could be accounted. "They don't pick up the camp because it'll only get dirty again."

"If you think that way then nothing ever get cleaned up," she pointed out.

"Exactly. That's the trap of despair. I suppose Michael's wings were meant to carry him far from it."

They were coming up on the first little knot of inhabitants. Zoë flapped her hand at Anatole to signal that he should be quiet now. Was it always his habit to speak of folk the same way whether they were there or not?

One of the knot walked toward them, a tall thin Cainite in the robes of a Greek monk. He had a mortal novice at his side.

"Michael sang a potent lullaby," the monk said. "A few have tried to lull them back to sleep since, but never with such success. And no one's been able to explain to them yet that dreaming and waking, agony and bliss are the rightful cycle of existence on this earth."

"Exactly," said Anatole again, looking somewhat surprised.

"The trash, I keep clearing it away. So do some of my colleagues. We just can't seem to outpace the chaos. There's too many of the despairing, as you say, in too small a space."

"You should leave them, or kick them out," said Zoë.

"Have you no pity?" the monk asked her.

"They are waiting to die. It would be better if they went alone to do it. They only stay because they like to make others suffer too."

"No, she hasn't much," Anatole said wryly.

"I see your face before," Zoë suddenly realized. The monk smiled and answered her in Greek.

"It hardly becomes me to say that I remember yours as well, but I do. One cannot help noting anyone who travels in the company of the Wonder-Maker."

"He is dead," she said, also in Greek, to forestall the obvious question.

"I see." The monk fiddled with the end of his prayer rope. The tic seemed vaguely sacrilegious to Zoë, but since he didn't seem even to be aware that he was doing it, she decided to extend speculative forgiveness for it.

"Once upon a time," the monk began again, "I would have said he'd met the fate to which his choice doomed him. We were such idiots. I can only beg pardon of you, his daughter."

No one had begged her pardon for anything in quite some time. She hesitated, then said, "There's nothing to forgive. My name is Zoë."

"My name is Brother Gerasimos. This is Nikodemos." He gestured at the mortal, who began an obsequiously deep bow. Gerasimos stopped him with a hand on the elbow.

"No, no—Nikodemos. Excuse him, both of you. I remind him again and again not to make the old reverences to Cainites anymore, but habits die hard. You," he said, turning to Anatole, switching back to the *langue d'oïl*. "You look like some sort of Latin clergy, but I can't quite make out. Forgive my rudeness in not knowing how to address you."

"Anatole, that's all. If I annoy you, you can call me sinner or wretch. It will do me good. But you, brother, are plainly a monk of some Greek sort."

"Yes." Gerasimos hesitated. "I... I believe that I am. The monks of my order were called the Obertus in centuries past, then the Gesudians. Of course, it—hardly matters now. There is no Gesu and no Obertus."

"Come," Anatole reproved him easily. "Every saint dies eventually. Don't lay your own doubts on the departed."

Sarah Roark   119

"I know." Gerasimos was staring at Anatole in a way Zoë had begun to recognize. "I think… I'm sure that I no longer follow my grandsire." The words seemed to cost him a great deal. "Yet I continue to wear the habit. I tried once to put it off, but the worldly garments felt like lye on my skin."

Anatole put a hand on his shoulder.

The sound of pounding hoofbeats arose out of the trees. A crowd of eight horsemen thundered up to them. Zoë stumbled back a step toward Anatole. The foremost of the riders was her exact vision of a savage young Turk: light golden-brown skin, a long thin nose opening into a pointed flare at the bottom, and narrow-slitted eyes set high up under the brows. His fur-lined coat and cloak splayed wildly back as he rode. Slung over his saddle lay a terrified boy, bound hand and foot, whose bumpings and jostlings the Turk steadied only partly with his left hand. One of the other riders looked like a Byzantine. The rest were assorted Bulgars, Slavs and Franks that the refugees must have picked up somewhere en route. They too bore prisoners on their horses. Zoë could see and hear, off in the woods, the beginnings of a contingent on foot arriving as well.

"Ah, Iskender," said Gerasimos in Greek. "I see the hunt was successful."

The Turk snorted. "By this time next year we'll have to ride to Aachen to find fresh vessels. This village had word of us, or at least they had pointed pikes set all around for us to run into in the dark. I lost two horses tonight. If Bardas doesn't start setting rations…"

"Bardas enjoys the influence he does partly because he refuses to set rations," Gerasimos interrupted.

Zoë found herself unable to look away from the blue stare of the boy. He had plainly cried multiple times in the last hour. His eyes and cheeks were red, swollen and windburned.

"You can hide the disease, but you can't hide the death." The Turk now reined back to look at Zoë and Anatole. "Who are these? More *Franj* rabble? That's the other thing to set a

120   Ravnos

limit on, I tell you. No more Cainites unless they bring five healthy vessels apiece."

"You can say it and I might even agree, but he'll never believe you until you fail at the hunt, and you refuse to do that. This is Anatole and this is Zoë, daughter of Gregory the Wonder-Maker. She was with the pilgrimage before you were, Iskender."

"And now she's back?" The acridity of the question snapped her head up to meet his curious gaze. She scowled.

"I belong here as much as you do," she retorted. "These are the survivors of Constantinople. Are you from Constantinople?"

"City princess, I *feed* this camp."

"Yes, I see how you feed this camp."

"And how would you do it? Send a letter to the French king demanding a blood-tribute, or else the might of Byzantium will sweep down upon him?" Iskender cast his hand across the unprepossessing scene.

"Come, Zoë." Gerasimos gestured for her hand. "Many things have changed since you left. Most of those whom you knew as leaders in Adrianople are dead or gone, and so you must be presented all over again. And your friend as well, of course."

"And who is leader?" asked Anatole—in heavily accented Greek, to Zoë's astonishment. "This Bardas?"

"I wish I could say there was one who truly led," Gerasimos answered as they began picking their way toward the center of the camp, where the decrepit hunting-lodge that the scourge had described stood. "Bardas has influence, yes. There are several others. Malachite and Verpus came back to us for a time. It was by their command that we left for Paris in the first place—"

"I know," said Anatole. "And now they have left again?"

"We tried to take ship in Ragusa." Iskender snorted; Gerasimos ignored him. "For months we gathered together all the money we could. Twice we found someone who took an advance fee and said he would carry us when the winds became favorable, and we would wait and wait for that, and then just when the weather turned he would go back on his word. The Venetians are against us, I think. And so we started up the coast instead. Then in Zara Malachite had a letter from someone, and he and Verpus left without a word that same night. Bardas says that Malachite chose him to lead the pilgrimage in his stead… but, of course, this appointment was not made before witnesses…"

Anatole nodded. A collection of sullen-looking mortals and Cainites sat on the ground or on crude mats around the lodge, several of them playing at dice and others sharing a wineskin, so that one had to walk through a gauntlet of wary glances just to get inside. Zoë and Anatole entered and waited in the cool dimness for their eyes to adjust. Gerasimos followed. Iskender dismounted outside and came in as well, still bearing his mortal prize.

Once upon a time this must have made a fine place for a minor lord's feasting. There was a great smoke-black hearth with a bit of a fire currently going in it—glorified coals, really; a bit of old scarred stump for fletching; quivers hanging on hooks and unstrung longbows in their sleeves propped up against the wall; and several log benches and trestle tables, only one of which was actually set up at the moment. However, the place had obviously been left to rot by its human masters some time hence. While its new denizens had tried to patch it up, particularly where sunlight could threaten, even Zoë could see that the daubing they'd used was poorly mixed and starting to crack. Someone had built a sort of brick vault on one end of the room, of the wrong shape and in the wrong spot to be an oven; she presumed it to be sleeping quarters for the undead, and hoped its mortaring was sterner than the wall-daub at least.

At the standing trestle table sat an informal assembly of four Cainites, before which Gerasimos and Iskender bowed. Zoë and Anatole followed suit, not having the faintest idea whom specifically of the group to direct their courtesy toward. Neither end of the table was occupied, only the long side, and with four sitting, there was no central place of honor there either.

"Gentlemen, milady," said Gerasimos to them in the *langue d'oïl*. "We have a pair of new arrivals who wish to present themselves."

"Plainly," said one of them. He was a stocky, curly-haired man of middle age and middle height, wearing what Zoë recognized (to her amusement) as Frankish garments that someone had tried to render more Byzantine by sewing panels of brightly colored fabric onto them. "What are your names?"

"Anatole of Paris, my lord, and this is my childe Zoë."

Gerasimos made a little murmur of surprise.

"Do you claim a clan?" the man asked bluntly.

"It rather claimed me, lord. My blood is the blood of Malkav. It was Gregory Lakeritos, a name I trust you know, who first Embraced Zoë; but since his death she has kindly permitted me to continue her education. She is pledged to me, and I take sire's responsibility for her."

"Gregory the Wonder-Maker… I wish you'd brought your real sire back instead, Mademoiselle Zoë. We could have found practical uses for that pretty craft of his. Well! You have company at last, Iskender. You're no longer the only Ravnos in the camp. I suppose congratulations are in order."

Zoë said nothing. She was caught perfectly suspended between annoyance at this man's belittling of both Anatole and Gregory in the same breath, and shock at the word *Ravnos*—a word she'd not heard since the night of her first rising in the Blood. Out of the corner of her eye, she saw Iskender turn to gape at her. She didn't turn toward him.

"Be welcome, both of you," the man went on. "Make yourselves comfortable however you see fit, so long as you make yourselves useful as well. I am Bardas, of the old Senate, and these are Helena of the Antonians, Urbien of the Baron's Gangrel, and Gallasyn of the Michaelites. What are you standing there fidgeting for, Iskender? Is something wrong?"

"I've just returned from the hunt, Bardas. We gained ten vessels but lost two horses."

Bardas sucked in a breath through his teeth. "Two horses! Was someone drunk? We can't afford such waste."

Iskender grimaced. "I'm glad to hear you say so. I came to tell you the kine are catching wise to us. They were ready for us tonight. They don't know us for anything but brigands yet, I think, but we can hardly keep on like this. If these villagers are setting traps for us, then I can guarantee you they're complaining to someone as well, maybe even to the king. There are some in this camp who—refuse to believe they don't dwell in the great city anymore." As he said this, the Turk minutely faced away from the Cainite at the right end of the foursome, the one called Gallasyn, a lank auburn-haired man who laced his spidery white fingers tightly together on the table, as though to keep them out of some mischief. But if an insult was meant, Gallasyn didn't respond to it. His gaze remained where it had been, turned downward. "They kill on a whim, and don't even call others to come lap up the cooling blood, but simply let the body fall where it dies…"

"Yes, yes. Old song, new verse. As it happens we've just been discussing these very problems, Iskender. We have new instructions for you. These mortals whose spines are stiffening, you aren't to raid against them anymore."

Iskender shifted. "Then where am I to obtain provisions? This time of year, the traffic along the highway is far too sparse."

"Further out. Range as far as you dare."

"But the Cainite lords."

"Let us worry about them. Meanwhile, the mortals near us are to begin paying tribute. You will let them know that for a modest annual tithe, we'll be quite happy not only to leave them in peace but also to protect them from any other brigands that try to begin operating in our area. They should find that both easier and more agreeable than trying to pursue their case with the king or anyone else."

"You want… coin from these people?"

"Yes. As much as you can get. We can also take a certain portion in food and goods. Try to look at the long term, Iskender."

"That's exactly what I'm looking at, sir—" Iskender tried to interrupt.

"As long as we remain in this hole, no one is going to take us seriously. No one is going to negotiate. What's a Cainite without a proper holding? A vagabond, a nobody." Bardas gestured to the others at the table, who nodded agreement with varying enthusiasm. "We need a real domain. We need a real house, and mortals who look to us for patronage. If they pay us tribute, they're ours. No one can say we're simply poaching on others' property then."

"Bardas, we've taken their *children*." The Turk jogged the arm of the boy, who let out a tiny noise of distress.

"And I'm sure they don't want to lose any more. Now are you capable of doing what is required of you?"

Iskender seemed to restrain himself for several moments before finally speaking. "Yes. Sir. It will be done. But even if we manage to buy or build some forest keep and fill it with cloth of Arras and golden candlesticks, it still won't *accomplish* anything except perhaps to lift our spirits. Alexander won't change his mind just because…"

"Prince Alexander is a great Cainite ruler, a scion of the ancient world." The woman called Helena stood, dark eyes ablaze. "You, Turk, understand nothing about how such men think. To him the color of candlesticks matters! We must prove ourselves worthy of his attention or we will never be able to continue the pilgrimage."

That was evidently the last straw. "Has it ever occurred to any of you people that *he* has yet to prove himself worthy of *your* attention?" he burst out.

"Bardas, do you intend to let this… youth stand here and blaspheme not only against the grandsire of the blessed Hugh, but against the very word of Malachite, Rock of Constantinople?" Gallasyn asked quietly, never looking up.

"Malachite is not here! Plainly he, unlike you, knows when to abandon fruitless pursuits! What is his word to us now? Where is your Rock, I ask you?"

"Iskender, trust me, you've made your opinions known," Bardas said, touching his index finger onto the table before him. "We've heard nothing new from you for months. You complain and complain, but you suggest no alternatives."

"I *have* suggested alternatives, Bardas. The rations, the—"

"Moreover, no one besides your own band agrees with you."

"They agree because they're out there with me, they see how it is."

"Yes, you're always out there and never in here. Look around you, Iskender. Does this pilgrimage need another prophet of doom? Is a full belly your sole concern in the world? We are here by the command of God and Caine. Did you think there would be no privations, no difficulties? Did you think we would never be tested? Now you have your instructions."

"Yes, Bardas." Iskender sketched a rather military bow, whirled on his heel and strode out.

"And the rest of you, that will be all. We do need to finish this council meeting some time tonight."

Zoë, Anatole, and Gerasimos all bowed and left, closing the lodge door behind them.

"Who do they think they're fooling, council meeting?" Gerasimos shook his head. His tone was ironic, but his eyes were hot with despair.

Anatole grunted meditatively. "And yet you follow them."

"I still try to follow God's will, and the will of Caine. It's not necessarily the same thing as their will, though they think it is."

"Are there others in the camp who feel as you do?"

"Yes. Most of them are not… members of the old Trinity families or their Scions, however. Some aren't even citizens. They don't have the authority of Malachite or the Dracon or anyone else weighting their words."

"That doesn't matter," the Malkavian assured him. "Come, Zoë. Let's build our shelters."

"I'll help you," Gerasimos put in quickly. "And Nikodemos will as well."

Zoë eyed both Greeks, particularly their elegant hands without a trace of callus, and wondered how much help they could really be.

"Good. Thank you, brother." Anatole swept the clearing with an evaluating gaze. "Over there, I think, out of the wind. Tonight we see to earthly needs, then; and tomorrow, Gerasimos, you must lead me."

"Lead you? Where?"

Anatole turned and fixed Gerasimos with one of his piercing gazes. The monk actually dropped the knot of his prayer rope. Zoë nearly felt sorry for him.

"Why, to my flock, of course."

***

It serves her right for nodding off over a book, she thinks grimly. Now she wanders its pages, trying to reach one cover or the other. The border grotesques laugh at her and offer up confusing directions; she pushes bristling ascenders out of the way and climbs up gilded trellises of acanthus. By some whimsical conceit of the illuminator, all the figures are masked and disguised: monks wearing the faces of goats, goats wearing the faces of sheep and sheepskins spread over their back, horses wearing the faces of donkeys with their tails braided partway down, and monsters with the faces of men, trying to conceal their misshapen forms under layers of finery.

John the Baptist leans down from his vantage point in the initial above, lowering his head on a platter to look at her.

"You should make for the page you were on," the head says. "That's what it's still open to."

"Ah, thank you," she replies.

"Do you frequently converse with the beheaded?" it asks. "You act as though you're accustomed."

She smiles. "In my dreams and visions I do. There are, after all, a number of such saints. You were only first."

"True, alas."

"Is there something you wish to tell me?"

"Yes. Do you see that figure over there, the man with the golden keys hanging on his belt, wearing the mask that looks like me?"

"I do."

"That is because he is my namesake. When he comes to you, do not defy him. It is his destiny to assemble the complete man from the parts; and when the man is finished he will put a sword in the man's right hand and a lamp in the left. And when he has done this the cracks in the rock may yet be mended, that is, until the appointed age when it must split forever."

"Teresa! You speak of her dream, the one she keeps having. What else do you know about it?"

But he simply raises his head aloft once more, turning back to his place in the miniature. As he does, she sees the flash of a fox's tail under his gray robes...

"Faustina!" Cecilia cried as she awoke.

Faustina started and nearly dropped her needlepoint. "What, sister?" she exclaimed.

"Please, I need a pen and parchment. I must write Abbé Gervèse. It's important..." But just as Faustina got up to obey, Cecilia stopped her again. "No, wait."

A fox's tail...

"Sister?"

"Never mind, Soeur Faustina. I want... I must ponder this a little more first."

Chapter Twelve

"It's the sorry end this Exodus has come to, isn't it?" Anatole pushed his hair out of his eyes and raised his hand to gesture toward the lodge under whose eaves they stood. "You circle the globe and yet you never manage to leave Egypt. Your Moses keeps climbing back up the mountain, and not a drop of manna in sight. What sign are you wretches awaiting? I tell you there's no smear of blood that will turn aside the coming scourge, and it profits a man nothing to be one of the nine righteous in Sodom."

"Haven't we already been judged and scourged?" Decius asked dryly. He gathered up the coins that lay in a semi-circle at his feet and then picked up the dice as well. Zoë watched his hands and sleeves carefully. Those dice had been rolled at least twenty times by each of the bettors now crowding around him before the game began, in order to satisfy everyone that they were quite honest. Zoë had privately resolved, however, that they couldn't possibly be—how could anyone turn the profit Decius did with honest dice? And so it remained only to try to find the trick.

"Yes, the Golden Horn is smelted into ingots to fill a robber's purse," Anatole answered. "And the rainbow glass is shattered. But this is nothing to the fire that smolders in the depths of the granary and waits only a breath of fresh air to leap on high. Listen!"

"I'm listening, but I'm not making much sense of you."

"When Eve bore Seth she said 'God has given me a seed to replace Abel whom Caine slew.' Do you remember when Moses parted the sea? There was a narrow path for the children of Israel to pass through safely and all else on either side was chaos. I am telling you that once again the safe and narrow path is open, but only for a little while. How many mortals were among the soldiers that marched against your city?"

"How should I know?" Decius tried to return to his game. "Tens of thousands. Zoë, his Greek's improving, but something's still getting lost in the translation. Bets, people, bets. Out on the ground where we can all see or it doesn't count."

"And Cainites?" Anatole pursued, undaunted.

"What?"

"How many Cainites among the invaders?"

"Again, how should I know?"

"But not tens of thousands."

"No. Maybe dozens. Enough, anyway."

"If you took away the Cainites, would the city still have burned?"

Decius paused, blowing out an irritated breath. "I suppose, yes."

"And if you took away the mortals?"

"You are *attempting* to get at something, I can tell…"

"And if God's face had not been set against you in the first place, then neither mortal nor Cainite would have prevailed, would they?"

"Ah. Now I see." Decius scooped up the dice and handed them to the next player. "We deserved it all. Yes, no doubt we did. And half the people here have flayed themselves with salted rope, beaten their breasts and sat in sackcloth and ashes for years now, and it hasn't made a damned bit of difference."

"And is it only your backs that awaited the lash? Do you think that God would empower the race of Seth to bring down the mighty Dream and then simply withdraw His hand again? Do you suppose He's through bestowing His gifts upon your prey? Did the plagues of Egypt get better or worse as they went on, I ask you? I am telling you that these Red Brothers will dye their habits in more than one kind of crimson, and it isn't them alone we should fear, though they're quite enough, as Zoë could tell you…"

"Speaking of prey—Zoë, be an angel and bring us a vessel," Decius interrupted.

Zoë looked at Anatole, who shrugged.

"One of yours?" she asked Decius.

"Of course. It's a host's duty to provide."

She made her way over to the western edge of the camp, where squatted the little cluster of wattle-and-daub domes that comprised Decius' encampment. A group of the mortals sat around a campfire toasting bits of game meat. On the skin between some of their thumbs and forefingers she could see the little serpentine brand that marked them as Decius' property.

"Your master wants one of you to attend him," she told them. They just snorted at her.

"I'll just bet," said one of the men.

"He sent me to fetch you," she said, clenching her fists.

"Fetch, Zoë, fetch!"

One of the women laughed at the man's joke and slid into his lap, making barking noises.

"Quiet, all of you." The voice came from off to Zoë's left, from an ascetic Frankish Cainite in a priest's cassock who sat mounted upon a fine palfrey. The mortals glanced up at him and fell dead silent as through they'd been struck.

"What is this place," the Cainite asked as he spurred his mount closer, "where a daughter of the shining blood itself is treated like a common strumpet by the children of Seth, the people of clay? Don't you know that when you mock her, you mock the very font of eternal life?"

The ghouls didn't answer; they huddled together uneasily, exchanging dark glances.

"Whichever of you still has a couth bone in his or her body—you will do as you are told, and show me moreover to the leaders of this camp."

"Decius… I mean, these mortals' master is at the lodge where the Council sits," stuttered Zoë. "I'll show you."

"I thank you, mademoiselle." He nodded at one of the men. "You. Come along." The mortal rose, still wide-eyed, and obeyed.

The Cainite rode alongside her back to the lodge. All along the way, curious mortals and immortals alike trailed along, whispering, staring at his spotless clothes and his mount's glossy coat.

"Thanks, Zoë, but I only asked you to bring a vessel," said Decius as they approached. He was the camp's richest dice-dealer and therefore determined to remain unimpressed. "Who is this?"

"Gentle folk, I am Father Folcaut," the stranger said as he dismounted, "of the Clan of the Rose. Is this where your leaders meet?"

They crowded around him.

"Did His Blessed Highness of Paris send you?" one of the Cainites interrupted eagerly. "He must have. Will he receive us at last?"

"Finally, a real priest in the camp," piped up a mortal Frenchwoman. "My son's been awaiting baptism since his birth last spring."

The door of the lodge opened and Bardas peeped around it, blinking as he emerged from the nearly lightless interior. "What's going on out here?" Then he spotted his elegant visitor and stepped out, a welcoming smile hastily pasted across his face.

Zoë sidled up next to Anatole. "This is no priest," the Malkavian muttered.

"He mentioned the shining blood," Zoë muttered back. "It's like what Isidro said to that Branoc in Arles, just before Gauthier shot him."

"Heresy…" Anatole sucked in a breath through his yellow teeth, which had already begun to lengthen.

"I thought I heard something about Paris," Bardas was saying as he took Folcaut's hand. "*Did* the court send you, Father?"

"Only in a manner of speaking," Folcaut demurred. "His Highness did not send me, but my venerable lord bishop is frequently called as an adviser to His Highness' privy council. Nevertheless, I don't come for the sake of politics. I come, instead, in search of those eager to hear the call of God in these troubled latter nights."

"Well! I can assure you, Father, if there's one thing to be found in abundance here, it's eagerness to submit to God's will… come in, come in and tell the Council all about it."

The door of the lodge closed again. At once the dicers gathered up their wagers, the game for the moment completely forgotten. Even Decius stood and followed them, at a reticent pace behind. Everyone but Zoë and Anatole crowded around the uneasy horse, stroking its coat, examining its furnishings and shiny bridle decorations and even poking at the saddlebags.

"You feel that? That's all coin right there, I'd stake eternity on it…"

"The finest, fittest gelding I've laid eyes on in years. Poor Iskender, he'll turn green with envy."

"Who is it? Who's come?"

"An envoy from the Blessed Alexander's priesthood!"

"But why is he *here*, do you think?" Zoë asked her mentor quietly.

Anatole shook his head. "Gambling for souls is to be the next pastime of the camp, I see. I didn't realize that the thrice-damned Heresy and its blasphemous assertions of Cainite divinity now infect even the vampire court of my native city… I must think what to do about it. Come, let's find Gerasimos, I feel the need for his counsel." He took her arm. She stopped him short.

"Anatole!"

"What?"

"We…" She amended. "I mean… you can't trouble yourself with the Paris court and what it does or doesn't tolerate right now. What about our mission? What about the Red Brothers? And Isidro?"

"We *will* strive against the Red Brothers, childe." He clapped his hands onto her upper arms and sought out a direct eye-to-eye contact. "But we must be patient about that. Their abbey is true holy ground. We can't simply storm it the way you and the caravan-master did the one at Bergamo. We must wait and seek our opportunities." Then suddenly he got a more faraway look. "Yes, yes, that is true. If it were given to fools and children to determine the order of things, much about the world *would* be improved. But it is set down that the Spaniard, the red pilgrim, will not fall until the prisoner is set free."

He listened to his private choir a few moments more, then smiled at her.

"Courage, Zoë. The justice of the Lord may wait a long time, but it can't wait forever. He will fail, he will fall, and I am told that you will be there when it happens… until then, be content. Now, Gerasimos. He must hear of this."

Chapter Thirteen

The Theodosian Abbey at St.-Denis
The Friday After Easter, 1212

"You were to bring a badge back from Tours, Isidro, or maybe a vial of holy water," said Gervèse. "Not a cardinal."

The two of them leaned out of the window, looking down into the cloister garden below. Frère Jaufres was still finishing up his tour down there, pointing out various plants and architectural features to the man who wandered beside him, hands behind his back, a stocky dark-haired man clad in a deceptively humble cassock.

Isidro shrugged, embarrassed. "Forgive me, *Abba*. But he's the one who didn't introduce himself properly."

"Well, what does he want?"

"I have no idea what he wants, only what he's interested in."

"Yes, and I have no idea why you had to go and *tell* him about it, now of all times. I would have thought this the worst conceivable juncture to start reminding Rome of certain activities of ours."

"Actually, it may be the best. Gervèse, I don't think he's here to condemn us."

"Then what is he here for? The letter didn't say."

"He's told me nothing that wasn't in the letter, so you know as much as I do. Now go on."

Gervèse put on what he hoped was his most perfectly abbatial manner and strode downstairs, Isidro falling into place a pace behind him on his right.

"Ah, Père Battista," he said as he came upon the two men in the garden. "There you are."

The "Father" bent to kiss Gervèse's ring. What looked like the faintest hint of a secret smile touched his lips.

"*Abba*. Your invitation honors me." His French was considerably salted with the accents of Italy, but he spoke it well enough.

"Not at all. It's I who must thank you for making the trip. Now come, you're needed. That'll be all, Jaufres, you can return to your duties."

"Thank you, *Abba*. Good day to you all. God bless."

Gervèse, Isidro and the "Father" then walked in silence along the dirt path to the abbot's house. Calling it Gervèse's "invitation" was at least as ironic as calling the man "Father," since the cardinal had ordered the meeting in the first place; but if such irony pleased his lordship it was certainly his to enjoy.

"Is this Soeur Cecilia that Frère Isidro spoke of here yet?" the "Father" asked.

"She should be, Monseigneur," Gervèse answered quietly. "I asked for her to be brought to the house when she arrived, and all the men of your company as well."

They opened the door to the house and went in. Almost as soon as it shut behind them, Gervèse and Isidro both went down on a knee and seized the "Father's" hand in turn.

"Monseigneur. You honor us so very greatly with your presence."

"Thank you, Abbé, but please, get up. I want you to understand something—well. You're both sharp men and you probably understand this already, from the simple fact that I'm traveling *incognito*. But this isn't an official tour. It's an investigation. Therefore the fewer know of my presence and my purpose in Ile-de-France, the better. And I'm afraid that includes men of the cloth just as much as laymen. Indeed I must ask you to maintain the charade even to your own brethren, until I give you permission to do otherwise."

"Of course, Monseigneur," said Gervèse, resisting the impulse to throw Isidro a look at the word *investigation*.

With a gesture, Gervèse invited the cardinal to go first. The cardinal indicated instead that Gervèse should lead the way to the hall, which he did.

136   Ravnos

Something like a dozen men waited there already—a few Benedictine monks, a couple of priests, two knights and several men in sober laymen's dress, one of whom had a pen tucked behind his ear. They hastily got to their feet as the cardinal entered.

"Gauthier!" exclaimed Isidro before he remembered not to speak out of turn.

Gauthier looked to the cardinal, who nodded. "Yes, his lordship has done me the supreme honor of asking me and Sire Jehan to accompany him as his guard on his travels. You see, God brings us together yet again, for a brief time at least."

"And that has to augur well, doesn't it?" the cardinal agreed. "Well. I see the nun isn't here yet."

"She is, Monseigneur," one of the Benedictines in the group said. "But she and her companion sister went into the chapel to pray for the good issue of this meeting."

The cardinal smiled. That a pair of nuns should wish to wait alone on their knees rather than in a roomful of men, some of whom were armed and not all of whom were bound by oaths of chastity, was certainly understandable enough. "That is kind of them, but they should come in now. Go fetch them."

The men assembled themselves at the great oak table. Gervèse called for more watered wine and small beer to be brought in, and a little toasted bread and cheese. Cecilia and Faustina followed in the wake of the food platters, Faustina looking as though she'd rather like to hide behind the brother who conducted them.

"Here they are," said Gervèse. "My lord cardinal, I would like to present Soeur Cecilia and Soeur Faustina of the convent of St. John the Divine in Tyre."

"Sisters, be welcome. My name is Battista Marzone, and I am here on a very important errand for the Holy Father. Word of your vision and piety has preceded you, Soeur Cecilia, which is why I've asked you to be here today. "

Cecilia ducked her head, discomfited. Faustina actually blushed.

"I doubt I am worthy of the faith you place in me, Monseigneur," Cecilia said, "but I will do my best to be of service."

"Good. Take your seats."

Once everyone was settled, the cardinal began. "Most of you here already know my purpose, but I see looks of total mystification on these other faces, so let me do a little explaining. Maffeo, begin." The man with a pen behind his ear hurriedly took out his wax tablet and stylus and started jotting. "It was my good fortune to come across Frère Isidro at Tours, where we were both making pilgrimage to the shrine. We fell into a most amiable conversation and, as has become my habit on this trip, I dropped a little lure here and there, hoping to turn up some rumor as to where in the Touraine or Ile-de-France the devil's most hell-touched agents might be lurking."

Gervèse felt his heartbeat suddenly throb in his throat, and his head actually went light for a moment. He told himself not to be stupid. This was not how an inquisition began, for God's sake, over toast and cheese.

"I quickly discerned that Frère Isidro knew more about such things than he cared to say. And I confess, memories of certain events of the past century came to me at that moment and piqued my interest in the Order of Theodosius anew. I trust, Abbé, that you know the events of which I speak."

"In the Pyrenees, yes, lord."

"Yes, in the Pyrenees. A certain unfortunate matter with a Frère Everard, as I recall."

"Yes, my lord." Gervèse did not look at Isidro directly, but he could see out of the corner of his eye that the other monk's face was downcast. As well it should be!

"Yes. And I've already sent to the Lateran for copies of those records, but just going on what I remember… it was discovered in the course of the ensuing investigation, was it not, just how broad and deep the learning of the red monks had grown?"

"I—I confess I'm not sure precisely what your lordship refers to," Gervèse temporized. The mood in the room shifted palpably.

"Come, come, Abbé. Don't play games."

"No, my lord. I..." He glanced around. His eye alighted for a moment on Cecilia, whose head seemed to twitch very slightly to the right. "I didn't mean to evade. My apologies. I know that the order studies many subjects, and that some in the Curia thought several of those subjects unbefitting to men of holy contemplation. And that the studies of Everard and his followers were condemned by all, even their own brethren. I just wasn't certain whether you wished me to speak to the miscreant's learning, or that of the current membership of our order."

"The deeds of dead miscreants don't at present concern me, Abbé. But wouldn't you agree that even now your Order pursues knowledge that some in the Curia would still find unfitting?"

"Well. Without knowing the Curia, it is hard for me to say, my lord, but... yes... I would imagine so."

"Yes." Marzone nodded. "And as I said, it soon became apparent to me that our Isidro, too, possesses a great breadth and depth of learning. But as I pressed, he became increasingly reluctant to discuss it."

"Your lordship, please, may I speak?" said Gauthier. He made as if to rise; his eyes were low, hidden under his thick brows, and his mouth contracted in a frown.

"In a moment, Sire Gauthier. It was then that I revealed myself to Frère Isidro at last, and bade him speak freely. He told me, Abbé, that he has devoted himself to the study of the heresy known as Cainism, and its priesthood— a flock of carrion-kites from Hell itself, or so my own researches have led me to believe."

The abbot took a deep breath. "He does study it, my lord. But only with the object of excising this vile cancer from the cheek of Christendom. Frère Isidro, I can assure you, has battled the Enemy's minions since he was a very young man. Whatever knowledge he has was acquired as a matter of utmost necessity, not morbid curiosity."

Marzone sat back. "Yes. That's precisely what he said as well. He also tells me that you, Abbé, know quite a bit about such things yourself. Is that true?"

All eyes were on Gervèse once again. "I know of the Cainites, yes, my lord. Several years ago we caught a few of them in Brittany, and then a good handful more recently in Savoy."

"Indeed. That was with the assistance of the priory at Bergamo, was it not?"

How much had Isidro *told* the man? "Yes. That is, Prior Ugo kindly allowed us to bring the demons to him for interrogation. We learned a great deal from that effort. Unfortunately, the demons that we hadn't caught staged a rescue, trespassing on the very grounds of the priory to do it. They were unable to free their fellows, thanks be unto God; we'd already destroyed all but one. But they did recover most of their possessions, which is a pity, since some of them were quite strange."

"Strange?"

"Things of dark cunning, Monseigneur. There was, most notably, a pale green box with an exceedingly complex lock on it, which took twenty learned monks the better part of the week to open." Gauthier snorted softly; Gervèse had no doubt that Gauthier would have proposed the Gordian-knot solution to that dilemma. "And then within that there was a sort of alabaster jar, and then within that, a heart."

"A heart!" the cardinal exclaimed. "Like a sort of… anti-relic…?"

"That's probably the way to put it, yes. The vile thing didn't rot, but it did seem to be coated in some brown tarry substance, perhaps to slow the putrefaction. I wish," he added, glancing at Isidro, "I do wish that we had burnt it at once… or at least removed it from the box entirely and kept it somewhere more secure. The fiends have it back now along with the rest."

"Yes, my lord. We are sons and daughters of the Church. What kind of children would we be if we should fail to do Her will?"

The cardinal drummed his fingers for a few moments on the table. Then, slowly, he smiled.

"That is the right answer, Abbé," he said quietly. "Yes, that is exactly the answer I was looking for. I told you that I come on the Holy Father's errand. That errand is to create, within the Church and yet without the Church's knowledge, a body of men—and women too, if God so wills—whom the Holy Father can trust to bring *inquisitio* against the very legions of Hell on earth. If you and your order have the courage, Abbé, and the necessary knowledge, *and* the humility to employ those tools toward a greater good without thought of glory or power, then your endeavors will gain the very blessing of the Vicar of Christ himself. Here… Maffeo, hand the Abbé the commission so that he can see I speak truly."

A not-quite-silent sigh of relief moved through the room. Isidro's and Gauthier's faces unknotted and slackened. A parchment tied in a silk ribbon with a heavy lead seal dangling from it was passed down the length of the table into Gervèse's hands.

From the pope's own chancery. His fingers trembled a bit as he took it. Here was an elegantly calligraphed pair of paragraphs in Latin, authorizing one most well-beloved son Battista Marzone, Cardinal-Deacon of SS. Johannes et Paulus, to form and prosecute a pilgrimage—a pilgrimage to free not the outward Jerusalem, but the very divine breath within each human soul in Christendom from the clutches of the devil's minions on earth; most especially that blot of demonic heresy known as Cainism…

"A secret pilgrimage." He looked up from the letter in awe, toward the cardinal. "The Holy Father knows, then."

"Yes, he knows. And what he doesn't yet know, he suspects. I am not the only reporter bringing words to his ears, Abbé. And he's now heard the account of what Sire Gauthier showed me in the emptied streets of Carcassonne." Marzone nodded toward Gauthier, who returned it grimly. "Even in the crypt of the church, I tell you… even in the church…" He shook himself. "You see why I have to be so careful."

"Yes, of course, my lord," answered Gervèse, his own passion stirring now. "But you will not be alone in this endeavor, I swear it. All the brethren in Paris I'll gladly place in your service, and I'm sure I can convince at least some of the other houses as well…"

"A moment, Abbé." The cardinal held up a finger. "I am not done being careful just yet."

Murmurs.

"You and Frère Isidro have both told me about your battles with the demons. Now I want to see them."

"See them, Monseigneur?"

"Yes. You are going to catch Cainites in Paris, you said?"

"Well, yes, my lord. Probably not for another several months, possibly even a year… we have a lot of investigation to do yet, a lot of groundwork I want to lay."

"Yes, exactly. That is what I want to see. I want to know how these things are done. I want to learn at the sides of men who have already done it. Sire Gauthier assures me that I am coming to the right place."

He paused, then, and looked Gervèse directly in the eye. "Am I?"

***

"He'll want to stay in a cell with the rest of us, I suppose," said Isidro as he and Gervèse led the two sisters back to the yard where their horses waited.

"Of course he will," Gervèse grumbled. "He's Père Battista, remember. No abbatial comforts for the simple Father."

"It'll be all right, Gervèse. We'll just go forward exactly as we planned and make a good showing of it. We weren't going to do anything less than our best anyway, were we?"

"That's hardly the point."

"What do you think, Soeur Cecilia?" Isidro appealed to her.

She seemed to consider carefully. "Every day and night, brothers, you pray for God's aid in your endeavors. What form did you hope the answer to those prayers would take?"

"There, you see?"

"Isidro, I'm not *saying* that the prospect of the Holy Father's involvement should be greeted with anything but rejoicing of the greatest magnitude. I certainly have no quarrel with the Curia. I just worry that they might have a quarrel with *us*, with the way we do things. It's not as though it hasn't happened before."

"If they do, then they do. You said it yourself, we obey the Church. Besides, the tides aren't so much against us as they once were. Abbé Bernard *was* exonerated."

"Well, we'll see soon enough." Gervèse got a wooden box, overturned it and set it down at the horse's side so that Cecilia could mount, then slid the box over alongside Faustina's horse. The young nun got up on it, putting a hand on one saddlebag to steady herself. As she touched it all of a sudden her mouth dropped open.

"Oh, no!"

"What, Faustina?" asked Cecilia.

"Sister, I'm so—I mean, I just realized I left your breviary back in the chapel. I'm so sorry—I'll just run and get it."

"Well, hurry."

Gervèse held onto the reins of Faustina's horse. "Oh, yes, that reminds me, Isidro. That fragment you brought with the story about Apollonius, Frère Guillaume finished reading it and wants to discuss it with you... Isidro?"

He leaned forward, looking between and around the horses.

"Where the blazes—" He glanced up at Cecilia, who sat gazing off toward the gate. "I mean, where did he go?"

"Over there," said Cecilia. "With Sire Gauthier."

Gervèse looked. Evidently the knight had been dismissed from Marzone's side for one reason or another; he sat already mounted and girded by the gate. He and Isidro exchanged a few words. Then Isidro raced off in the direction of the stables.

"I see." Gervèse stroked the nose of Faustina's horse and patted its shoulder. A few silent minutes went by.

"What story about Apollonius?" Cecilia asked suddenly.

"Hm?"

"Apollonius."

"Oh. Yes. He once had a student Menippus who wanted to wed a beautiful lady that was far more than she seemed. Apollonius warned him repeatedly not to proceed, but the youth insisted. And so Apollonius arrived on the night of the wedding feast. He caused all the wedding food and other luxuries to disappear, thus proving that they'd only been evil illusions, and then forced the bride to confess herself a *lamia* who meant to fatten Menippus with pleasures and then consume his flesh and blood."

"Does it say how he broke through the creature's enchantments?" she asked.

"Not much about it. Most versions of the tale don't say at all. It's sorcery, after all."

"I see. Then he was not a saint."

"What? No. No, no, he was a sorcerer... supposedly a virtuous one, but... that was by a decidedly pagan reckoning."

"And does Frère Isidro have such skill, so as to dismiss evil illusions?"

He looked up at her in surprise. "Why, no, lady. I mean—that is, Isidro's no sorcerer. He is one of our more learned monks, but there's nothing to condemn in his learning, just as I told the cardinal."

"I don't condemn. When I was a little girl there were those that thought I might be mad, or worse. I couldn't say how I knew things, and my visions were not like Hildegard's, all warmth and light and color."

Soeur Cecilia a child (perhaps with hair the color of honey? Or of varnished wood?), bowed and cowed by a terrible, divine gift she didn't yet understand: It was impossible to credit and yet at one time it must have been so, just as the oak must once have been an acorn.

"Sister," he began, "I wouldn't have you think I esteem your gifts lightly, or imagine they're lightly borne either— Isidro!" he broke off to exclaim as the other monk rode up. "What on earth is going on?"

"Nothing," Isidro returned, taken aback. "Gauthier says the cardinal gave him permission to see the sisters home, and if you'll permit, *Abba*, I'll constitute the other half of the honor guard. Not that my coming along is much honor of itself. You see, this way I can press Gauthier for the details and he can't get away. Plainly he's up to much more than he's been letting on. He never told me he was planning to take a *cardinal* into Carcassonne once it fell! I would have gladly stayed to help, if he'd only mentioned it; but in fact now that I think about it he rather bustled me away, once I'd blessed the oils for him…" He frowned then.

"Ah well, he was probably trying to protect you."

"Protect me?"

"From *yourself*, you…!" Gervèse restrained himself for the sake of Cecilia and of Faustina, who came puffing up just at that moment.

"Gervèse, look, I—" Isidro's expression collapsed into bewilderment.

"No, no, go on. Don't keep the sisters waiting. The daylight burns." Gervèse held the horse steady for Faustina's ascent and saw it off with a pat on the flank.

***

Gervèse turned the page back again for the fourth time. For the fifth time he lost the sense of the paragraph mid-sentence.

"*Abba?*" A young lay brother of the house stood with one foot in the door, murmuring. "Frère Isidro is here to see you. Will you receive him?"

"Of course."

"Don't say of course," came Isidro's voice. The Spaniard entered the room. His face was so grief-stricken that Gervèse immediately put the book down.

"What do you—"

Isidro went down onto his knees at Gervèse's feet, clasping his hands together. "I mean I don't deserve to be received by you tonight. I can only hope you'll allow me regardless, so that I can beg penance from you."

"Penance, my old friend?" Gervèse turned his chair toward him, already feeling three times kinder.

"*Abba*, please don't call upon friendship just now, I implore you. Treat me as though I were the wickedest of your erring novices. I assure you I deserve it. I have sinned."

"Very well." Gervèse quirked a brow at him. "Let me just get my stole…"

He took it out, kissed it, and put it on. "All right. Let's do this properly. *In Nomini Patris, et Filii, et Spiritus Sancti.*"

"Bless me, Father, for I have sinned. It has been two days since my last confession."

"And what are your sins, my son?"

"I have had uncharitable thoughts towards others, Father, including a superior in the Church—"

"That you're hardly alone in today, I'm afraid."

"I was later to the Divine Office than I strictly needed to be upon returning to the abbey. And I have had a lustful dream."

"Not again."

"I can't help it, Gervèse. When my mind slumbers it wanders abroad without my will to curb it. Nonetheless it is my great fault. I—I pray God's forgiveness day and night for this."

"I don't understand how anybody who dreams like you do manages to live as such a chaste monk. Anything else?"

"Yes. I have vexed my abbot multiple times today, through my incredible thoughtlessness and weakness. "

"Isidro."

"I didn't *mean* to attract the attention of one such as Marzone. Even if it turns out for the very best, as I hope I will, it was an inexcusable lack of caution on my part. It could have been so much worse."

"Well, what on earth did you think you were doing? Why were you even hinting of such things?"

"I was… well, he hinted first. And then I thought it necessary to determine just how much he knew."

"Obviously he's much better at that than you are."

"Yes. Obviously. Please forgive me, *Abba*. It's been haunting me all the way back from Paris."

"My son, if it is God's will that some great good come about from a mistake of yours, we must be thankful for it. Don't worry, you'll still get your penance."

"Not yet.—I must also beg pardon for my utter breach of decorum." Isidro paused. "I… didn't realize I'd left you alone with her. I wouldn't have even for a moment, if I'd seen Soeur Faustina run off."

Gervèse sat back. "Yes. You should have looked before you left. You know the Rule of our Order that always governs such situations."

"Yes, I should have. I should certainly know better by now. Such things should be uppermost in my mind. To have placed you, my brother and superior, in such a vile position—oh! Not that she herself is vile, of course, of course not, forgive me… But you know what I mean, an embarrassing position, one unbefitting an abbot's dignity. And it's worse than that. It was a trespass against our friendship as well. That is beyond price to me, Gervèse, God save me from ever offending you even for a good reason, let alone an ill one."

"Well, I don't—" Gervèse started to demur, and then wondered what exactly he was trying to demur about, and then decided to abandon the sentence altogether. "Never mind. It's done and past. Are you ready to hear your penance, my son?"

"Yes, Father. I am truly sorry for these sins. Please."

"You will hear each of the next three Offices prostrate on the floor with arms spread out; and you will also say a Psalter. Very well, two Psalters."

Isidro bowed his head humbly, and his eyes were as contrite as any confessor could hope for, but a smile of vast relief spread across his lips. "Thank you, Father, thank you, *Abba*… and thank you, Gervèse. *Deus meus, ex toto corde poenitet me omnium meorum peccatorum…*"

Chapter Fourteen

The Bière Forest
The First Monday of May, 1212

She wondered if the moon was full. It probably was the first night of the full moon. She hadn't looked the night before, so she wasn't completely sure, but it probably was.

"Here's another piece," said Isabel, handing her a long strip of red samite. Zoë took it with smiling thanks, looked it over, then examined her creation for a good deal longer. Finally she made the strip fast to one end of the twig-hoop and wove it through the star-shaped portion of the pattern in a tight spiral.

Isabel looked over her shoulder, admiring it. "What is it supposed to be?"

"I don't know yet." Was the moon full or not? No, it didn't matter. "I'm only playing with techniques. I began with no idea what I was doing at all."

"I see. Then this isn't something your mother taught you?"

Zoë turned to her in surprise. "No. No, my mother never had a chance to teach me anything. She died when I was very young."

"Oh, I'm sorry. So did mine. It was just that it's so pretty. I can hardly believe someone didn't teach you."

"That's good of you to say."

"Well, it is."

"My sire taught me how to make many things," Zoë answered. "If we had brass or silver or gold that I could work…"

"If we had brass or silver or gold to spare for you to make pretties with, many things would be different," the young vampire interrupted, and squatted down on her haunches to watch in earnest.

"If you could have met my sire, you wouldn't worry whether it was to spare or not. You'd give it to him regardless."

"Oh no I wouldn't," said Isabel flatly.

"Oh yes you would." Zoë meant that to come out more playfully than it did. She glared up at the sky again for a moment, hoping to catch a space between clouds as it flew overhead.

Isabel studied her curiously.

"Why?" she asked at last.

"Gold or silver in coins isn't half so valuable as what he'd do with it. He would make a fish, detail it down to the last scale and set in little cabochons for the eyes, and then he would put it in the stream and cause it to swim so that with every flash of moonlight it would look like a zigzag of lighting in the water."

"Why, what's the good of that?"

"You'd know when you saw it." Zoë tied off the strip, increasingly annoyed at what, to her, were patently ridiculous questions. "The others would watch it wiggling and cavorting and at first they'd only stare. Then, after a little while, maybe it would leap up shining and flick its tail and splash someone, and he'd laugh."

"I suppose…"

"And it would be the first laugh he'd had in years. Then the others would begin to laugh and smile too, and talk excitedly about how it was done. And they'd argue about it as well. But they wouldn't hurt each other the way they usually do when they argue, because their hearts were already so much lighter, and who could hurt anyone over such a silly argument? Anyway, part of the fun is in not knowing entirely how it's done, but being able to go to sleep still wondering about it. And for that evening and maybe many more afterward, we wouldn't all be what we are. We couldn't possibly be, because we had such a wonderful, pretty, useless thing to amuse us."

Isabel took a stick and traced a crude attempt at her own name in Latin letters into the dirt. "I think I understand what you mean," she said at last. "But it still wouldn't be as good as having a real home."

"No, I know that." Full. It *was* full. Swollen to its peak. Zoë stood.

Isabel stood too, springing to her clawed feet. "I'll bring you more tomorrow," she said, talking quickly now. "I know where I can get blue and green, and white and maybe even one with a bit of gold thread."

"Why, what does it matter?" Zoë retorted as she turned away.

"No, you're right," Isabel called after her. "You're right. I'll bring you more… I'll bring you more tomorrow!"

Zoë ran through the camp into her hut and virtually slid to her knees onto the dirt floor, scrabbling in her make-shift chest for the knife. She lifted it, tip downward, and was momentarily disappointed as always. It looked so heavy and dingy and utilitarian, even in the lane of moonlight that fell through the door. She wanted it to be mirror-bright, honed to a cruel parchment edge, like a presentation dagger. She wanted it clearly marked as a weapon and not a utensil.

She scuttled over against the wall into a dark niche, out of sight of the doorway.

Zoë, my Zoë, what are you doing?
—Shut up, father.
It's the first Pillar that we let our Beast protect us. The Beast is wise. It remembers for us that we eat when hungry, sleep when day comes, and refuse to suffer ourselves to be hurt.
—Shut up, all of you.

She bunched up her skirt and stared at the white flesh of her inner thigh. It often seemed to her that all her skin had grown tougher since the Embrace, but this here was still smooth and soft and round. She hooked the tip of her knife into it and dragged it down, watching the flesh open wetly and spill out its blood. It was dark, thick, slightly warmer than the skin surrounding it. Both the sight and the sensation cheered her. She carved a second line parallel to the first one. As the curdled streams dripped down and pooled in the dirt she felt some of the tightness in her chest melt away, and she took several deep, long breaths. A pleasant chill traveled down into the core of her body. She wrapped her free hand around her upright knee and hugged it.

There, does that anger you, Beast? See how I can make you bleed?

She could stand a little more pain yet. She was stronger than it was. It would want revenge, reward and she would deny it. She made another slice, even deeper, gritting her teeth to restrain the cry. With each cut she felt larger and wiser. Yes, out with this vileness. After a little while the dark gouts thinned and turned red, flowing like a clear river. She stifled a little sob of gratitude. Anatole insisted God was always listening to her, but it was only now, in these moments, that she could actually feel His kindness near.

"You see, it was just a mistake, like Meribah said," she whispered. "I didn't mean to wake his Beast, and he, he never meant to put it into me. That thing that tore my throat, that was not my father. I didn't want to disobey. You have to understand us both, You must."

The compulsion came constantly. Sometimes it gripped her in the middle of talking to someone or even in the middle of feeding. But if she gave in too often then she had to feed even more. She wasn't so stupid that she didn't understand that. And so it was only once a month that she gave herself permission. Even though the relief was so brief, and even though the next evening when she awoke she'd see her thigh unmarked, and know that the poison was building up again. Twenty-seven nights of twenty-eight she endured the pollution, bore her cross with humility. The other was her remission. It was her own arrangement and it was no one else's business.

She took a cloth out of the chest and carefully wiped both the knife and her leg clean. The rest of the weaving could wait now. She hadn't paid Anatole or Gerasimos good evening yet. She smoothed out her skirt and left the hut smiling. On the way she stopped to gather up a bunch of primroses that had had the audacity to start growing at the base of Bardas' wall.

Chapter Fifteen

The Bière Forest
Feast of Mary Magdalene, 1212

"And so you see, little brothers and sisters, that though it was given to the children of Caine to be the replete vessels of His shining blood, it was given to a simple monk of the children of Seth to herald the true faith in the Occident. Let those of you whose souls still strain to breathe through the heavy clay of earthly flesh take heart." Folcaut shifted. His intonation, Zoë noticed, always subtly changed as he moved from one subject in his sermon to the next. Anatole could take a lesson from that. Wise as his words might be, the sense of them tended to get lost in the flood of unmeasured syllables. That most in the camp didn't speak French as their native tongue didn't help either. Folcaut took great care to enunciate his *langue d'oïl* succinctly, and sometimes he would also throw in a phrase in Greek to clarify himself.

"Now it's come to my sad attention that some of the Cainites are doing a terrible disservice to the mortals whom duty calls them to shepherd ever towards an admirable rebirth. When you take your offering from the Sethites, brethren, you must treat the sacrament with its due honor. Even the blood of a mortal must not be let to waste, not so much as a stray drop upon the ground. In this way the Sethites will learn from your example. For if you revere the spark of the Pleroma which gutters even in their blood, then surely they will know that they must revere the coursing flame that dwells within the shining blood sevenfold above that."

At that a crashing and thrashing came from the upper branches of the tree below which Folcaut preached. Anatole slammed feet first into the ground next to the Heretic priest.

"Brothers and sisters," he cried, "listen to this wretched madman if you must, but don't credit his words an ounce. Just because a faith calls itself Cainite, that doesn't mean it carries the Dark Father's seal and blessing! Brother." Anatole laid a hand on the shoulder of a ragged vampire youth who stood near the front of the throng. "Have you ever cut yourself on the skin, or been cut? Yes? Then tell me, does the blood shine? Does it shine?"

The vampire opened his mouth, but no immediate answer came out. The Frenchman cast his gaze fiercely over all the assembled. "Our blood does not shine! Your own eyes will easily tell you that it is dark and thick like old bile! Brethren, this false prophet would lead you to a false glory, a glory based on pride in the self, pride in the very curse laid on us. I beg you to seek a lower and yet a higher glory, a glory hidden from the eyes of the proud. The children of Caine serve their purpose under God, yes, but it is *not* to pretend to divinity and lead mortal souls astray from the true worship!"

The crowd seemed to waver. Folcaut stood stoic.

"And you would yoke them to the altar of the Church of Pilate instead?" he returned when Anatole had finished. "The abattoir Church?"

"Ah, Folcaut. The abattoir lies not in the Church Herself, but in the hearts of Her misguided shepherds. Do not speak to me of abattoirs when an abattoir dwells within the heart of each Cainite here! Tell me, Father, what of the Beast? Is a Cainite angel in most parts and devil in only one? Is it possible to Fall *partway* from Heaven?"

A tumult rose from the edge of the gathering. Zoë hauled up on tiptoe to try to see. She caught a glimpse of Iskender's fur-lined hat bobbing along among the tops of others' heads. The folk who'd so avidly watched Folcaut and Anatole argue a moment before pressed forward as a mass to get the best view of what turned out, at last, to be an even more dramatic scene.

Iskender grimly elbowed the onlookers aside. He supported one of his Cainite raiders on his shoulder—Mátyás, if Zoë remembered the name correctly. The man's left leg hung uselessly underneath him, riding-trousers shredded. The limb was charred black down a long strip of flesh and blistered red around the edges of that.

"Let me see him," said Folcaut, coming over and kneeling down to get a better look at the wound. "Stand aside, please, let me see."

"It's a burn," said Iskender. "Out of the way."

"Yes, so it is. Ditmar, bring me my ewer and my basin."

"It's a *burn*," Iskender repeated, scowling.

"Why, what are you going to do?" Mátyás asked Folcaut.

"If you will permit me, I'm going to wash your wound."

The Hungarian made a painful, questioning grimace at Iskender, who waved his free hand.

"*I* think the thing to do is dangle it in the stream, but it's your leg…"

"What happened?" Zoë asked.

The Turk's eyes flashed over to hers. "What do you care?"

She stared at him, wanting to get angry but too horrified at the man's wound, which stank like a roasting-pit.

"I ask the faithful here to come to me," Folcaut said as he took up the pottery ewer in his hands. Several of the Cainites in the crowd obeyed. Each he blessed with a hand on the head. Each bled into the ewer, biting a gash into the wrist to do so and then licking it shut again afterward. Then Folcaut bled into the ewer himself.

This display caused much quiet consternation among the rest of the crowd. In the always-parched economy of the camp, even a momentary use of one's blood powers on another's behalf was a boon as precious as a gold ingot. Yes, mortals were drained dry as their owners wished; but most of those owners guarded and maintained them as jealously as prize livestock (there were, as Iskender had pointed out some time before, notable exceptions). None here watching were so full that the smell of the spilled vitae didn't sharpen their senses and cause their lips to open slightly. That these devotees could shed their own blood so ungrudgingly, to what seemed a largely symbolic purpose, held them all in a moment's honest awe.

Folcaut raised the ewer up toward the heavens.

"O True Creator," he intoned, "we offer of ourselves in humble remembrance that the shining blood belongs to You utterly, that all things of *pneuma* proceed from You and thus are due unto You, and that without this the gift of your most beloved Son's sacrifice, we would be utterly enslaved to the torment of matter. We beseech You to imbue our blood with all the replete virtues of the Caine-Christ, that we may refresh ourselves in His most sublime purity. In Your ineffable Name we pray."

"Amen," echoed his knot of congregants, bowing their heads. Then Folcaut began to pour the vitae carefully over Mátyás' leg, letting the runoff spill into the basin below. He swabbed gently around the wound with his finger. Mátyás sucked in a hissing breath. Then after a moment some of the tension began to melt out of his face.

"It feels cooler," he said in surprise.

"It does?" Iskender echoed.

"Yes. It feels... I think it's better than it was."

"Look!" cried the youthful Cainite whom Anatole had challenged with his question. "Look, the blackness has faded."

"No, it hasn't," said someone else irritably. "Let me see."

"It has," exclaimed yet a third. "See, the blister that was there is gone."

"It does feel better..."

"Of course it feels better," the Father said with a gentle smile. "That is the virtue of the shining blood. There is no sweeter elixir, no other cure or nostrum needed. It restores you because it is the very essence of *pneuma*. Drink now, my son, and receive the full *consolamentum*."

"Mátyás—" Iskender began, but the Hungarian stopped him.

"I know, captain, but it's not the bond... surely one drink does little enough harm."

"Little harm and great good," answered Folcaut. "In any case this is no longer the blood of Cainites, but something even a degree beyond that in purity, indeed the fount of all shining blood."

Mátyás willingly allowed Folcaut to tip the mouth of the pitcher against his waiting lips. He swallowed in desperate gulps.

Anatole moaned and clutched at Zoë's upper arm. "Oh, wretched man, how cheaply you're sold."

Folcaut ignored him. "Let's try that leg now."

Zoë unconsciously shook her head—maybe the burn did look a little better, maybe it didn't, but it certainly didn't look better enough to stand on.

"Yes, Father." The very color of Mátyás' eyes seemed to have changed. They'd always before looked quite dark, but just at the moment they were a warm auburn. He rested his hands on Folcaut's forearm, and with the Father's help he creaked back up toward a standing position. Gingerly he tested his weight on the injured side. Then all at once he straightened completely.

"Father," he said again, triumphantly. Sighs and gasps arose from the onlookers.

"A miracle!" "A sign!" "We are witnesses!"

"Are you sure you can walk on that, Mátyás?" Iskender frowned. "We don't want you re-injuring it."

"I'm positive, captain. Look!" He paced easily round in a little circle.

"Good, well… then let's go down to the stream now."

"The stream? But that'd rinse off the blood."

"Console us also, Father," one of the Cainites in the crowd begged Folcaut, seizing hold of his cassock. "What Mátyás suffers in the flesh, we have suffered in the spirit for so long." Another Cainite darted forward to take hold of the spattered basin and thrust her face into it to drink up the dregs; several more tried to seize it from her, and a struggle ensued.

"No!" Anatole stepped forward. "Listen to me, you miserable people! You must listen, but your ears don't hear because your eyes are dazzled."

At once a dozen hostile gazes bent upon the Frenchman. "Anatole," Zoë whispered to him urgently, trying to take his elbow. He shook her off.

"Even Pharaoh's conjurers could turn staves into snakes," he pressed on. "And the Beast's own prophet will tell you he is sent of God. Do not give yourselves over so quickly to the one who promises ease and peace!"

"You said yourself to take note of what our own eyes tell us, Malkavian." This came from a new voice, smooth and cultured. Zoë looked up. It was Gallasyn, the councilor. Taller than most in the crowd, he rose through them like a white peak among storm clouds. "I don't know what *you* see, but I see Mátyás walking again."

"Anatole," Zoë whispered again.

"What you see is a blasphemy, not a miracle!"

"*You* are the one who blasphemes," one of Folcaut's followers, a haggard man in a richly embroidered but threadbare dalmatic, hissed at Anatole. "You blaspheme against the shining blood of Caine, you spit at the very face of the One who gave us all immortality!"

A clod of mud sailed out from somewhere among the throng and struck Anatole on the cheek.

"And he that shall blaspheme against the Holy Spirit hath never forgiveness," Folcaut murmured. He stepped aside, out of the path of any further missiles.

Zoë searched among the faces for the guilty one, baring her teeth. Next someone threw an old gristle-covered chicken bone, and next a rock. She ducked away. Then she saw that Anatole still stood unmoving under the growing hail of filth and tried to go back, but the crowd poured forward to surround him.

"No!" she screamed in Greek. "No, leave him alone, you animals!" She tried to pull back the shoulders of those standing in her way. A hand fell on her shoulder.

"Zoë." Iskender's voice was low in her right ear. "Come away."

"They're killing him," she protested, straining at his grip.

"They will not kill him," he said firmly. "Don't rile them up further. Let them have their fun."

She rounded on him, aghast. "Their *fun?*" But despite his words, the Turk's face was perfectly serious, even worried. She glared at his hand lying heavily on her shoulder. He removed it.

She stood there, clenching her fists.

"It'll be over in a minute," he said. But a long minute went by. Gallasyn extricated himself from the mass and walked away in the direction of the lodge, his cloak wrapped close around him and a peculiar look on his face. She heard the noise of mortal snot being hawked and spat, and once a crack of bone. The top half of Anatole's impassive head could be seen for a little while, but then it disappeared, dragged under.

"They're killing him, I know it!"

"Give it a count of forty. If they haven't stopped, we'll drive them off together. I promise! Now count."

"One. Two," she counted, feeling perfectly idiotic. Why forty? It was already horribly like counting the lashes upon Jesus' back. She could make out nothing of Anatole's voice, not even a shout of pain.

"Twenty. Twenty-one." For a moment the clamor seemed to die down, and she thought perhaps they'd disperse; but then something stirred and swelled in the center of the group and another cry went up. She saw Anatole bob limply up to the surface, borne on a dozen hands. Dirt, slime and worse substances literally covered him, and his face was crisscrossed with fingernail scratches. As one they rolled outward toward the edge of the camp, still holding him aloft.

"Iskender!" she growled. He nodded in silent accord, breaking into a half-run alongside her. They followed the mob out to the most ramshackle of the camp's day-shelters. The cesspit lay just a bit further beyond. The instant she saw it Zoë realized what they planned to do, and put on a burst of speed, but it was too late. The frontmost pair of the throng hefted Anatole in their arms and flung his unresisting body into the yard-deep stew of ordure.

160   Ravnos

Zoë and Iskender ran up to the edge, pushing aside the crowd, which settled back uneasily now, unsure whether to stay and watch or not.

"They've killed him," she wailed. She saw no sign of movement within.

"Wait, wait," he said.

"No! I'm going down."

"No, I'll go down." Iskender started to unbuckle his sword. He eyed the pit, as though if he looked hard enough he'd find some way down that wouldn't involve wading through mortal excrement.

One of the two who'd thrown Anatole in came up behind Iskender. "Here, I'll help you," he said with a grin, and shoved Iskender forward. Iskender almost toppled but recovered himself, grabbing the hilt of his sword. In the next instant the other Cainite's neck was stretched out to its full length as Zoë's knife flashed out and caught him directly under the jawbone.

"You move again and I take your head clean off," she snarled, quite delighted to have someone to vent her fury upon. The crowd protested, but they drew back another step or two. The Cainite held up his hands.

"So… I see our great bandit-chief has a new protector," he said, covering up his sudden fear with mockery.

But if he was hoping to inflame the Turk, it didn't work. Iskender glanced at Zoë, then gave her a nod. "The bandit-chief is always grateful to find someone watching his back," he replied. "As you should be, Mihai."

Zoë let Mihai unhook himself from the point of her blade and escape.

"Did you see where he fell?" Iskender asked. Zoë shook her head.

"In the middle, I think."

"Of course. Maybe it'd be better to get a rope—wait! There."

The surface of the muck stirred near them, rising slightly. The little disturbance moved up to the edge of the pit. Then Anatole's head burst out. The Malkavian reached his hand up toward Zoë, who took it. Slipping once or twice on the steep side of the hole, he clambered up to stand at the pit's edge.

A tide of gasps and exclamations greeted him as he emerged. Iskender, too, fell aside, gaping. Zoë was so relieved simply to see Anatole walking that at first she didn't realize what the fuss was about. Then it struck her.

Not a drop of filth was on him. His clothes were once again the soft dark-gray they showed only after their occasional washings. His hands, arms, legs and even feet were white as snow. Of the scratches on his cheek no trace remained. Even his hair, which had been hanging in its usual rattails just a little while earlier, lay askew but fine and clean on his shoulders. He leaned on both Zoë's shoulder and Iskender's and allowed them to help him past the staring bystanders back towards his shelter.

"Why do you stand amazed, fools?" the Malkavian muttered at them as they clustered round, some seeking to touch his robe. "Haven't you been told every day and night since you were born that God washes away our blackest sins in the blood of Christ? Doesn't He spin the stars round the earth and speak life itself into being with a word? What is a little dirt?"

Then he stopped and turned toward Folcaut, who stood removed from the rest by several yards, his princely face wreathed in bewilderment.

"Christ's blood," he added. "Not Caine's. Even the Dark Father himself would tell you this, if you troubled to ask him."

***

Zoë came to Anatole's shelter later that night. She was more than a bit disturbed to see a half-dozen Cainites and mortals kneeling in silent prayer-vigil at various spots in the vicinity, the men bare-chested and all penitently unshod. Still, her own need impelled her forward, and she knelt herself to knock softly at the wooden flap-door. She could hear mumbling within. Usually that implied a vision, not a guest, but it was impossible to tell. No answer came. She knocked again.

"Anatole. May I come in?"

She thought she heard the word "yes," and opened the door a crack. The Frenchman crouched on the floor, head bent to touch the ground before him—he looked like a Saracen praying toward Mecca, except that his hands weren't placed palms-down but clasped together underneath him.

Was he in pain? She came all the way inside and shut the door. "Anatole?"

"Oh yes, of course," he murmured into the dirt. "When a woman thinks alone she thinks evil, it hasn't been written in so many words yet but it will be. And then what, I won-der, will be made of you, long dead and past defending. Whether you wore black, red or white, homespun or pearls from Cathay, will make no difference to them. It all chars to black in the flames. And that too burns easily. Scribble away. Hildegard will stand a thousand years from now, but not you. No, not yet… not yet, my child, the puppets must fin-ish their dance, no poking. Yes, he is there, but is he *with* you? Any of them. Are you sure? Oh yes, that, I feel that too, it frightens me as well. The devil doesn't take bets any-more, after Job; God must rely on the unwilling and the unwitting to do His dirty work now. Myself, I'm both, why should it surprise you that I fear? But I would no more refuse my cup than you would yours."

"Anatole?"

He sat up and gazed at her. She could see, even in the dark of the shelter, his pupils contract as he refocused from within to without.

"I don't mean to interrupt," she said.

"Oh, we weren't talking about anything important," he replied cheerily. "Besides, you're my childe and my first duty. What is it?"

There wasn't really room to stand in Anatole's shelter. It was well built and well sealed, having just one tiny win-dow with a sturdy inner shutter to allow for night visibility; but it was no taller than absolutely required for day-shelter. She arranged herself in a kind of side-saddle sitting posi-tion. Then she hesitated for a long space. Anatole waited.

"Anatole," she said at last, "about the, the miracle earlier tonight."

"There was no miracle," he said flatly.

"No miracle—" she began to argue, but then remembered what he'd said at the cesspit and took his meaning. "Whatever it was that happened, then."

"Yes?"

"How did you do it?"

He crooked a smile. "I didn't."

She scowled in return. "No, I don't mean that. Not that part of it. How could you stand there and let them treat you like that? You—you didn't even flinch…"

"What else would you have had me do? Keep talking on, when my words went unheeded? Fight back? What would that have accomplished?"

"I know, but—" She wished she could stand, to pace. "Doesn't something in you rise up in fury? Have you no Beast?"

"Of course I have a Beast. We all have one." He took her chin and looked her over, as though he'd never seen her up close before. If it had been anyone else she would have recoiled.

"Then how do you make it stay down?"

He released her. "What you're talking about, child, is not the Beast. The Beast may seem like a wild creature, but really it's more like a well-trained hound. When its mistress is hungry, it tries to feed her. When its mistress is frightened, it leaps to protect her. And when its mistress' pride is hurt… then it moves to avenge her."

She nodded, blinking back the start of tears. "I know that pride is a terrible sin."

"But?"

"But… sometimes I feel like there is nothing else."

He absorbed this. Once again he was doing that terrible *listening* of his. She knew that her words were being turned in his mind like one of Gregory's crystals, examined from every facet, their depths fully scried.

"You've had to let go of so many things over the past several years," he said finally. "Small wonder if you wish to cling to whatever's left."

"But you, you don't need to cling to anything."

"What I have is such bounty that other things seem very insignificant and easy to do without by comparison."

"I'm not that way."

"I don't ask you to be."

"No, I ask it. I can never *rest*, Anatole." Her voice dropped all at once, into some bitter adult register. "My pride won't let me. I've done so many stupid things for its sake. Sometimes I even knew they were stupid and yet I did them anyway. You see, tonight I'd die to avenge Gregory. But when he was here I used to say such horrible things to him… I hurt him on purpose. I don't know why. Something in me drove me to defy him. If he were still here, I'm sure I'd still be doing it. And now, now I hurt day and night. I can never stop thinking of all that I've suffered. Thinking of what I once had, the chance I was given—and what I am now."

"And what is that?"

"Nothing." The word was thick, tarry. She fairly vomited it out.

"Nothing is nothing."

She shook her head. "That's not true! Or maybe it's true, maybe nothing is nothing. But some things are no *good*. What good am I? Who needs me now? The world would just be better off if I died, wouldn't it?" She dashed tears out of her eyes with her sleeve, then cursed herself for soiling it.

"No. Everything that is, is because it must be," he said. "But be honest about what you really ask. It's not the world's need that torments you, but *your* need to think well of yourself, and your fear that you will never be able to do so. This is the obverse of pride, childe, not the reverse."

"But what can I do about it?" she protested.

"Accept that God alone is good, and rely on His strength and dignity instead of your own."

"But how do I *do* that?"

He seemed to ponder this. Then, slowly, the little smile came back.

"Do you truly wish to learn?" he asked.

Chapter Sixteen

The Bière Forest
The Following Night

"Quiet, please. Quiet," called Anatole as he climbed up onto the wooden pallet that served as the camp's announcements platform. "I see that not everyone is here. If someone could pass the message on to the absent later, I'd be most grateful. Most of you know my childe, Zoë."

A minor din greeted this: mutterings of "Ravnos," a catcall or two.

"Unfortunately, my little love-light, my daughter, has disobeyed me most grievously. Much as it pains me, I find myself needing to punish her. And so I call upon you, our extended family, to assist me in her correction."

The mutterings quickly turned to snorts, chuckles and outright laughs. Zoë tensed her jaw, feeling wave after wave of prickling shame wash through her body.

"Yes, she must learn better than to get caught!" someone shouted.

Anatole held up his hand. "I've informed her that for the rest of this week, I am setting her out as servant to the rest of the camp. If any of you have chores that need doing, feel free to command them of her. I can tell you that she's especially adept at building and fixing things."

This both amused and gratified the crowd greatly. Zoë could see crafty looks descend on a number of faces. Even as she stood there suffering she understood the lesson in it. She *had* been a bad daughter to Gregory. Everyone in the old caravan had known it, too; they just didn't usually say anything. And though she'd felt terrible about it, she hadn't felt anywhere near as terrible as she did now. Why should that be? Why should the public exposure of the sin trouble her so much more than the sin itself?

"You mean any of us at all?" Decius asked. "I can get her to patch up my roof?"

"Of course," said Anatole. "Any of you at all."

"Do you really mean that?" Gallasyn called. He leaned against a tree, crossing his arms. "Shall she even wash out Father Folcaut's offering-bowls?"

"She'll wash out the Father's bowls, if he asks it of her," Anatole answered firmly, "she just won't fill them."

Zoë looked at him, the word "no" forming on her lips. But Anatole only nodded.

"Well! I'll be sure to let him know," said Gallasyn, and he left.

Anatole saw Zoë's expression and murmured in her ear, "Be patient."

"I can't," she murmured back. "Not with him."

"'There shall be false teachers among you,'" Anatole quoted, "'who privily shall bring in damnable heresies, even denying the Lord that bought them, and bring upon themselves swift destruction.'" He stared after Gallasyn's retreating back. "Their time will come as well, I promise you."

***

"Anatole was right," Iskender said that Sunday. He looked over the bridle and pulled on it to be sure the new fittings were solid. "You are quite the tinker. You'd better watch out. Once the word spreads you'll never be able to escape again. Bardas might even appoint you to a post, Caine forbid."

"Oh, like he appointed you camp pantler?" Zoë asked, putting her shoe up on a stump to retie it.

"Exactly." The Turk made a wry face. "So I know whereof I speak. What did you do, anyway?"

"What do you mean?"

"How did you disobey Anatole? It must have been pretty bad. He hadn't struck me as the harsh sort."

"Yes, it was pretty bad."

"But of course you're not going to tell me."

"I don't see how it's your business," she retorted, and then immediately regretted it. It wasn't a very humble answer, and humility was supposedly the point of this exercise. "I—went out without his permission," she amended herself. That had been one of her more common offenses against Gregory, after all.

"Over-protective, eh."

She was silent.

"Well, thanks in any case," he went on. "It's good to know someone around here has such skills. In my line of work, things do break."

"You're welcome." She wiped the remnants of polishing-oil off her hands with a chamois cloth. "I must be going. Gallasyn's not satisfied just watching me wash out the Father's bowls, now he wants something done for himself as well."

He clucked and chuckled. "Well, don't do a better job than you must, then." Then he gave a short farewell wave and left.

Gallasyn smiled about as broadly as he ever did when he saw Zoë, which is to say, not very, and crookedly. "Lakeritos' daughter has certainly performed her own share of wonders this week," he called. *Humility*, she thought, *humility*.

"There are no more wonders anymore, messire," she answered. "Only work."

"Somehow I doubt that," he said, and then paused. He stepped closer and lowered his voice. "In all seriousness, mademoiselle…"

"In all seriousness?" she echoed.

"Yes. Actually, I'm curious. I mean, if there *were* anything left—here or back East—I'd assume you would be the one to know about it."

She fought the urge to edge away. "Anything of what?"

"Of the *wonders*, of course," he returned angrily, a hard light kindling in his eyes.

"No, there is nothing left," she said hastily. "I'm all done with such things. Would I be here otherwise?"

"Of course." He straightened and withdrew. His face was cool and statuesque once more. "You follow the mad prophet now. You have no part in such vanities anymore."

"And neither do you," she reminded him. "You follow Father Folcaut."

"Yes. Come, mademoiselle. Can you saddle your horse quickly?"

"Why, where are we going?"

"To where your chore waits, of course."

"But isn't it in the camp?" she frowned.

"No, I'm afraid it's a short ride from here. That's why I was hoping you'd be along a little quicker. In any case, you're here now."

"Well, all right… let me get the rest of my tools, then… messire…" She turned and headed in the direction of her shelter. He fell into step beside her.

Suddenly Iskender was running on pounding feet up to them. "Hoy! You bitch!" he shouted, putting his fierce countenance an inch away from hers. "What do you think you're about? You think you can work this kind of deceit on one of your own blood?"

He thrust the bridle up at her. She took it with an unbidden cry of disgust. The bridle rings she'd just gotten done laboriously repairing a few moments ago were once again broken and twisted.

"You are supposed to be playing servant to everyone in the camp who asks it… everyone!" he went on bellowing. "Is this how you honor your sire? What do I ride with tomorrow, eh?"

The furious words *You must have done something with it!* tumbled right up to the back of her lips before she remembered. With the greatest effort of will she subdued herself, drawing in a deep, unnecessary breath purely to chase the tremor out of her limbs.

"I—I'm sorry, Iskender. I'll try again, right away."

"Now wait a minute," began the councilor.

"Sorry, Gallasyn. She has to finish one job properly before she gets to start another. I don't know what made her think I wouldn't see through the trickery, but I won't be cheated so." Iskender seized Zoë by the arm and dragged her away. Halfway across the camp, he ducked to the right and behind a hut.

"Why did you break it again just after I fixed it?" she asked, humility now straining a bit at the edges. "Does it give you—"

He looked at her strangely. "What on earth are you talking about, woman?" He took the bridle back from her. It vanished out of his fingers. Then he reached into his coat and brought out the real one, still clean and polished. "I'd never break my own horse tack. I live by the saddle. Why are you looking at me like that?—Listen. I was walking away, and I thought about what you said about Gallasyn. And it just came to me that whatever he wanted, it couldn't be good. Now, I'll certainly apologize for interrupting your punishment, if you're enjoying it so much…"

She started to reply and then stopped. Yes, she was supposed to be performing every task without question, but in all honesty the part about having to leave camp had excited her suspicions as well. Whether the scorpion actually meant harm or not, Iskender was no doubt right: It couldn't have been pleasant. In any case, it wasn't she who'd refused Gallasyn's request. Iskender had saved both her and her conscience in the matter.

She bowed her head to him then. "No. No, there is nothing to apologize for. Thank you," she said. And for once the words came quite easily.

***

"That's it!" Later on that evening Zoë flopped down beside Anatole where he sat trying to build a miniature castle out of pebbles and mud. "One hour to dawn and no more requests!"

He nodded. "You're finished, then."

"I'm finished. I think I've done more real work, helped more people in the past four nights than I have in the past four years. Thank you, Anatole."

"Don't thank me. What did I do?" He grunted as an attempt at a corner tower collapsed into shapeless muck. Zoë pulled up some blades of grass and started to help him. "And did you succeed in your real endeavor?" he asked.

She sat up excitedly. "I did. I actually did—almost completely. I was even polite to Folcaut, and that beastly Urbien who just stood there and *sneered* at me the whole time, I just smiled back. And when Decius' people made fun of me, I thought of you and the cesspit, and of the Beatitudes. It was hard at first, but it got easier and easier as it went on."

"Hm." He stood. "Plainly I didn't choose the task very well. I'll have to think of something better, if I can…"

She stood too, in dismay. "What? Anatole, what do you mean?"

He smiled at her. "Childe, what does it profit your soul to learn humility if you're simply going to take pride in the fact that you've learned it?"

Her mouth fell open.

"You see, our deepest faults are deep-rooted indeed, and prolific. They can't be gotten rid of so quickly. We must be like careful gardeners, first weeding in the spring and then in the summer searching out those that we missed regardless, and the next spring starting all over again nearly from scratch, and so on. I'll see what I can think of. But I fear that your devils, like much else about you, are clever."

Chapter Seventeen

Paris, St. Merri Quarter
Two Nights Before the Feast of St. Faith, 1212

"Ite, misa est."

In Crespin's benighted youth, these words had always been a source of great joy. He'd had no idea what they meant, other than that his time in pious bondage in the nave was over; that he could once again go out into the sunshine and enjoy the remainder of his Sabbath in whatever street amusements might present themselves before his mother hauled him back inside the master's kitchen to stir a pot or turn a spit.

Tonight it was just as great a joy, but for a very different reason.

"Deo et Cain gratias," he responded along with the rest.

The angel smiled upon them benevolently as he walked back through their midst, causing the base of Crespin's stomach to glow again with that remembered warmth, like a swallow of spiced wine. Crespin roused himself. He felt eager, now that the mass was over, to escape the oppression of close-packed bodies in a narrow room. He headed toward the door along with the rest. But Garnot took hold of his elbow.

"Don't run right away," the brewer exclaimed. "You realize this is an occasion, after all."

"It is?" he asked, still feeling a bit dazed.

"Yes. Your third Communion. Come, come." Garnot propelled him out.

There the angel waited beside the "chapel" door. Periodically he made the peculiar sign of blessing, which Garnot said was meant to represent the star that heralded the birth of the Second Caine and the radiance that proceeded from the heart of the Pleroma. The merchant stood just behind the angel, puffed up with velvet and his own importance; the key to this door, the warehouse proper and all the rest hung prominently on his belt. Crespin tried to control the trembling in his legs as they approached the tall, elegant, white-skinned being in purple robes.

"Your Grace?" At the angel's tacit nod of permission, Garnot went down on his knee, as did Crespin. One at a time they kissed his ring.

"Forgive my disturbing you, Your Grace, but this is Crespin's third Communion and I was hoping that you would favor him with a blessing."

"Of course, Garnot." The angel laid its cool hand upon Crespin's sweating head. "Once honors the First Caine, twice honors the Second Caine, and the third is a prayer in hopes of seeing the Caine who is to come," he explained. "Now you are a full partaker in the shining blood, my son. Rise."

"I… I hope for no honor other than to serve you and the other perfect well, Your Grace."

"The True Creator bless you for your devotion, my son." Now the hand slid down around his ear and to his neck. "It is… traditional for the convert, upon his third Communion, to offer of himself in repayment to Heaven for the blessings he has received. If you feel that you are ready."

"I am ready, Your Grace."

The others in the storage room, who had gathered into little conversational knots, suddenly fell silent as they realized what was going on. Crespin bent his head away from the angel's descending lips, which fastened upon him at the base of his throat. He felt the burning puncture of the twin teeth and almost at once he thought he could fairly *see* Heaven. Forms and outlines dissolved into blots of color and then into misty lights. He ascended through the roof of the warehouse and floated far above the city. He was delightfully bodiless, a thing composed solely of warm air and love: love for the angel, for God, for the stars and the streets, for every leprous beggar and whore crawling the alleyways. He felt that he could speak a word in benediction and lift all the world out of its sublunary misery forever; but the same ecstasy that gave him that belief also stopped his tongue. The angels often spoke of taking the shining blood into one's belly as *consolamentum*, the "consolation"—the act that made mortals temporarily perfect in Caine. This, however, this was every bit as deserving of the word and the praise. He wished it to go on forever. He didn't want ever to return to his human flesh, to that clunking assemblage of ham-hocks and tears.

And then the stiff little bone-shards were withdrawn from where they lay so deliciously lodged in his flesh. He gave a groan of regret. The angel's tongue lapped at the edges of the piercing and the skin smoothed out again under the healing balm of his saliva.

"You have done well, my son," the angel murmured.

"Your Grace." He went down on his knee again, rather less steadily than before. As one the other parishioners sighed in sympathy and envy. Many pairs of eyes turned hungrily to the angel, who simply smiled again and withdrew to the upstairs offices with his deacon to unvest.

"You see?" said Garnot, clapping him on the shoulder, then holding him up by the elbow when that nearly sent him stumbling. "Now aren't you glad I stopped you? You want to listen to old Garnot. My family's been in the Faith since it first came to Paris."

Crespin only nodded. He didn't yet trust himself to speak. The congregants left in pairs and threesomes, stealing out into the night and leaving by different ways.

"Let's go back to the tavern," Garnot said as they in their turn stepped out into the night air. "You needn't return to wife and marital bed tonight. I'll send you off to dreamland with a mug of my best beer, and then you can doss down in one of the guest rooms."

"No… thank you…"Crespin gently disengaged himself. "Actually, it probably sounds funny, Garnot, but I… I want to have a bit of a walk and a think."

Garnot nodded. "I quite understand, my friend. I felt the same way my first time. Just be careful where exactly you choose to walk. Your heart may be in Heaven still, but your body is down here on the same streets with the robbers and *ribauz*." He embraced Crespin in a huge, enveloping hug and headed off towards home.

Crespin stood a moment, savoring the evening coolness on his damp forehead.

Then he ducked into the alleyway across the street. One of the shadows unfolded itself and separated itself from its fellows, resolving into the shape of a pale man in a dark gray robe.

"You see, it *is* the same place every time, Reverend Brother," Crespin said, ducking his head. "Between fifteen and twenty come. That's as many as will fit within. It's not always His Grace that officiates, though, sometimes it's the other priest instead. And I'm a bit surprised he came alone tonight. Usually he brings his two deacons along, they're both Cainite as well…"

"Thank you, Brother Crespin," said Anatole. Then he drew aside the collar of Crespin's chemise, frowning slightly.

"I see they took from you. You're not hurt, I hope."

"No, Reverend Brother. It was no worse than when you take me—and no better, of course."

Anatole smiled and released the fabric to its place. He laid his hands on Crespin's shoulders.

"You've done well, brother," Anatole said. No heretic bishop could hope to match the warmth, the loving-kindness of it. And Crespin had pledged himself to God's Own Fool in three "communions" long ago. The mortal's face split wide in a grin of relief and pleasure.

"Now home, quickly and quietly as you can." The gray-swathed form moved to the alleyway's mouth and disappeared, leaving Crespin vaguely disappointed that that was all he was to have of his prophet's company that evening.

Well, he'd said he wanted a walk and a think.

Chapter Eighteen

"Anatole!" Zoë found her mentor at last. It was one of his several favorite spots, a little projection of rock and earth just over the stream-bed. He sat cross-legged on the rock, the cowl of his robe pulled completely over his head. Only the dirty bare feet identified him.

"Anatole," she repeated, coming to sit beside him. "A chance!"

"A chance for what?" he asked, not raising his head.

"At Gauthier! I've had your Anna watching the St. Martin gate."

"I have no Anna."

"What do you mean, you have no Anna? Anna who's been with you since I met you, Genia's sister."

"I have no Anna. I have no Genia. I have nothing genitive about me, nothing that conjugates. I am the world's dangling participle. It dangles, too, never did me a bit of good. Tonight I'd give up the whole thing for one more night in the field with Marie-Agnes, one more chance to sow. An ordinary immortality. My nose on the face of a little girl somewhere." He sniffed. Zoë became aware, from the smell of it, that he was weeping. "God help me, I don't even want to talk to her anymore, except perhaps to tell her to sin with her body and not just her heart. One night in the field and God won't be the poorer. But that's not my argument. I have no part in Seth. I understand why it had to be so, of course. How could the root watch its branches burn and still praise God? But it doesn't feel like a mercy, not now. Leave me, whoever you are. Leave me to my weakness. The Devil is tempting me."

"Anatole." Zoë shook him. "Hush. Look at me. It's Zoë. Look at me!"

Slowly, almost fearfully, he brought his head up. His cheeks were streaked with red.

"Do you understand? It's Zoë. I need you thinking sensibly now, Anatole. It's important. Your Anna says that Gauthier rode into Paris *alone* day before yesterday. If you carry me we can get back tonight and maybe catch him while he's still away!"

Anatole flopped down on his side. "I have been waiting," he said. "The wick is trimmed, but the oil's run out. I thought I brought plenty. In the east they blow trumpets and in the west they beat drums. And in the plain the golden calf. You tell me which way to turn first."

"Ohhh…" Zoë tried in vain to turn him over. He had become heavy as lead. "Stop arguing with Belifares, or Uriel, or whoever it is tonight! We don't have time for this, Anatole. Talk to *me*. Listen to *me*."

"Would you like to buy some oranges from Chambery?" he muttered. She leaned forward and shoved him, pushing him slowly off the rock and into the water below. He made an enormous splash. Then his head broke through the surface of the water and, coughing, he climbed back up onto the bank and sat there.

"The others in the camp throw me into stinking offal when I offend them," he said once he had recovered the use of his lungs. "But not my Zoë. She simply baptizes me anew."

"Are you going to listen now?" Zoë asked hopefully. She went down to join him.

"I *was* listening."

"But are you understanding? Did you hear what I said about Gauthier?"

"Yes, his right arm hurts."

"No, he's in Paris."

"Of course."

"Alone. Does his arm really hurt?"

"It must not have been you that said it."

"I'm going into Paris."

"You're not supposed to go into Paris. It's the gardener's decree."

"Oh, don't play innocent, Anatole, I know *you* go into Paris. Please come with me. The two of us together could take him hostage, and then we could draw the Red Brothers out, we could lure them anywhere we liked."

"Yes, that's a good idea." He stood and began to wring out his robe. "But I have a better one. You told me, didn't you, that Isidro once tricked a Heretic Cainite to his death by speaking secrets of the Heretic church?"

"Yes, I saw him do it. He knows about Folcaut's ilk, plainly he just doesn't know about Folcaut yet. Which I suppose we should be thankful for, even if the scoundrel does deserve a good thick stake in the heart from a Red Brother…" She frowned, connections already forming in her mind. "Why do you ask?"

"There's a kennel for God's own hounds inside the city walls—little sister to the Templar mother-house outside. We'll look first in that quarter. But we must leave quickly. Are you ready?"

"Of course."

***

There's always a high road and a low road to get there. It was originally a Leper saying, but it had become popular in the camp as a handy phrase for the many little compromises and sins that even a Caine-appointed pilgrimage must tolerate in its time of need.

Ironically enough, the "low road" into Paris was actually a high one, namely the St.-Jacques gatehouse. A fishwife's market call was evidently the signal for those within to let a little basket down on a slender thread of yarn. Anatole counted some coins out of his purse and dropped them in. The basket snaked back up the wall again. After a few moments one of the guards appeared at the window, nodding and waving. Now a knotted rope spooled down into their waiting hands.

The guards let them down the other side of the tower with barely a word exchanged. Even their appreciative glances in Zoë's direction had a quality of boredom, as though this sort of clandestine nighttime toll-traffic were no more remarkable to them than that which passed through the gate itself during the day. Perhaps it wasn't.

"We'll have to take the long way round," Anatole explained once they were safely inside, "since you can't hide yourself from sight as I do. Try to remember the turns. If you ever come back on your own, there are certain areas you must avoid at all costs."

She nodded and tried to take careful note as he led her through the warren of the Left Bank and then across the river, but he zigged and zagged like a weaver's shuttle. Only the moon above kept her sure even of their overall direction. At last, however, they arrived at an imposing house hard by the Grand Pont and its money-changers' stalls.

"A kennel for God's own hounds, did I say?" the Frenchman murmured wryly, gazing up at it. "A counting-house for God's own bankers, would have been at least as accurate. Many a great lord whose lust for war outgrows his purse must come begging to the Poor Knights, hat in hand. They say a mountain of gold and treasure lies in the vaults of the Temple itself. How much do you suppose they might have squirreled away here, perhaps under our very feet?"

Zoë could conjure no such amusement. Civilian as the place might look from the street, any counting-house of the Templars must surely be guarded even at this hour. "Who cares about treasure?" she replied impatiently. "How do we get in?"

"We don't."

"But, Anatole…"

"If the fox goes where the hound isn't, we won't have much of a chase."

"Gauthier's not inside?"

He shook his head. "He might have been, earlier. But our pilgrim arrives at the house of his city brothers, and they embrace him, and light a sweet beeswax candle and show him to a soft safe bed with garnet-red blankets, perhaps even intimating that if he still finds it too cold, something lovely can be brought in to warm it further… no. It's simply not in him to sleep well under such conditions. Here." He handed Zoë a large square of fine blue cloth and a pin. "Put that on your head for a wimple, and fasten it as the French matrons do."

"Why?"

"So that he won't recognize you. You remembered to bring along your little burglar's friends, didn't you, the things for picking open a lock?"

"You asked me to bring them, didn't you?" she retorted, irritated to be reminded as though she were a careless child.

"I know, I'm only making sure. It's far better for our purpose if we don't have to break the doors open."

"What doors? What purpose? Anatole!"

"It's simple. You'll see. Now quick, jump into my arms. And go limp, like you're a mortal I've just drained."

Distaste rose in her gullet at the very idea, but she did as he said, letting one arm swing down like a pendulum and resisting the urge to tense her neck and lift her head so she could see better.

Just a few moments later, the sound of iron-shod hooves on paving stones echoed up from their right. Gauthier rode up the street toward the entrance. He was armored but bare-headed. His eyes seemed a bit puffy and tired, and his horse looked weary as well. Clearly whatever sort of lonely vigil-round he'd gone on that night had been a long one. But he sat straight as ever in the saddle, carrying his lantern on a pole.

Anatole stepped out into the moonlight. Gauthier hadn't even been looking in their direction, but at once he froze and turned his head. The fatigue fell from his eyes in an instant; they opened wide, as though to swallow up the sight of the vampire clutching his helpless prey.

Then a dry snaking utterance, lashing out toward them. "*You.*"

Anatole grinned. It was one of his very best lunatic grins. Zoë herself felt the passing urge to strike him.

"Me," he agreed beatifically, and took off running.

Gauthier cursed and spurred his horse into pursuit. Zoë found it difficult to stay convincingly dangling and loose what with all the jostling, and she wanted desperately to glance back and see how closely the knight followed. It sounded like he was right on their heels.

"Run faster!" she hissed.

"No. Mustn't lose him right away," he said.

She groaned. Once again it seemed as though Anatole were trying to trace out a minotaur-maze with his feet. But after a small eternity of chasing through the narrow streets and alleys, the hoofbeats finally receded and became more distant. Then they faded entirely. Soon afterward, Anatole pulled up short at the door of a tall wooden building and tipped Zoë without ceremony onto her feet.

"Hurry, the lock. Hurry."

She fumbled in her purse for the lockpicks, inserted them into the keyhole and worked at the tumblers for a few panicked moments until they gave way.

"Good. Perfect so far, in fact." He lifted the latch. "Let me go first, then come when I call."

What, wait outside while Gauthier thunders down upon us? Zoë thought, distressed. But Anatole opened the door and slipped into the darkness. A little while later she heard a murmur, then the thump of something falling. Then came the whisper of her name. She carefully stole inside. Anatole looked up from the body of a guard who lay sprawled out on the floor under him. He dragged the man off to one side of the room, tucking him behind a low table loaded down with fabric-bolts.

"He'll live," Anatole said, mistaking her consternation for concern. "I'm sure he'll be sacked tomorrow, but he'll live. Now do you see that stack of crates up against the wall? Move them aside. Try to remember how they were arranged because if all goes well we'll be putting them back. There's a door behind them. I need you to pick its lock too. Then you go upstairs and hide. Above all stay *quiet*. The merchant who owns this warehouse lives just next door, and we don't want him waking if we can avoid it. Don't come down till I give you the all-clear."

"What?" As much as Gauthier frightened her, the idea of sitting out the whole episode annoyed her immensely. The knight was her nemesis as much as Anatole's, after all. "Why? What are *you* going to do?"

"Go and fetch Gauthier," he answered solemnly. "Hopefully he hasn't gotten himself too lost."

Zoë found that lifting the crates was never a task meant for one as small as herself. But once her arms were engorged with blood-strength, she could move them easily and quickly enough. With an occasional glance at the unconscious guard (who luckily did not stir) and at the outer doorway (which remained thankfully empty) she laid them neatly out in the reverse order of their original placing. Then she unlocked the inner door that now stood revealed.

She'd be damned if she wasn't going to at least see what lay within this hidden room before she ran and hid herself. She gingerly tried the latch. The door swung open easily. She went inside.

She still didn't quite have Gregory's senses, but any vampire had a keen nose for the smell that greeted her as she walked in: mortal blood. Old and stale, and a remnant only—no visible traces of it remained in the room—but unmistakable. In the gloom she could make out a single piece of furniture, a low cabinet of wood, a little longer than most men were tall, with a slab of marble laid across the top. At one end of the slab were score-marks, as though from a blade. Behind the altar (she was now quite sure that was what it was) lay a huge copper bowl with a strange star-shaped design worked into its base. The smell of blood rose especially strongly from it, and if she peered she could see that the crevices hadn't been completely washed clean.

Anatole, she knew, could sometimes touch a thing and summon a vision of its past. What if he were to touch these score-marks? What in God's name had intervened, however fleetingly, between metal and stone? Folcaut bled

182   Ravnos

mortals for the sake of his heretical offices, she knew, but sentiment in the camp wouldn't permit him to take the lives of precious feeding-vessels. Yet. Perhaps in Paris they'd become more prodigal in their bounty…

She shuddered and moved away. At least Anatole's purpose was now clear. Kill two birds with one stone. Or, more properly, kill one bird with the other bird. She supposed she approved; but she still wanted to be there herself when Isidro died. The last time she'd asked him to re-prophesy on the subject, he'd again assured her that some night it would be so.

As she drifted from the altar she saw the first of several Frankish-style devotional paintings festooning the wall. They were laid out just like the stations of the Cross, except there were too few of them. She examined them curiously. Here was a picture of Adam and Eve being exiled from the Garden of Eden, only Eve and the serpent both wore gilded halos. Here was another haloed figure with red hair and the robes of an ancient priest, bringing a huge rock down onto the head of a lad in shepherd's robes. Two beings that seemed meant to be angels, except that they had no wings, bore up the lad's dropped crook and hovered nearby, holding it out as though for the haloed figure to take when he was finished. Of course. The heretic re-imagining of Caine and Abel, wherein Caine earned neither curse nor infamy for his cowardly act, but went on to usurp his brother's place as Godly shepherd, and later the very glory of Jesus Christ…

Barely in time she heard the faint noise in the street outside, and fled upstairs into the offices.

"Come out, demon." Gauthier's voice sounded from below, muffled by the wooden floor. She put her ear to the floorboards to hear better. "If you think I won't disturb the neighborhood's peace to find you, you're wrong. I'll tear this place apart if I must. In the name of the Father, Son, and Holy Spirit, I charge you to reveal yourself and face your punishment *now*… Holy Mary, Mother of God."

The last was an exclamation, not an invocation. Straining her senses, she could hear his footsteps move into the other part of the downstairs, into the hidden room. They paced around in a circle. Then they stilled for a long time. After that came several extended scraping and sliding noises. She waited, tightly coiled.

The footsteps started again. They headed toward the door and out into the street, where they turned once more into hoofbeats and slowly retreated.

Another set of footsteps came up the stairs. She bolted to duck behind the writing-desk, but then Anatole said softly, "All clear."

She came out. He was smiling. They went downstairs, where Anatole checked inside the "chapel" to make sure it was undisturbed. Then he shut the door and had Zoë work the lock closed again.

"He left," she said, half-wonderingly, as they began to replace the crates.

"Yes, he did. Thanks be unto God."

"For a moment I was sure he'd burn the whole thing down."

"I'm sure for a moment he was tempted," Anatole chuckled. "But no, he's clever, like us. He can wait till the crop is ripe to harvest. He'll probably set a secret watch on the place starting tomorrow. He'll ask questions, find out who lives here and what goes on in the neighborhood—he knows this merchant can't possibly be ignorant of what takes up a portion of his own warehouse. He'll bring in the cunning aid of the Red Brothers. And on a night not long from now, when the time for Heretic rites comes around again, he'll come back together with his men. Now *our* task is to tidy up very carefully, so that the idolaters are indeed still here when he returns."

She nodded, though as she worked this through in her mind, agreement soon turned to doubt. "But Anatole... surely he noticed that the way was cleared for him, that the doors were unlocked. Surely he's going to suspect. Or else the Red Brothers will."

"Childe, it doesn't matter if Gauthier or the Red Brothers suspect. They'll still come back. Nothing could stop them from doing it now."

He looked around the now-restored room in satisfaction, brushing the dust off his hands. "It only matters that the Heretics don't suspect. Ah, I forgot to look, is our friend still out cold? Good. Now, Zoë, I ask you one last time tonight to play to the outlaw legends of your blood. Run upstairs and unchain the office strongbox from its moorings. Then let's see what else down here a bold and fleet-footed thief might think to make off with."

Chapter Nineteen

The Theodosian Abbey at St.-Denis
The Following Monday (Holy Week, 1213)

"And you confirm, Frère Isidro, that this is the same blasphemous iconography you've seen in other 'sancta' of the Cainites?" Only Marzone's eyes moved, but the regard in them was quite sharp.

"Even leaving aside everything else, Monseigneur," Isidro replied, "the halo around the head of Caine would settle it. And the star etched in the offering-bowl: the thirteen-pointed star, whose dimensions, I assure you, are not selected at random—though I confess I don't yet know their meaning."

"You counted, Gauthier?"

"I counted," Gauthier said eagerly. "Thirteen. Monseigneur, Messire l'Abbé, brothers, I put it to you that we at last have definite Cainite spoor. And it matches up nicely with some of our other evidence. Remember that strange murder on the Left Bank. The hue and cry was raised and the killer pursued over the bridge into that very same quarter; even at the time we thought to look around there, but obviously we were looking in the wrong *sorts* of places. That wine-dealer who had the mysterious 'miracle' cure from leprosy? He's a friend of the merchant who owns the warehouse. That priest who was garbling his Masses in suspicious fashion, I just learned this morning that his mother wet-nursed the merchant's last daughter."

"Yes, and it's good to see you're checking into it further, Sire Gauthier," broke in Gervèse, leaning forward. "But what about all the other bits that don't match up? Up until this happened, you were almost positive we should be looking in the Rue St.-Jacques among the students."

"Gervèse—*Abba*, I still think it's quite possible we're looking for *multiple* parishes, as it were, with a smaller attendance each, the better to hide the true numbers. And the space Sire Gauthier describes certainly sounds quite small." Isidro glanced at the cardinal, who nodded for him to go on. "So I say, let Sire Gauthier keep poking around the student and faculty houses if he likes, and you can likewise pursue your theory about the Ile de la Cité. But it's as our knightly friend says; this is different. This is definite. We must act as one."

"I know, I know it's definite," Gervèse grumbled. "That's what worries me. It's a little too definite. Now Sire Gauthier, this mad creature you chased into the heretic sanctuary. You said you'd seen it before, interrogated it."

"Yes. And Frère Isidro saw it also, more briefly."

"So there's no question at all that it knew precisely who and what *you* are. Why would it run right into its very own church, knowing you'd chase it inside and very likely act on what you found there?"

"I don't know, Abbé. I thought at first there might be a secret passageway, like the one Monseigneur and I found in Carcassonne, leading to a crypt for the unhallowed dead. But I could discover no such cache. The infamous thing simply disappeared, in that maddening way of theirs."

"Yes. And what about the woman?"

"Woman?"

"You said it was holding a woman at first, and then it wasn't."

"Ah yes. Well, no doubt it dropped her to get rid of the ballast."

"And has that ballast turned up again? Another mysterious corpse found in the city, there will be talk."

"Well, no, not yet. But he might have dumped her in a well, in the river, in a cesspit, who knows."

"And then when it did run into its sanctorum, in the warehouse, it didn't even stop to lock the door behind itself?"

"My lord abbot, if you have some supposition about these things—"

"I have no suppositions, Sire Gauthier." Gervèse sat back again. "Only suspicions. I'm afraid it may be a cunning trap. I put nothing past these devils."

"It may well *be* a trap," Gauthier countered. "That I'll allow. But if so, what are we to do? Sit by? Pretend we didn't notice?"

"I wouldn't suggest that, in any case," Marzone put in dryly.

"He's right, *Abba*. There is no choice." Isidro caught Gervèse's eyes. At once Gervèse saw the Spaniard's mind; his argument was all but written on his forehead. The good cardinal had been waiting with them a good year now, and they'd promised him in no uncertain terms that he would see Cainites spitted on stakes or cloven and melted to ash before he left. The honor of the abbey, and quite possibly of the Order, was at stake. "Trap or no, we must go forward regardless. But at least we have a little time to think, to gather our strength."

"What time?" Marzone wanted to know.

Gervèse cleared his throat. "According to what Isidro and I have gathered, Monseigneur, these Cainites don't hold their unholy rites as often as we in the Church have Mass. No doubt this helps them keep their blasphemous activities secret, and perhaps it's also done as a concession to the sheer difficulty of making frequent blood-sacrifice. Most likely they're meeting perhaps once a month, if even that."

"In Toulouse, the Cainites preferred to meet on the first night of the waning moon," Isidro added. "It may be the same here. We can certainly have the place watched and find out. Or if they do decide to pack up and move quarters, perhaps we'll at least see where."

"The place is already being watched," Gauthier assured them. "I do have one or two friends left in Paris."

"Very well," said Marzone. "If it is the waning moon, that'll give us a few weeks anyway. In the meantime, we spy, carefully, and marshal our strength. Myself, I should write a letter or two. The collection of holy relics which you and your band have acquired is most impressive, Sire Gauthier…

but we'll see what the word of a Roman cardinal is good for in France these days, and whether it might not be possible to acquire something especially—shall we say, appropriate to our endeavor."

***

From Gervèse, abbot of the Order of St. Theodosius at St.-Denis, to Cecilia, most worthy colleague in the Lord's service in obedience to the sisterhood of St. John the Divine, fondest greetings and blessings in Christ.

Alea jacta est, my fellow-servant of Heaven, and I pray that Heaven may indeed smile favorably upon our fortunes. The place is set, and, we believe, the time as well. Gauthier has the services of Sire Jehan, of course, and this week gained the aid of yet another longtime stalwart of his. He has also brought in a pair of young knights from Champagne who impressed him favorably when he stayed at the commandery there. Let us hope that his judgment in this is keen, as I imagine these lads will likely see much that both we and our enemies normally struggle to keep quite secret.

As for Isidro and myself, once again we turn our library upside down. I especially comb through those volumes he saved from the Laurendine, hoping that some new vital fact about these creatures may leap gleaming off the page. Isidro claims he has found an ancient Aramaic prayer in a book his old teacher brought back from Antioch, which when properly rendered will consecrate a bit of onyx to the archangel Raphael. Raphael being—according to Isidro—the angel whom the Cainites most despise and fear because he ushers the revealing light of the Sun into the world, we reason that these stones may if carried against the enemy act as most potent talismans in our defense.

And now I come to the true subject of my letter: your own contribution. Has the curtain of Heaven rolled down before your Sight recently? Any inkling, however small, might speak to the issue of our struggle. I realize that your visions are not your obedient handmaids, to be called at your whim. But even upon my dull soul a feeling of foreboding descends, and I must ask whether it be the same with you. Whatever earthly advice you may offer us is, of course, as very welcome as always.

Sarah Roark

I pray that this letter finds you, Soeur Faustina and our holy sisters in the Order well and happy. It cheers me to think of that house of peace, charity, order and serenity even in the midst of the evils of Paris (human and otherwise); of the sisters embroidering and sewing together in the common room, or planting and weeding, or reading books in the little garden (never mind that some of those books I daresay Rome would still see burnt). I likewise humbly ask for their prayers, and yours, since peace and order may well prove elusive for their brothers over these next weeks. May all our labors redound to the eternal glory of the One who redeemed us!

I am today and ever your faithful brother in Christ. Given by my hand at St.-Denis this day the xvii Kal. Mai. MCCXIII.

With all blessings,

Gervèse, Abbot, etc.

***

"Peace?" murmured Cecilia, in the sisters' cell at the Theodosian convent inside Paris's walls. It was the Tuesday after Easter and she had just received Abbé Gervèse's letter. "He thinks we'll sleep in peace now, knowing that they're soon to ride against a den of serpents armed only with faith and a few pieces of blessed onyx?"

"And with Gauthier and several of his knights," Faustina demurred. "It will be all right."

"It will?" Cecilia looked up with a wry expression. "Can it be the 'ungifted' sister is receiving a premonition at last? I'd be glad to hear it, especially if it's an auspicious one."

"Not a premonition, sister," answered Faustina, equally wryly. "It's called 'hope.' It's all those of us who don't see the future have to rely on."

Cecilia chuckled. "Sometimes I envy you it. I'm sure you get very tired of hearing me say that."

Faustina shook her head. "I know your suffering all too well, sister. I assure you I don't usually feel called to ease nonexistent burdens."

"You are the most faithful easer of burdens I've ever known, Soeur Faustina."

"Pish. Have mercy on my attempts at humility, Soeur Cecilia…"

"He is wrong about one thing, at least," Cecilia said, returning now to the letter. She walked over to her desk and put it down.

"What's that?"

"They can be called. It's not… usually wise, but they can be."

"Soeur Cecilia?" Faustina folded away the last of Cecilia's needlework for the day and turned to look directly at her, frowning.

"You've always attended my fevers in the past, when they descended suddenly at any time of day or night. If I were to ask you, humbly, to please be so kind as to see me through a bout of deliberate illness now…"

"Sister," Faustina pleaded, "if you haven't seen anything about the Red Brothers lately—what I mean is, surely if God intends for you to receive a premonition, you will."

"God works His wonders through human hands and hearts," said Cecilia distantly. Already her gaze was diffusing, turning inward. "I cannot just stand by while they go to face the very Pit."

"Do you think the Red Sisters wish to stand by?" Faustina argued. "But they do. And do you know why? Because that is the place their brothers have ordained for them. Cecilia, please, this is vanity. I beg you, do not do it. You aren't acting from devotion to God—"

Cecilia, trying to walk toward her bed, stumbled and fell with a cry; Soeur Faustina at once broke off her recriminations and sprang out of the chair with a doe's athletic grace in order to catch her.

"No, no," she soothed. "*Pobrecita, alma mia*, come. Come, let's get you into bed. Lie down. I'll get some cool water for your forehead…"

***

From Faustina, humble handmaiden in the service of Our Lord under the obedience of the sisters of St. John the Divine, to my most honored lord Gervèse, abbot of the Order of St. Theodosius at St.-Denis, greetings and every fervent wish of fellowship in Christ.

My lord abbot, I regret to inform you that our beloved Soeur Cecilia is presently too ill to reply to your letter as speedily as you or she would ordinarily wish; but, knowing the full urgency and import of your request, she has entreated me to write you in her place and tell you the issue of the several visions she has had this past week, of which I have taken the most faithful notes that I could.

She tells me that overall the signs look more favorable for the group effort than she had at first feared, but that it is possible great hurt will come to one or more individuals. She has said that we are brass tigers that one hand forged and another tinkered, and that we should fear the one who does not hate us more than the one who does, and the orthodox more than the heretic. She has said that we will be most sorely tempted not by the fruit but by the sapling.

She also asked me to repeat this to you, word for word, for it came directly from the lips of her namesake saint: "When you find yourself suddenly abandoned, take heart. The pilgrim returns to the beginning of the road, yet he is far from home. Bitter truths in the garden, fallen by the source of the scream." She regrets that as yet she has no theory as to the meaning, but if it comes to her she will no doubt bid me write again.

Hoping this finds all of your lordship, his lordship and all at the brothers' abbey well, in good spirits and filled with hope and courage in its usual abundance. Given by my hand at Paris this day the xii Kal. Mai. MCCXIII.

I am ever your most humble and faithful servant in the Lord's service, taking refuge in His strength, wisdom and mercy,

Faustina of St. John the Divine

Chapter Twenty

It had taken a fight to be here tonight. Zoë didn't often fight with Anatole—it was dismally like trying to beat back the tide—but on this occasion she'd decided to brave it regardless.

"I refuse to let the damnable Heretics deliver all my justice for me," she'd insisted. "Besides, if Decius were to open a pool on it, I'd give the Heretics the far longer odds to win. And anyway, Isidro will probably be there. How can you possibly expect me to stay home?"

"But I've told you many times before that Isidro's hour is not yet come, child," he'd protested. "What do you hope to do to him by being there?"

"What if your prophecy comes true that very night, and I'm not there? Have you thought of that?"

"No," he'd said, "actually I hadn't." Then he'd sat a while and conferred with what Zoë gathered to be the ghost of Abel himself. In the end he had finally relented. "It might be that the appointed hour will come that night," he'd admitted. "And in that case I won't deny you whatever your destiny in the matter might be. But on the other hand, what if it doesn't come?"

"Then we'll simply test whatever Inquisitors survive to be tested, just as you always do," she'd assured him.

And so here they were. Anatole had found them a fine seat from which to view the proceedings: a garret just across the street that served as storage attic for the wealthy family below it. Fortunately the warehouse only had the one outer door, so they needn't fear missing the outcome of what they devoutly hoped would be a rout one way or the other. Crespin, of course, would not be attending the services this evening, having come down with a most convenient cold.

They watched the merchant carry a candle downstairs through his house, then come out and unlock the warehouse door. A little while later, in dribs and drabs, furtive-looking burghers and burgesses of various stations came to it from the surrounding streets and knocked upon it in a certain pattern, and were just as furtively let in. Most of them carried unlit lanterns. The best of both worlds, no doubt. If the watch caught them, they could claim their light had just that moment gone out, damn the luck—and most of them looked respectable enough to carry off the lie; on the other hand, in the more likely event that they eluded the watch, their passing would be far less noticeable to whatever decent citizens might remain up at this hour.

Next a greater darkness descended on the street. Zoë craned her head around to see if a cloud had sailed over the moon, but no, the sky was quite clear. This was something taking place on the ground.

"The shadow-shepherd arrives with his fellow angels," Anatole whispered very, very quietly. "You see, it's in his very blood to cloak himself, now in false darkness, now in false light."

Zoë studied the gathering gloom. It did seem to gather more in one particular spot than others, and it moved at about the speed of a horse's easy walk. In fact, now that she strained she could hear the hoofbeats, unnaturally muted. Somewhere in the center of that black roiling mist were mounts, which meant there were also riders. She saw a sliver of light momentarily reach through the patch of darkness as the door opened and shut. Then the whole thing dispersed. She saw the three palfreys clearly now, saddles empty, standing by the door. A moment later a pair of mortals appeared from within to lead them round to the merchant's stable.

Then there was a long silent stretch. Zoë fidgeted, feeling cramped among the piles of old broken furniture, and looked periodically over to Anatole, who sat very straight and alert.

"Well, what's going on?" she whispered at last. "Can you hear anything?"

"Yes," he said. "They are singing. They are re-crucifying Christ."

"They are?" Zoë could by now believe nearly anything of Heretical liturgy, but this sounded like the outer edge of blasphemy even for them.

"Yes. They are lifting vinegar to His lips and thrusting a spear in His side…" Anatole bit his lower lip—it began to bleed a little—and shook his head. "O Lord, I beseech thee. Suffer not your Son to endure such insults any longer. Send your scourge in judgment, I pray."

"They are literally crucifying someone in there?" she pursued.

"They don't believe in the Crucifixion."

"Never mind…"

She tried to settle down again.

"There goes the spy. Not long now," Anatole said, pointing at a shadow that lengthened down the street as its owner pattered off westward. "They can't be far off."

"If that is a spy. If they took the bait at all," she reminded him.

"Don't worry."

And indeed it now appeared that a new congregation was coming, somewhat late, to Mass. Zoë moved to the side of the window and peeked out with a single eye, gripped by what might or might not be an unreasoning fear that someone would look up and see her. The first to arrive was a small company of six men on foot, unarmored except for dark padded tunics and bearing between them two heavy trunks and a large sack, which they carefully set off to the side along the front wall of the house. One of the men wore a bow and quiver. Silently they arranged themselves in a large semicircle around the front door, with the archer at the far end. Then came another group of four men, carrying a short, thick wooden beam with handles mounted along the side and shod in iron on one end. A miniature battering-ram, she guessed immediately. Next she heard several horses clattering down the street toward the warehouse, but they stopped something like halfway down the row.

Moments later she was rewarded with the sight she'd been waiting for: Isidro and Gauthier, and—there! The monk that had ridden out of Bergamo with Isidro so long ago, looking a bit stouter perhaps but otherwise exactly the same. She thought she might remember one of the other Templars from the night she'd rescued Anatole, as well, but it was hard to say. She counted four Templars in all besides Gauthier, and two more monks in addition to Isidro and his companion. All the monks had swaddled themselves in thick black cloaks, the distinctive russet of their habits visible only in occasional glimpses. A stocky man in a dark priest's cassock brought up the rear; in his hands he held a cushion with a little inlaid wooden casket set atop it. The priest strode to the center of the semicircle. All present bowed their heads, and the knights and monks each in turn wordlessly kissed the casket. The priest seemed to pray, but nothing audible escaped his lips. He then withdrew to the edge, taking his place in between two of the men making up the perimeter.

"I am pleased," murmured Anatole. "I'm very pleased. I believe they've thought of everything."

"Shh," said Zoë desperately. The quiet in the street seemed—well, unnatural, if the word could apply. Zoë was used to such silences breaking out wherever Cainites gathered in a group. After all, no one breathed, few twitched or fidgeted, not a single heart beat. But for so many of the living to glide along with so little audible report of it was absolutely eerie.

A low-shaded lantern was opened and its flame used to light a torch from the sack. That torch lit another, and another, and another. Each in turn was passed along the semicircle until it was completely ringed in fire. Even the priest held a torch aloft in one hand, the casket in the other. The monks all took one as well, and so did Gauthier; the other knights apparently preferred to carry a shield instead. Finally Gauthier nodded to the men with the iron-shod beam. They positioned themselves in front of the door. With a collective grunt of exertion, they barreled full-tilt into it. It gave way completely under their blow.

And then all hell seemed quite literally to break loose.

The sound of screaming arose from within the building; it grew even louder as the knights and monks charged over the fallen door. Zoë saw candlelight flare up in the neighboring houses and faces appear in the windows. Someone along the street began shouting for the watch.

Some of the Heretics ran outside and were chased down by the knights and the ram-bearers, who now brandished unlovely but well-sharpened swords. Those who tried to fight back received no mercy. She saw one bearded, staid-looking man in scholar's robes pull his eating-knife out of his belt and slash at one of the Templars; the Templar buried his sword in the man's belly and then slid his body back off it again with a shove of his booted foot. But others of the Heretics, men and women both, took one look at the fence of torch-bearers and went down to their knees, covering their heads with their hands. These were made at swordpoint to huddle in a tight bunch at the far end of the semicircle, and as their number grew from a few to a handful and then a double handful two of the ram-bearers left off fighting to stand guard over them instead.

A pale man in deacon's robes appeared at the upstairs window. He balanced himself on the sill, crouching for stability, and glanced downward, evidently gauging the distance for a jump. Zoë wondered if he possibly meant to jump clear across the street into *their* window, and started to hide her face again; but in the next instant a flaming arrow slammed into the creature's chest. He screamed horribly and toppled down to the street below, landing with a crack of broken bones. Almost immediately he stood back up again, batting in panic at the fire at his breast. One of the knights came up behind him and in a single neat blow chopped off his head.

"Deo gratias!" the knight shouted as the head flew up and landed a little more than a yard away. He let the fountaining body fall where it stood. Ignoring the spatter of vitae that streaked his white overtunic, he speared the head

on the tip of his sword and brought it over to one of the torchmen to set it afire. The horrible smell of burning hair wafted up to the garret. Zoë looked to Anatole—but the mad prophet was gone. She hunted around in a panic.

"I'm here, childe. I only wanted to keep my view without giving them one." The voice was soft, reassuring, and came from exactly where he'd been sitting all along, directly in front of the window. A shimmering in the air, like a heat wave, disturbed the spot for a moment and then died away. Zoë knew that Anatole possessed the art of vanishing, but it always bothered her when he used it, because he was also quite in the habit of wandering off unexpectedly, and she usually couldn't tell the difference between the two.

She nodded and re-stationed herself along the edge of the window where she thought she could find the best compromise between concealment and vantage. It occurred to her that she should have darkened her face and hands with lampblack; well, too late now.

Now Gauthier chased another man in robes out of the warehouse. The man, whom Zoë quickly identified as another Cainite, fled out toward the edge of the ring but then had to stop, fangs out and snarling, before the torchbearers in front of him. He whirled, effortlessly picked up the battering ram that had been dropped and drove it into the two nearest men, smashing one's chest and crushing the other's jaw. They dropped like stones. The priest ran towards the vampire, holding up the casket and bellowing in Latin. The creature shrieked like a Fury and recoiled. In the next instant he was on the wall of the warehouse, climbing up it. Zoë saw, dumbstruck, that Gauthier already hung from the vampire's leg—much like in Arles, where he'd somehow covered several yards in a single step to block the Toreador's escape. He'd dropped his sword in order to grab hold but still had his torch in his left hand.

The Cainite stared down at the knight. *"Drop it,"* he growled in a sepulchral tone, and for a moment the torch fumbled in Gauthier's grasp. But then he caught it again. The Cainite pulled his leg away from the wall and tried to snap Gauthier off with a kick. Gauthier swung out nearly horizontal and crashed back into the wall. Then he thrust the torch up under the Cainite's robes, setting them alight. The vampire curled up like a dying spider and fell, taking Gauthier along. Gauthier rolled and jumped up, but discovered that his own overtunic's hem had caught fire and had to scramble to unbuckle his belt and pull it off.

All at once a burst of light erupted within the house and spilled out of the door into the street—not the yellow light of torch-flame but the clear brilliance of sunlight itself. Zoë stumbled back with a cry as it burst into the garret. The skin of her arms and face bubbled up immediately into blisters. She stumbled blindly out of the lancing radiance and fell headlong into the furniture. Her hand brushed across the cool fabric of an ancient moth-eaten hanging; grasping at it, she pulled the cloth to her and rolled into it like a burrowing worm.

It took several long minutes of whimpering before she found the presence of mind to call out softly through the pain. "Anatole?"

No answer.

"Anatole, are you still…"

Then she heard a scraping of moving furniture.

"Anatole! That had better be you. Please, God, oh Mary Theotokos."

Someone touched her through the fabric. "You can come out now, *enfante*. The terrible light has gone away for good." It was his voice. She gave a sob of relief.

"Are you sure?"

"Well, not completely, but one of the knights just told your Isidro to 'for the love of Christ drop a lantern-shade over that thing—never mind the Cainites, it's terrifying all the rest of us'…"

Zoë hesitated, then with a burst of courage extricated herself from the heavy folds. It was once again the correct shade of darkness for the hour. Still, little scatterings of glowing dots spread across her field of vision now and again when she blinked.

Gritting their teeth in pain from the blisters, they went to the window again. Much had happened while they'd hid. Several of the torchbearers were now fastening manacles on the kneeling Heretics and chaining them together. Zoë counted fifteen of those, including the weeping merchant himself. Three others lay dead or unconscious in the street. Someone had set the beheaded Cainite's body on fire; now it lay there assiduously burning down to ash. The horses had been brought the rest of the way up, and the monks busied themselves with repacking their saddlebags. Bumps, thumps and the occasional crash of something falling could still be heard within the warehouse. Neighbor families stood meek and terrified outside their front doors, watching, parents' arms securely wrapped around their children.

And the watch had arrived at last. Their commander was in deep discussion with Gauthier and the priest; the rest stood nervously by their horses, weapons out but not aloft.

"It doesn't look like they're getting into very much trouble," said Zoë.

Anatole gave a quiet snort. "What sort of trouble would they get into, childe? The secular law can't touch them. The Church won't convict them."

"The perfect assassins," she realized.

"Very true…"

"I think they must have killed the bishop with that light."

"Possibly, but I wouldn't assume." The Malkavian's searching gaze swept up and down the street. "There—that shadow."

"What shadow?"

"Shh. It's the only one not flickering in the torchlight… no, I think we'll be hearing from the bishop again. But he must not hear from us, or see us. Stay still, childe."

Suddenly one of the kneeling Heretics knocked down the man who leaned over him to fasten his manacles. He reeled to his feet and dove away past Gauthier and the watch captain. An encouraging shout went up from the rest of the captives. The ram-bearers shouted much less pleasantly, drew their swords and gave chase.

200   Ravnos

"Anatole!" Zoë nearly broke out into full voice in her excitement, but she quickly strangled it down to an excited whisper. "Anatole, look!"

"Yes. He might outpace them, if he's clever."

"No, don't you see? 'The prisoner slips free.' That's it! It *is* time!"

"No." He blinked, then frowned. "No, that's not right…"

"It is. Look with your own eyes."

"No, it can't be."

"I'm going to try."

"Zoë, childe, it's not wise. They're all down there."

"They're tired."

"I don't know how tired they are really."

"And anyway, I'll get him alone."

"I still don't think it's the right time for—"

"I'm going," she interrupted, and even she was surprised at the finality in her tone.

There was a silence.

"If you must," he said slowly, "then yes, you had better get him alone. Two streets to the south of here, not far along, there's a fine old house with only an elderly caretaker and a cook to look after it, and an overgrown garden. Perhaps you could lure him within its walls."

"How many times have you *come* to Paris and not told me?" She shook her head. "Very well. The garden."

"I'll be with you," he said. He laid a hand on her shoulder. Then he ducked away behind the clutter and disappeared.

She pulled Gregory's ring out from where it lay on its chain under her shift and stared at it thoughtfully.

***

"I wonder how long it'll last," Isidro mused as he hung the shuttered lantern from a strap on his horse's pack.

"I can't imagine it would last for very long," said Gervèse, "although it'd certainly be useful if it did."

"Is the other one still in the chapel?"

"It must be, unless one of the men moved it. I'll go get it."

"All right."

Something flashed and twinkled at the edge of Isidro's vision. He blinked and shaded his night-accustomed eyes from it; then he became curious and lowered his hand again. It drifted closer. A flying insect with scintillating wings. With a sudden decisive movement it lighted on the pommel of his saddle.

He stared at it, fascinated. It was the most beautiful such creature he'd ever laid eyes on. Its body was pearlescent blue and purple, its beetle-wings shimmering green, its eyes like miniscule drops of jet. Its legs were the warm color of rose-gold…

No. Not the color of. He had seen such a thing before.

For a moment he froze, afraid to disturb it, enchanted by the gentle fanning motion of its wings as it rested. Then he realized his opportunity and reached for it.

It fluttered away. He made another grab and almost caught it. It spiraled further off.

"Gervèse…"

But Gervèse was in the warehouse. Isidro glanced over at Gauthier and Marzone, still reasoning with the watch captain, and then peered back toward the insect. It had landed on the wall of a house. If it took flight again he'd lose it.

He muttered a mild Spanish oath for which he immediately felt guilty, then started off toward the thing.

***

"Thank you for inviting me to dinner," he says. She still can't see his face beneath the gray cowl.

In some part of her mind she realizes she never invited him, but in the logic of the vision he is due the returning courtesy nonetheless. "You're welcome." She ladles him out a bowl of soup. He takes a huge gulp from it. Then he sets it back down on the table, chewing. Suddenly he stops, half-gags, and removes a human finger from his mouth. It has a fine jeweled ring on it. He chuckles, pulls the ring off and sets it on the tablecloth, then pops the finger back into his mouth and swallows.

"Never let it be said that you don't provide richly for your guests." He tears off a hunk of bread and butters it.

"I don't know how that got in there."

"Don't you?"

"I don't know. I didn't cook this." She stirs through the rest of the soup and begins finding ears, eyeballs, pilgrim's badges, bronze seal-stamps, thimbles. She takes the slotted spoon and begins straining them all out.

He just shakes his head and takes a bite of the bread, spitting a button out next to the ring.

"You'll never find it all," he says.

She gives a cry and dumps the entire tureen out onto the table. The flood of ordure pours out without ceasing. Fingers and ears are followed by entire hands, some still clutching daggers, and heads that roll down onto the floor. One she recognizes just as it begins to tumble downstairs.

"No!" She chases after it, but slips in the soup and falls. The stream continues to wash down upon her, growing into a torrent, flooding the stairwell. She accidentally swallows a mouthful of the brackish water. Then she tries to swim. Books and spinning wheels and drowned Red Sisters float past her in the gloom. She manages to pull her way along the wall to the door and open it. It's all ocean outside as well. She flails up toward the sparkle of moonlight.

Her head bursts free at last. The marine breeze is stinging cold, but she's grateful simply to breathe. Everyone is walking effortlessly on the face of the water. The fishwives sit by their wagons on the water and the housewives drag screaming children across the water to buy from them. A king is having his feast on the water. Jugglers tumble across the water to entertain him. Monks in procession chant and trudge penitently across the water. She weaves through the passersby, the only person not walking on the water, trying to avoid being stepped on. She can see no land anywhere between here and the horizon. But a bed with red velvet blankets floats by. Her arms and legs trembling from the exhaustion of treading water, she climbs onto it. It drifts and drifts for what seems like many miles, far away from the other people. She snuggles into the down mattress against the cold.

Finally, after the moon has tracked more than halfway

across the sky, the bed drifts into the bay of a distant shore. She washes up by the mouth of a vast river. She gets out of the bed and follows the riverbank inland, hoping to find some sign of habitation. But the wilderness only grows more lush as she fights her barefoot way upstream. Parched, she tries to drink out of the river and finds that the water is salt. A tarred basket floats by among the reeds. She splashes out to catch it and unwraps the blanket bundle within to reveal the broken pieces of a polished silver mirror. Each edge of each shard has been whetted keen like a scissor-blade.

Then an enormous voice speaks out of the sky above her. "Why did you leave it out of your letter to Bergamo?" it demands. "Was it given to you to judge?" She looks up in terror. The words are coming not from a thundercloud or from the mouth of some giant being, but from a swarm of insects—shiny scarabs, locusts and gnats, which descend upon her and envelop her…

She woke to find herself standing in the common room downstairs. Her veil and wimple were pinned on, a bit askew, and her shoes were also on and laced. Her feet pointed toward the door.

Her heart pounded and her mouth felt dry as alum, but she knew what she must do. Stopping only to cross herself and murmur a quick prayer before the painting of the Madonna and child that hung on the far wall, she hurried out into the night.

***

The false beetle was only visible when it moved—its wings glittered under the moonlight when they beat—and so the pursuit went in fits and starts. The light from his lantern seemed to disturb it and send it flitting, so a few times when he thought he might have lost it he succeeded in finding it again by walking along the sides of the buildings and shining the lantern into nooks and crannies.

At length it lit on a high ivy-covered garden wall.

"Oh no," he pleaded with it in the *langue d'oc*. "Not after all this." A moment later it flew up and over.

He stood at the garden gate, berating himself both for wanting to go in and for not going in.

Then he heard a man's voice within the garden, singing and humming rather tunelessly. He couldn't quite make out the words. If some inhabitant of the house was still up, perhaps he could ask to come in. True, it would no doubt strike whomever it was as a little odd, a monk knocking at the gate in the dead of night, begging leave to follow a beetle round the garden…

He knocked tentatively.

"Hello? Messire?"

There was no answer, but the humming continued.

"Messire?" He knocked again, a little harder. The latch on the gate was rusted half away, and almost gave under his knocking. If he pushed on it a little harder, it would swing right open.

He hesitated again. Then he pushed it open. "Excuse me, messire? I beg you, forgive my intrusion… hello?"

The garden was lovely under the moonlight, but as wilderness, not as garden. Clearly nothing had been trimmed or pruned in many years. Weeds grew interspersed with the flowers, overrunning them in many places. A scattering of rotted apples lay under the trees. Still, there was a man walking the garden's paths, his face turned away from Isidro's. His legs and back stooped slightly under a long green tunic edged with narrow strips of silver-threaded brocade. Yet his hair was black, without a trace of gray or white that Isidro could see. Perhaps he was a cripple or an invalid, Isidro thought suddenly.

"Messire, I am sorry to disturb you…" Could the man be deaf also? Or was he simply ignoring his trespasser's incredible discourtesy? "This is going to sound very strange to you, I'm sure, but I am a brother of the Theodosians at St.-Denis, a, a scholar in my way, and… I take quite an interest in zoology, botany too. Messire?"

"Very interesting," the man said softly. He stooped to sniff at a rose, never looking at Isidro.

"Yes," half-laughed the monk, relieved. "And, well, again, it's strange, but I just saw a certain insect fly into your garden, a very beautiful and rare insect that I've hoped to have the opportunity to look at up close."

"There were once many rare and beautiful creatures in my garden," the man replied. He eased himself down to sit on a stone bench, his long black locks tumbling down over his cheeks and shoulders.

"Ah." Isidro frowned. "Were there?"

"Indeed. There were even some who called my garden and its animals a miracle. Great lords and ladies often came to visit, their hearts heavy with affairs of state and whatever sins their consciences bore, and they departed again with souls refreshed in the clear water of delight."

Isidro stepped closer now, his curiosity and sympathy both piqued. "Then—then what happened?" he asked.

"Every paradise must come to its end," the man answered. "Thieves and murderers pillaged it. They destroyed my little menagerie, laid waste to the fragrant bowers, and all but killed my young daughter with grief. Now it's all gone for good..."

Isidro came up beside what had probably once been a fishpond and settled himself on its cracking edge.

"Men can be so needlessly cruel…" He shook his head. "What you say, it's heartbreaking. I'm so very sorry."

"Yes." The man's long-fingered hands folded in his lap. "Yes, you should be."

That confused the Spaniard. Had he just missed something?

"Yes, messire—?" he prompted after a moment.

"You see, brother, those thieves and murderers did their plundering in the name of God."

"Oh." The logic of that much clicked into place, but a question yet remained. "Yes, in my old home we've seen… very similar evils. You mean that—that here in Paris, men claiming to do God's work rioted and destroyed citizens' homes? When was that?"

The beetle flew out into the open and descended toward the man's hands, alighting on one of his fingers. He didn't start or exclaim, simply studied it meditatively. "I never said it was in Paris."

And then he looked up. It was a fairly young face after all, or at least no older than Isidro's, with a short neat beard and dark Byzantine eyes.

Isidro tried to get up on suddenly nerveless legs, but tripped on a crumbling flagstone.

"Dear Holy Mary, Mother of God and Our merciful Christ," he moaned. "Not you…"

"I have been awaiting you, brother, for a long time," the man said. He pushed himself to his feet in a graceless but undeniably powerful motion. His voice was no longer low and sad, but fierce. He stepped toward Isidro, and as he did his face began to change.

***

"Is that that, I hope?" Gervèse muttered to Gauthier as the latter came back to his horse.

"I believe that is that," Gauthier answered. He stroked the stallion's nose affectionately and then swung up into the saddle.

"Our two dead?"

"Have been laid as much to rest as they can be at this hour." They both crossed themselves. "My men have wrapped them in cloaks. The rest must wait till we get in."

"All right. Then let's get Isidro and get out of here."

"Where *is* Isidro?"

"He was here when I went back in the house. You didn't see where he went?"

"No. I assumed he'd gone in with you."

They both stared at each other as their hearts went gelid cold.

"Isidro!" Gervèse called out loud.

"Isidro! Has anyone seen Frère Isidro? Hellfire and damnation…" Gauthier circled his horse around fretfully. "All right. Panicking does you no good, Abbé. I'll take Sire Jehan and go that way, you take Sire Lion and go that way. He can't have gotten far."

"Right." Gervèse mounted his horse as well, nowhere near as easily as Gauthier. He felt the piece of blessed onyx where he'd secured it in his purse to make sure it was safe and sound. Then with a word and a jerk of his head he collected Sire Lion, who (to his knightly credit) didn't even ask what the errand was.

They rode for what seemed like eternity to Gervèse, but in reality could only have been a few minutes, alternately calling out Isidro's name and listening intently.

"Where would he have gone, do you think?" Sire Lion asked.

"In this neighborhood? I've no idea. The only place I can think of his *wanting* to go to is one of the churches. More likely he spotted some devil that escaped our noose, and ran off to chase it without saying a word. It never fails to amaze me how a man so wise can be so impossibly hasty at times..."

Then all at once he stuttered to a halt.

"Wait," he said.

Lion shifted in his saddle, his ears immediately pricked for some warning of danger.

"What?" he returned after a silent moment.

When you find yourself suddenly abandoned, take heart. The pilgrim returns to the beginning of the road, yet he is far from home. Bitter truths in the garden, fallen by the source of the scream...

"The road to Compostela," Gervèse exclaimed. "It begins just near here, at the church of St.-Jacques."

"Yes, it does, but...?"

"Quickly. We must make for it."

***

Long dead as she was, Zoë could feel a flush of triumph in her cheeks as she watched Isidro scuttle back from the seething, shifting apparition of Gregory, his mouth hung wide open in horror and his breath coming in gasps.

"Now," she whispered.

208   Ravnos

"Wait," came Anatole's return whisper. "I just heard something—odd. Let me look and make sure you weren't followed first."

"But—"

"One moment. Continue to… amuse him, I'll be right back."

***

Hildegard gives her a pitying look, then comes over and closes the book before she can even finish her page.

"This is not an age for visions," the saint says. "There are few who will listen anymore; and however valiant they may be, the times are against them as much as they're against you. Black and white is the new habitude. There are no golden birds in silver trees anymore, no brasswork cats."

"Still I'll do what I must," she answers as bravely as she can.

"You are like a mute who hears the very hymns of the angels and cannot sing them, or like a man who could be the greatest sculptor in the world if he had hands. To be able to act in full on what you know, that is to be truly blessed."

"It is my test," she argues, but she weeps…

In her moments of half-waking, Cecilia wished she'd remembered to wear a cloak. It wasn't very cold, but the fever chills still raged through her frame every now and again, making her teeth chatter. She looked up to see where she was. St. Catherine's hospital. She chuckled grimly. No road was ever free of temptation. She was closer, but she was not *there* yet.

"Just think whom you might save," he whispers. He should know better by now than to come as Hildegard, she's long past being fooled by that trick.

"Only God saves." She turns from him but finds her way blocked with sheets of white linen gauze, and as she tries to brush them away they only circle around her tighter.

"Let Him save you, then."

"Demon!" she shrieks. "I name thee Beelzebub and Belial, enemy of God. In the name of the Father who has all power to banish your kind, I charge you to release me!"

"Release you?" He grins and fingers the horns that poke

*through the top of his cowl. One at a time he savagely yanks
them out, licking their bloody stump-ends, and throws them
away.* "Child, it's not I who has trapped you. This day will
come in truth on earth, and who will you curse then? Or who
will you call on to stay the killing stroke?"

*The strips of linen knit themselves into a braided tube,
enclosing first her legs and then her belly.*

Left foot. Right foot. In her youth she'd seen soldiers
marching and singing as they went along. Didn't it go something like that? "Left foot, right foot take me there; left foot,
right foot take me back; left foot, right foot draw your sword;
left foot, right foot now attack…"

She couldn't remember the rest of it. Maybe there was
a psalm, a hymn that would do for a nun's cadence.

*He holds her close. She struggles within the winding, but
to no avail and silently; her head has been wrapped and something leaden stuffed into her mouth beforehand. Through the
gauze she can still feel his breath in her ear.*

"How about this," *he says,* "it goes: 'Once were we three,
with but one heart among us. Scarce are we two, now that
the third is fled. Fled is he, fled is he, but the grief remaineth;
bitter the weeping, for so dear a head…'"

She stopped at the intersection of the streets.

A moment later he was there. He didn't look as he
usually had, not quite like any of the forms he'd taken. Not
a fox-tail in sight. He did wear the robe, a blasphemy on a
monk's habit, dark-gray sackcloth belted with a bit of frayed
rope. She was at first dismayed and then gratified to see that
he was young and beautiful. In a way, it would make it easier.

"You're not just a dream, then," she said.

He shook his head. "No." The look on his face was
indescribable. He stepped toward her with the same expression of awe she'd once worn as she approached the altar to
take her final vows.

"No wonder, then," he said. "No wonder. Or… just the
opposite… I can't decide."

She folded her hands over her heart. For some reason
it felt like the right gesture.

"I refuse."

"Obligatory." He nodded. "Let us proceed with the proprieties. I will kill him. I will kill both of them, in fact. It may take a long time, but I possess that."

"It's as you told me. That day will come because or in spite of you. This is not the way to bargain."

At that he suddenly broke into a little smile. "Is there still a way to bargain then, Cecilia, virgin martyr?"

"When Our Lord prayed in Gethsemane," she said, "for a moment He was unsure of His own strength. But the Devil watched Him and shook his head in wonder at the endless folly of Man, that even the Messiah could so doubt Himself."

"Yes, because of the episode on the pinnacle of the temple," he finished. "The Devil invited Him to cast Himself down and thus verify that He truly was the Son of God; but He was able to deny the temptation to put it to the test. His own trust in the Lord already sufficed. So it wasn't possible that He could pass that first test and fail the second…"

"Since they were essentially the same. As you've said, you have your cup and I have mine, and I thank God mine isn't yours. You already have your answer—I don't know what name to call you by."

The little smile twitched. "It's not Beelzebub."

"I know."

"Very well. I've finished one duty, then. I go to fulfill the other." He turned to leave.

She stopped him with a word. "A moment."

He faced her again, reluctantly, as though compelled.

"I may be rid of you now," she said, "but what makes you think you're so easily rid of me? If one body of water runs into another, the reverse is just as true."

He walks barefoot up the mountain, his staff plunging into the crumbling rocks ahead of him. It is a long, lonely trudge, and in his belly and in his throat the dry thirst burns; dust fine as ash enters into his mouth and eyes and nose and makes it even worse. He comes to a crevice in the rock and squirrels himself within it just as the cloud descends.

Sarah Roark   211

The voice is a voice he has heard before, but only in phrases of two or three words, disjointed half-sentiments. Now, however, it speaks in full sentences. With every sentence the reverberation on the mountain grows until he is certain his eardrums will burst and every drop of blood he has ever stolen from the flesh of innocents will pour out onto the cracked earth—a fitting sacrifice to that ground, that holy of holies and unholy of unholies, which will never be sated.

THOU HAST DESIRED TO KNOW ME, ANATOLE; THOU HAST PROCLAIMED MY WORD AND MY LAWS FAITHFULLY AND FOUND GRACE IN MY SIGHT. WHEN THE TRUE MOSES ASKED IT OF ME I COVERED HIM WITH MY HAND AS I PASSED BY, THAT HE WOULD NOT SEE MY FACE AND DIE.

BUT THOU HAST NO MORE NEED OF SUCH PROTECTIONS, SON OF PETER. THEREFORE I WILL DO FOR THEE THIS THING THAT THOU ASKEST. LOOK UPON ME AT LAST, THEN, AND KNOW A PORTION OF MY WILL CONCERNING THEE AND THE FARMER'S OTHER CHILDREN…

***

"Well, the church doors are shut," said Sire Lion, bringing the reins up short, "though that can be changed, if absolutely necessary…"

"No. He's not in the church," Gervèse returned. "I think we may be looking for an actual garden. *Bitter truths in the garden*, her letter said. Sometimes a thing referred to in her prophecies is exactly itself, nothing more or less."

"Then let's look in the churchyard and the garden."

"Right."

They wheeled their mounts around. Gervèse breathed a brief prayer to St. James to show him the right road. Then they heard the scream. It didn't sound like Isidro's voice, quite, but it was certainly a man's scream, someone's scream—

He didn't even need to call Sire Lion. The man was already spurring his horse into a charge, determined to be the first to danger.

***

Zoë's smile chilled over. Inspired by exactly what—stories of Constantinople's Trinity or something else—she hadn't known, but she'd decided that Gregory should shift into the shape of an enormous dragon and coil around Isidro roaring. Unfortunately, the sight of monstrous beast actually seemed to trouble the monk less than the vision of her sire had. At any rate he recovered his wits. As she watched seething, he called upon St. George and the Virgin Mary. Then he stretched his thin hands out toward the twisting scales. His fingers passed right through the illusory flesh. At once her apparition disappeared without a trace or sound.

She growled. "Anatole... Anatole?" But he didn't answer.

"Enough *amusement*," she told herself. She spread out her hands and closed her eyes. She hadn't realized it was possible for blood itself to tire, but it was tiring now. She forced it regardless. Think what it was to be a child, waking at night to a strange noise. Think what it was to be an old man long past working age, not a friend or relation left, and to find one's eyes milking over with cataracts. Think what it was to be a sailor steering into a rocky bay when suddenly a fog arose from nowhere. She imagined herself in these places until that fear, that terror of the sightless dark threatened to gnaw her innards apart, until she literally felt sick—and then she bestowed it upon Isidro. He gasped and fumbled around the path-stones with his hands, rolling forward onto his knees. A rim of sheen too bright to be reflected moonlight began to gather around his hands and legs, then to leak through the cloth of his habit. She dashed out from behind the tree towards him, her dagger upraised.

The scream rent the air outside the north garden wall, passing in a line from east to west.

"Anatole!" she shouted. She gazed down at Isidro, gathering more supernal brilliance into his ascetic body with each passing moment, and her blistered hand trembled and squeezed the pommel tight for a blow. Then suddenly with a cheated cry she flung herself through the gate and ran out, chasing after her fleeing mentor.

***

"Down this way!" Sire Lion shouted, turning down a narrow street. Gervèse nodded and thundered after him; when it came to heat-of-battle instincts, he would never trust his own above that of one of Gauthier's knights.

But then he called forward. "Lion, stop! Look, there's a garden wall! Raise your lantern high."

The knight did as instructed, lifting the end of the pole far above his head so that the angles of the shadows all changed. Together they surveyed the empty street. One black lump in the center gutter didn't shift.

Gervèse spotted it first and fairly leaped out of the saddle. "Isidro…" He fell to his knees beside the crumpled form, turning it over. The face that greeted his searching, agonized gaze was not olive-skinned, however, but the deathly white of milk.

"Cecilia!" He seized her cold fingers in his right hand. His left he cupped behind her neck to lift her up. Her throat was unmarked, but her closed eyelids didn't flutter.

"Soeur Cecilia…?" Sire Lion was at his side immediately.

"What was she *doing* out here?" Gervèse moaned, rocking back to sit on his heels.

"I don't know. Is—is she—does she live? Hurry, man, tell me!"

Gervèse bent and put his ear by her lips. For a moment he was despairingly certain that the slight stirring of air was only his wishful thinking at work. Then he heard a soft inhalation.

"Cecilia… oh, thanks be unto God…"

Now her eyes opened. They were sleepwalker's eyes, full of vague horrors brought back from the other side of waking. Then they emptied, cleared and saw him.

"Brother Gervèse," she managed. "My lord abbot."

He sat up again. "Yes, it's me. Sister, good news. We've triumphed against the Cainites, at least in part, with the blessed strength and aid of His Holy Name… You, you're out of cloister."

"I know."

"And you are not well. Your forehead's burning up and your fingers are like ice. Where are your gloves?" He laid her hand gently down on her lap. "What on earth happened?"

"The demon. He came to me, with his deceits and illusions…"

"God preserve us." Sire Lion crossed himself. Gervèse absently echoed the gesture.

"Then that scream—"

"It was the demon. The Lord preserved me even in my unworthiness and put the unclean spirit to flight. My lord abbot, I… I believe I'm all right, or will be. Don't trouble yourself further." She pulled herself up to sitting.

"I will never forgive myself," came a sorrowful voice over Gervèse's head.

Gervèse started violently, his head jerking up.

"*Isidro!*"

The Spaniard stood over the three of them.

"I fear she's suffered on my account," he said, "and I'll never forgive myself for it."

"Nonsense, Frère Isidro," she returned. "From what I can tell, it might be as fair to say you've suffered on my account. It's all tangled together. Let's just own that we were both tested tonight, and that the Lord carried us through safe and sound, and count ourselves blessed, and be content. Sir Lion—" She extended a hand to the knight, who took it to help her to her feet. She toppled a bit but remained upright.

"Tested?" Gervèse pinned Isidro with a keen gaze. "Why, what happened, brother? For what possible reason could you wander off like that? Speak."

"*He* appeared to me, Gervèse. He led me into that garden and sought to torment me." Isidro gestured at the wall.

"What *he?*"

"One of the ones from Chambery. In the devil-caravan. The first that we questioned. I'm positive it was him, or his ghost… if Cainites can have ghosts…"

"Let's not make the holy sister stand in the street," Sire Lion broke in. "You can talk on horseback just as easily."

They mounted up, two on a saddle, and began riding back.

"I shudder to think that killing them *once* might not be quite enough," Gervèse commented.

"Yes. Gervèse, I… he…"

Gervèse quirked a brow at him. In the wake of so much fright that had come to so little relative harm, he felt almost unspeakably lighthearted. "Yes? What is it?"

Isidro reached forward and took hold of the reins ahead of Gervèse's hand. He pulled them back so that the horse dropped behind, out of Lion's and Cecilia's immediate earshot.

"He spoke of having a daughter," Isidro said quietly. "A young daughter in mourning."

Something tugged at the bottom of Gervèse's buoyant spirits then, trying to drag them back down. "Don't be ridiculous, Isidro. Demons don't have daughters. Not human ones, anyway."

"I know. And yet."

"And yet what?"

"Well… he spoke of it in Bergamo as well. And now I'm wondering. You remember their would-be rescuers."

"Exactly. If he spoke of a daughter, I'm sure he meant either that little hellcat-creature or something exactly like her."

"Yes, probably. I only… well, never mind. I'm sure you're right."

They rode on a while in silence. Then Gervèse heard Isidro grunt.

"Yes?"

"Nothing."

"What is it now?"

"You know there's a very strict Rule of our Order governing such situations," Isidro said.

Gervèse felt heat rising in the skin of his neck. "I know," he said. "And I will mention it at my next confession. But you didn't see. For a moment she really seemed to be dead... and Sire Lion bade me find out if she breathed. We were in a perfect panic over the both of you."

A long, low chuckle. "Brother. *Abba*."

"Isidro—"

"Can't you tell when you're being mocked? Forgive me. Of course I mean no reproof. You've committed no fault."

"No, you're right. I forgot the Rule. And I'm abbot, so the fault is that much the greater."

"*Abba*." Isidro sighed. "There are times when our Rule must give way to one far older and more divine yet."

"Oh?"

"Yes. The Golden Rule. Never belittle the kindness of your heart."

***

"And so it was in obedience to one of her visions that Soeur Cecilia came to be in that place?" Marzone glanced at the men still loading the remaining prisoners into the back of a wagon, then turned back to study the four of them. His horse shifted from one side to another, eager to get home to a nice sleep in the stables. Gauthier sat beside the cardinal, white-lipped and white-knuckled—angry (fortunately) not at Isidro or Cecilia but at whatever hellspawn could have the blasphemous audacity to try tempting the soldiers of Christ into perdition on the very heels of their great victory.

"Yes, Monseigneur," Gervèse hastened to answer. "Indeed, she arrived just in time to drive forth a demon that doubtless planned to assail either Isidro or the rest of us. And it was one of her prophecies that enabled me to find her and Isidro. Clear as the very daylight in retrospect— thank God the meaning came to me when it was due. I will show your lordship the letter."

Marzone smiled keenly at the nun. "Soeur Cecilia."

"Yes, Monseigneur?"

"Tell me something. Has your abbess ever said when she plans to call you back to your house in Outremer?"

"I…" Cecilia stuttered, and then recovered. "I have written her a few times to ask that, Monseigneur. She will only say that the time is not yet."

The cardinal nodded. "And after tonight, I'm inclined to agree. That is the wisest course, I think. I'm afraid I must move on tomorrow… with the deepest gratitude for everything you all have shown me… and complete my tour. But it'll comfort me to know that you and Soeur Faustina remain to assist the brothers in their godly work."

Cecilia bowed her head low, causing her face and eyes to fall into shadow. "Yes, Monseigneur."

"Frère Isidro, I look forward to receiving your notes accounting the events of this evening, particularly those I wasn't privy to. For all this," he gestured around, "it seems nonetheless that I managed to miss the night's chief miracles."

"I will attend to it at once, Monseigneur," Isidro murmured.

"And now homeward with all of us," Marzone finished. "I won't go so far as to say we deserve a long sweet rest, but doubtless we've come as close as we're going to tonight."

Chapter Twenty-One

Zoë arrived in the camp bleary-eyed from an ill day, passed in the cellar of a ruined little basilica by a cave where (if villager legend had it right) some ancient local girl-saint had fled to escaped the awful fate of being married off to an Arian, the forest creatures themselves feeding her on honey and berries. No animal had brought Zoë such sustenance; although on rising she'd found a young rabbit straying unwisely near the stones that didn't hear her approach until too late.

Anatole's shelter was empty, the door left open. But when she went to that of Gerasimos she found the Byzantine monk seated praying over a lump in coverlets.

"Brother Gerasimos."

He looked up, blinking. "Zoë! Thank God above, there you are…"

"I'm sorry to interrupt, brother—you're tending someone ill?"

"Not ill." He drew aside the blanket. There lay Anatole, still deep asleep. The Frenchman's mouth was partway open. A peculiar expression knotted his pale forehead and pulled at the flesh beneath his eyes, making him look far older than usual. His hair was choked with leaves, and all over his face and arms were tiny scratches, as though he'd dived into a patch of brambles.

"What's the matter with him?"

"I was hoping you would know," Gerasimos answered grimly. "He came back just before the crack of dawn and fell asleep standing up in my arms, and this evening he wouldn't wake up even when a vessel's vein was opened before his lips."

"Well, how long can he go on like this?"

"Childe," he shrugged, "our kind can sleep for days, weeks, centuries… without knowing the reason behind it there's little way to tell."

"I don't see any deep wounds, and yet he screamed so loud…" Zoë touched his scraped and blistered cheek. He was as one truly dead. His head lolled under her hand but did not move on its own.

"Did Iskender find you?" Gerasimos asked.

"Iskender? No, why?"

"He volunteered to look for you when Anatole arrived alone, so I sent him out."

"Oh. No, I didn't see him."

"Zoë, what happened? Did the brothers in red find him?"

"They must have, or one of the knights. I don't know… he left me very suddenly. He'd promised to stay with me and help finish Isidro."

"Isidro? You actually did attack the man?"

"It was time," she retorted, not quite sure what about his question set her on edge. He asked it without malice. "*He* wouldn't agree, stubborn *Franj*, but it was just as his own prediction said it would be. 'The prisoner slips free,' and we saw it happening right there before our very eyes.'"

She gritted her teeth. The shaking anger was back upon her, the anger that could kill mortals. She tried with all her might to tamp it down. "And then he ran away just when we had the murderer cornered. I don't know why. Why he had to choose then of all times to break a promise… oh, maybe it wouldn't have done any good anyway. Every prophet can be wrong sometimes, I suppose. Maybe I was the fool really, for putting so much stock in his words."

Gerasimos said nothing for a long moment. Then, very hesitantly, he spoke.

"Wasn't it… the prisoner is *set* free, not the prisoner *slips* free?"

She didn't answer for a long moment.

"If he's not going to wake soon," she said at last, "then we must find a good place for him until he does. Somewhere the Heretics can't find him."

"And then what do we do?" he asked her softly, despairingly.

"We wait. And we guard. And we carry on as he would wish us to do... you are still his priest, aren't you?"

He turned and looked again upon the face of his Cainite saint. As he did, something like resolve entered back into him.

"Yes," he answered. "Yes, I am."

Chapter Twenty-Two

Somewhere in Paris
Feast of the Holy Innocents, 1218

"Ah, my little shepherd comes to me properly arrayed in the blood of the lamb. Most pleasing."

"Madame Comtesse."

"And how goes it with the good work?"

"It goes, madame, gradually."

"Gradually?"

"It takes time to soften hearts long hardened to error, madame. We have nearly half of them now, including one of the leaders."

"I'm afraid half is not enough, Your Grace. You see, the vassal lords grow impatient with His Highness on this matter. They tire of being poached upon. And the mortal nobles complain as well; they don't hold with murder and extortion that doesn't line their own purses. Now some refuse altogether to be soothed. One even talks of raising a mercenary band to go out against the Bière robbers. I think you understand the several reasons why this cannot happen."

"If His Highness sees fit to cleanse the woods, madame, I won't argue. Give me one night to remove my converts, and the rest can go to the flames in body as well as spirit—
"

"Your Grace. Don't be foolish. A clutch of some twenty-five, thirty Cainites, however bedraggled? And three times as many kine? Who's going to 'cleanse' them? If it could be done so easily, it would have been by now. No, they must be brought under *control* instead—our control. It's the same here in the city. If all here decided to rise against His Highness at once, he'd be deposed in a night. But they won't, because his skill at *controlling* them guarantees his throne."

"Of course, madame. Control, yes."

"Now I distinctly recall your assuring me that you could have the entire camp converted to your faith, and thus in your hands, within a very few years."

"And I still believe that should have been so. But there have been obstacles."

"Obstacles always have names, Your Grace."

"Yes, madame. Anatole. The Malkavian."

"The Madman, yes..."

"Madame?"

"Mm? Forgive me. I was wondering. I'd thought the miraculous Madman hadn't been seen in some time."

"He slumbers, madame. But it doesn't matter. He still has a band of followers who agitate against us with, if anything, greater fervor. The rest simply waver. The eternal clash of rhetoric confuses them."

"Plainly either this Anatole or his followers—preferably both—must be eliminated. Can't your Folcaut see to it?"

"He's objected, on the laudable grounds that faith shall conquer. And I've felt that it would be unwise, madame, to start a civil war within the camp. Even if it succeeded we might only gain the ill-will of all."

"Then think, my little shepherd. I know you're no courtier, but pretend along with me for a moment. If you cannot do it yourself, then someone else must do it for you."

"Someone whose hatred of them burns as brightly as ours."

"Exactly. Now you show sense."

"Madame, I believe I may have just thought of someone. It will take a little time to arrange, because I must place a spy or two."

***

To my resplendent father in His Name,

My doubts are answered. I venture out into the wilderness frequently enough for meditation and prayer. But I think we had best not meet too close to here—there is a cave near the Saturnine chapel that will do for our purpose. Among the procurers there is still only one who has embraced us. However, that one should be able to acquire a fit subject easily and discreetly enough on his own. I will so instruct him when your lordship has chosen the time.

Given by my hand this pridie Non. Feb. MCCXIX.

**

To my well-beloved son in His Name,

Much has transpired since your last visit to me. Our cassocked convert tells me he has finally made himself a close enough acquaintance that he may usher the chosen one unto them without arousing suspicion, and moreover that circumstances are propitious. Therefore have your procurer set about his procuring and let us make arrangements to meet. I trust I need not instruct you that the subject should be of such an appearance and manner as to win beating hearts and soothe the doubtful thoughts of minds still surging with imperfect humors. For this purpose one of simple birth actually would, I think, suit perfectly, and the younger the better.

Given this viv Kal. Oct. MCCXIX.

**

To my well-beloved son in His Name,

I am told that the kid-goat bleated most admirably and preparations have already begun, but we do not yet know the precise day when things shall come to pass. Even your most faithful must not see traffic between us so close to events; and so the best signal I can give you is that the Compline bells at St. Martin's will ring a full quarter hour early the night before. I trust that will be sufficient. May God be with you and yours, my son.

Given this Non. Oct. MCCXIX.

Postscriptum—Acknowledge receipt as soon as possible.

**

To my resplendent father in His Name,

I acknowledge receipt and will faithfully attend the signal you describe, so that like Noah I may populate my ark before the northern flood descends. I also pray God may smile upon our endeavors and tear up not only the branches but the very root of the evil we have endured for too long. Yours in reverent devotion.

Given by my hand this vii Id. Oct. MCCXIX.

Chapter Twenty-Three

The Bière Forest
The Ides of October, 1219

Iskender plucked the staff out of Zoë's hands and tossed it back to Tomasz, who grinned and caught it.

"Was I that bad?" Zoë asked challengingly.

"Actually, not at all, for a complete novice," Iskender replied. "Maybe if you ask Tomasz nicely he'll show you how to use it in earnest."

Zoë relaxed. But her smile faded somewhat as Iskender gave her a hand up into the saddle behind him and her eye fell on the pair of young villagers she'd subdued with the bulky stick. One grimaced as his bruised wrist was bound; the other cursed the mortal bandit who herded her toward the handful of other weeping women. The look in the bandit's eyes was one Zoë had seen more than once.

Iskender spurred his horse. He and Yosef rode well before the other men and the prisoner-train on the journey home, far enough ahead to learn of upcoming trouble.

"They're going to rape those women," Zoë said after they'd ridden in silence a while.

Iskender looked at her curiously. "Yes, I know."

"And you'll let them."

"I can't control them if they think I'm cheating them out of their rightful plunder. Besides, worse will happen to most of them in the camp."

"Yes." Zoë considered this. "In your mortal tribe, was it the same?"

"Did we take women, you mean? Of course. That's the first thing to do after any victory."

"Why?"

"Because it humiliates all the tribe at once, men and women," he answered quite matter-of-factly, "and you plant

Sarah Roark

the seeds of the conqueror in the soil of the conquered. Many mothers won't kill the child they bear even if it belongs to an enemy."

"Then I suppose you've been with many women."

"Yes, many," he grinned. Then he hesitated. "You, I can't tell if you have been with men before..."

"No," she said.

They rode on for a little while. Her conversations with the bandit-chief often went this way, bursts of exchange followed by silences in which both chewed over what had been said.

"Is it always so?" she asked at last, a bit unsteadily.

"Is what always so?"

"When a man and a woman are together."

"You mean—oh!" He looked back at her. He picked his next words more carefully. "No... that's only one way. It's a very different thing, and much pleasanter besides, when the woman knows your name and calls it out, when she wraps her arms and legs around you."

"And you've been with women many times this way. When they called your name."

"Oh yes."

"Then what is a woman's natural desire?"

"What, are you testing me?"

"I am asking you!" she retorted, her voice rising in anger and embarrassment.

"Well, it depends on the woman, of course," he began.

Zoë felt dumbstruck. Then it was as though some evil enchantment under which she'd unknowingly labored forever suddenly lifted. *Of course*. She laughed.

He didn't understand, and stiffened in umbrage. "What, you ask me something you say you don't know and then mock me when I try to answer seriously! I'm being serious. There was one woman who liked me to go quickly, and another slowly, and one who liked to scratch at me with her fingernails, and—stop it! Stop laughing at me!"

But she couldn't help herself. The bubbling cauldron of her mirth boiled over. It was a bit like when the knife opened her flesh but even more so, a feeling of largeness and lightness in which joy momentarily had room to expand to its fullest dimensions.

Iskender clenched his fists and cursed her under his breath the whole time. But then, to his plain surprise, she drew her arms close around him.

"Go faster," she said in his ear.

***

By a couple of hours later it was obvious that the mortals simply couldn't travel in the dark and wet any further, and so they all made hasty camp under the thickest bower of trees they could find. Iskender's tent was of plain, dark material, but he took a brightly colored Eastern carpet from his packhorse and spread it inside so the floor would be dry.

"Come, come in," he beckoned her from within, holding out his hand. She eyed the tent doubtfully. It was quite small.

When she didn't speak, he finished, "Or stand in the rain if you want," and ducked back behind the flap.

She came in. Iskender lay on his side. She sat beside him.

"What shall we talk about now?" he asked amiably.

"Your homeland."

"Only if you're going to tell me about Constantinople." He fished a cloth out of his bag and moved toward her, holding it in one hand. "Now…"

"What?" She turned on him.

"Your hair is dripping."

"I don't mind."

"Then do you mind if it's dry?"

She smiled and let him towel off the ends of her tresses and blot the rain from her forehead. She took it from him to finish the rest, then offered it to him as well. He mopped himself as clean as he could.

No, talking about Constantinople was still impossible. Not because of the grief; her grief for Gregory was deeper, and yet she could speak of that. It was simply too enormous. Nothing she could say would convey the scale.

"Your sire, then," she said. "I've already told you a little about mine."

"My sire was a great witch. She called herself Ambika Yogini, but she liked me to call her Amlika when were alone…" He lay down and gazed up at the roof of the tent. She lay down on her side beside him. "She was clever, like you. A rival of hers tried to denounce her to the elders, saying that she'd taken me into the Blood when I wasn't her kin. Now, years before she'd had me name my ancestors for her as far back as I knew—ten generations. At the time I had no idea why she asked it of me. Then when her rival accused her, she went before the elders and recited every generation necessary to prove that my eight-times-great-grandfather was actually the brother of her niece's six-times-great-granddaughter."

This news troubled Zoë. She certainly had no intention of seeking out her clan's elders, but it made her uneasy to think that if she did, they might destroy her out of hand as illegitimate. "Was that true?"

"I don't know," he said, smiling. "If it was a lie, it fooled the elders."

"Tell me more."

He sighed. "How much more? Um, she followed the way of our people, but she did it in her own fashion."

Our people. "And what is the way of our people?"

"You mean your Gregory never explained it?"

"No." She reared up on one elbow. "He just said that both his mortal order and his immortal kin had it wrong. That if one was going to spend one's existence distracted by illusions, they should at least be happy ones."

"I can see that way of thinking."

She found herself watching his moving profile as he talked. It was elegant, well-cut. It would have done nicely on a coin.

"Our people," he began, "believe that the world is an illusion, both a dream and a nightmare from which we occasionally awake… when we die, I mean. Then most of us fall right back asleep again, into a new earthly life. And we believe that in each life everyone has three things: a great virtue, a great fault and a *svadharma*—a destiny for either good or ill. But this destiny isn't something that happens by itself. You must seek it every day and night. You must accept it bravely no matter what it holds. And you must help others to their destinies as well. That increases your soul's honor and readies you for a wiser existence in the next life, and the next. Then someday, perhaps, you'll wake from the illusion forever, into something beyond imagining."

"But how does one learn one's destiny, or another's?" she asked.

"Eh. That's the difficult part."

"And do you believe it?"

He rolled over on his side to look at her.

"Yes, I believe it. I don't believe it every moment of every night, of course. I have sinned against *svadharma* in the past."

"When?"

"Well, for example, when my sire was murdered, and I killed her rival in revenge."

He couldn't possibly know. Not unless Anatole told him. Zoë's next words tumbled numbly from her lips, like blood spilled in careless feeding. "But… for all you know, that *was* her destiny…"

"It might have been," he said, oblivious to her shock. "But I didn't act for the sake of destiny, only out of my own rage. That's my great fault."

"Wrath?"

"Yes. I'd ask you what yours is, but I fancy I know."

"You do not. Tell me." When he only smiled she shoved him. "Tell me!"

"Now, now, easy. You don't want to make me angry."

She threw herself flat on her back with a thump.

"It sounds like she deserved to die, in any case," she said irritably.

"Yes. She did deserve to die. I remember how good it felt to kill her, sinful though it was." Indeed, she could hear the old coagulated rage in his voice as he went on, so like that always flooding her own heart. "I seduced her into bed and then pinned her heart so she couldn't move, so that she could watch the blade as it came down. She denied me that last pleasure, though," he added. "Instead she turned her eyes aside to look at the beautiful lamp at our bedside. It must have taken every last ounce of will she had, but she did it."

"Why?"

"It's another belief of ours. Whatever you last see before death, that's what you take with you to be guided into the next life. So when you feel the end coming, rather than spend the last moment fighting destiny, you should instead use it to choose something good to bring, something good or fine or beautiful."

"I see."

"At the time I was furious. I wanted her to see my blade, my rage, my hate. But perhaps it's better this way. I trespassed greatly enough as it is."

"My sire too was murdered, and I seek revenge on the man who did it," she told him.

He pondered that in silence for what seemed like a very long time.

"Well, perhaps that is your destiny, and his," he said at last.

She nodded and exhaled. When she exhaled she realized she'd been holding her breath. How stupid for an unbreathing immortal.

"Yes," she answered. "It feels so heavy on my soul sometimes that I think it must be fate."

"Then I must help you."

That surprised her. "Why?"

He smiled again. "I told you. It's my duty to help others to their destinies. Especially others of my own kind."

She leaned over and kissed his forehead. It was an impulse, just an urge to bestow some kind of thanks. When she rose, however, she was halted by the sight of his staring eyes, only a few inches away from hers. They were still narrow and slanted in their outer shape, but the dark irises suddenly seemed thrown wide open to her exploring gaze. She read all the desire, fear and

hope of his soul in that moment with the same spirit of respect-
ful violation in which she'd once dissected Gregory's gear-work
birds. Then she threaded her fingers into his black-silk hair and
kissed him again.

He craned forward to meet her. He seemed to want to
taste each portion of her mouth, upper and lower, center
and corners, and she let him, supporting the back of his
head on her hand. Then she buried her face in the top of his
coat-collar, overcome by a need to discover his smell. It disappointed her that she could detect little that seemed
actually his—he was a vampire, after all, so there was no
expiration of body-scent from his skin; but the smells that
were there, aging leather and fur and forest loam and the
faintest hint of sweet Cainite blood, were all pleasing to her
enlivened senses.

She felt his lips on her neck now, searching out the
vein. She rolled on top of him, restraining him with her
hands on his chest. His arms slid up her trunk and pulled
slightly. He opened his mouth and she saw the little tri-
angles of his white fangs peeking out from underneath. Hers
had come out as well, almost painfully taut.

A questioning noise, something between a complaint
and a moan, escaped him.

"Shh—shhhh," she said. "I am not one of those women
in the ropes."

"No," he agreed desperately.

"You would not take me against my will."

"No. Zoë, in the name of everything holy, I wouldn't, I
never would…"

She slid his hands back down and placed them on the
rug at his sides, laying her own hands over them for a moment and then letting go to see if they stayed. They did.

"Prove it," she whispered.

She framed his face with her hands and kissed him all
over, eyelids, cheeks, hairline, then found her way down
the chin to the base of the jaw. As she did she unfastened
his coat and reached under his shirt. The shape of skin and
muscle and bone there was so like and yet so fascinatingly

unlike her own. His chest in particular startled her, being neither bone-flat like a little child's nor rounded into woman's breasts. His ribcage squirmed under her touch, nipples contracting at once into hard little buds as her fingers ran over them. Just the way hers had done on certain mortal nights in bed in Constantinople, when—without ever understanding why—she ran her hands over and over her own flesh, wondering what the God- or Devil-given purpose of each response could possibly be.

His fingers dug into the carpet. She nipped at his throat and collarbone, letting her hair fall in a cloud over his face and chest. He took one deep, gasping breath after another; the streams of air passed through her hair and across the skin of her scalp, cool at first and then progressively warmer.

He began to plead with her. "Zoë—little witch—oh Shakti, mercy on your captive Turk, please—"

Mercy on you? Mercy on myself rather—

The blood-thirst was a haze in her head. She realized she'd roused it too far. She couldn't put it back to sleep now. She could only obey it and trust that he would stop her if she failed to stop herself—and that until that point, he would keep his hands down as she had told him to.

She plunged her fangs into his supine neck. He tensed, barely strangling a cry of pure ecstasy.

* * *

"Captain." The voice outside was aggrieved. The thump of a finger against the taut tent fabric made a drumlike noise.

Iskender growled and started to get up, but Zoë laid a finger over his lips.

"What is it?" Iskender called.

"Captain… there's not enough time anymore to make it back to the camp before dawn."

"Has the rain stopped?"

The voice didn't answer, instead letting the near-silence of the forest speak for itself.

"Oh. I guess the Cainites will be camping then. But you men go ahead on with the captives. You can handle that sorry bunch, can't you?"

"Of course." The voice sounded less aggrieved now.

"Good. Move out.—Little witch. All that time wasted for nothing," he complained to Zoë.

"Nothing?" she echoed warningly.

"Well. Not nothing. But when is it my turn?"

"When I say it's your turn." At his look, she added, "You're just as free to refuse me."

"That's what you think, woman..."

Zoë changed the subject back. "She promised for thirty years and still she never took you?"

"I'm sure she thought we would have a lot longer together."

"Maybe she never really went herself."

"Oh, she went. Look." He rummaged in his pack and brought out what looked like a leather pen-case. He opened it up and unrolled a square of silk. Inside the square was a large yellow tooth strung onto a leather thong, with several beads alongside for decoration. The square itself bore a painting in a style Zoë had never seen before: a beast somewhat resembling a leopard, but painted the fire-orange of a fall leaf and then covered over with swirling stripes. It didn't stand stick-stiff like a mosaic figure or rear up pompously like a lion rampant on a Frank's device, but circled fiercely around itself, as though just turning on a pursuer. Every line was a powerful, fluid exertion.

"What is it?" she breathed.

"It's called the *tigris*. I'm told they still roam the wilds of Cathay, and also the lands of our ancestors. This tooth came from one."

"I wish I could see them." Just imagine what Gregory could have created on such a magnificent model. What she could have created. Glossy enamel on the brass, of course, to make the stripes, and carved topaz for the eyes.

Iskender gazed at her for a long moment. Then he took the tooth necklace and looped it over her head.

"We can go," he said. "After you've gotten your revenge. Then we'll leave all these parasites and ragamuffins behind."

"Yes, after that." She nodded eagerly. Yes, leave it all behind. The very idea of exploring new lands where neither Greek nor Frank walked seemed to wake something deep in her blood. But then a panging thought came. "And… after Anatole wakes. Then perhaps."

He absorbed this with evident difficulty. After all, who knew when or if? At last he nodded as well.

"After Anatole wakes, then."

***

Zoë smelled it long before they broke into the clearing the next evening. So did Iskender. He shouted at the other Cainites to ready their bows and whipped his horse on ahead, but it was far too late. The whole camp lay enwreathed in smoke that stank of burnt hair and blood. At first they heard nothing as they rode in. All the huts on the outskirts had been broken apart, stove in like rotten eggs. Nothing stirred anywhere.

Then the sharper-eared among the bandits said they could hear voices at the eastern edge of the camp. They felt along in that direction and soon discovered the mortals busy digging a burial pit. Most made not a wail or moan as they went about stripping their kin of anything worth salvaging. It was hardly possible to take a deep breath for whatever reason without breaking into a coughing fit.

Zoë got down from Iskender's horse and helped them toss in the corpses. It was what Anatole would have done. By the time they'd gotten in ten of the thirty or so it became painfully apparent that not enough pit had been dug, and so she took up a shovel and began to help with that instead. But Iskender came up behind her a little later and tapped her on the shoulder. He had the chief of the bandit-gang's mortals with him; the man was literally ashen-faced.

"You should see," Iskender said.

They turned and walked toward the center of camp. "They knew what they were doing. They attacked during the day, and look… they went out of their way to open as many shelters as they could to the sun's rays. If I hadn't sent the mortals ahead I think everyone would be dead. They arrived in the middle of it all and put the attackers to flight."

Zoë peered inside first one hut, then another. In some she could see charred bits of bone and clothing; in others there was nothing but a dusting of ash.

"How many dead of the Cainites?"

"I count eight so far. Two of the leper-kind, Decius and his childe, that Komana who was almost as mad as Anatole, and three more that I can never remember what they were, if they were anything in particular… but I haven't checked the lodge yet."

"All right."

The lodge, at least, was still standing, though it looked like someone had tried and nearly managed to set the thatching ablaze (evidently the rain had soddened it somewhat). The door stood open a crack. Iskender gave it one perfunctory knock and pushed in; Zoë followed.

In a flash Iskender was flat on his belly on the floor. One of the camp's most bestial Gangrel crouched atop his back, naked, shaggy haunches trembling.

"György." Urbien's rock-rough voice. "Release him."

Zoë looked around. The rest of the council was here as well, except for Helena. Bardas had a chair but he couldn't seem to sit in it. Gallasyn stood next to Folcaut rather than his council colleagues, and the other Heretics huddled around their priest as well. After another moment, Zoë spotted Gerasimos in the corner. He had his arms wrapped tight around himself.

"What the hell is going on?"

"Yes, you might ask that, Iskender," said Urbien. "You might need bringing up to speed, given that you were out…" He glanced at Zoë. "Just what *was* it you were doing?"

"Provisioning, of course!" *Wrath*, thought Zoë, watching the tension in Iskender's frame as he dragged himself up to his feet and threw a warning look at György, who only reluctantly backed off. She could feel her anger boiling as well—at the intimation, at the indignity; but she was too busy feeling guilty about her part in Iskender's tardiness for anger to take the fore.

"But your kine were here," pointed out Gallasyn.

"We all got caught in the storm and had to camp for the day. I told the mortals they should go ahead."

"Of course."

"Would you rather he didn't send them ahead?" Zoë broke in. "Would you rather Iskender were here sleeping so he could be killed too?"

"Come to think of it, Gallasyn," said Iskender, "I'm looking around this room and noticing something much more interesting about who is and isn't dead. I see the entire membership of your little cult made it through all right."

Gallasyn stiffened. "We had Mass up on Lookout Rock last night, and passed the day in a nearby cave," explained Folcaut. "Caine be thanked for thus sparing so many of our number, though of course we grieve for the murdered nonetheless."

"Fair enough." Iskender shifted. "But I wouldn't be throwing stones from Lookout Rock, in that case."

"No, I agree," Folcaut agreed smoothly. "I don't think Iskender's actions need examining, Gallasyn. He's always acted in the best interests of this settlement, after all."

Then he turned to look at Zoë, as did the rest of the room.

Zoë suddenly felt rather like a cornered fox. "What?" she blurted.

Bardas leaned over his chair. "Zoë, mademoiselle... the men who attacked our camp were monks robed in red, along with a band of men-at-arms. They deliberately destroyed havens. They even brought hounds for the express purpose of sniffing them out. They got into the lodge, and burned our Helena..." He shuddered. "I'm sure I'd have joined her, if the tide hadn't turned. Now, you can't pretend that Anatole hasn't made a particular bugbear of the Red Brothers. Even I've heard him preach against them."

"But Anatole is asleep, how many times must I—"

"And the rumors aren't new either, rumors that you've both gone well beyond preaching on this matter. Some say you've made many trips to St.-Denis, and also sent kine out there to spy on your behalf."

"Not only that, but you were gone last night as well," added Urbien with a scowl. "You've never gone with Iskender on one of his raids before, have you?"

"I invited her," protested the Turk. "It was my idea."

"I'll just bet."

"You think I would bring the Red Brothers down upon this camp, the men I hate above all else?" Zoë cried. She took a couple rushing steps toward Urbien, for what possible reason she couldn't have said—but a growl from György stopped her.

"I certainly don't suggest you'd do such a thing on purpose, childe," said Folcaut. *Ever the kindly Father*, Zoë thought bitterly. "But where there's a sting there's bound to be a slap. If you have troubled the Red Brothers, and if you weren't as careful as you thought…"

"I have barely *looked* at them in five years!" It was essentially true. Just the occasional spy to make sure that Isidro hadn't either died or left. She whirled to stare at Gerasimos. "Brother, please. Tell them it's true."

Gerasimos looked up. He hadn't yet dropped his arms. "Yes," he said in a low voice, "it's true. We've busied ourselves with our work here. We've felt it best to leave the Red Brothers alone awhile." Then he lowered his head again.

"Brother? Is something wrong?" she asked. Then, suddenly, "Where's Nikodemos?"

He put his head in his hands.

"It seems poor Nikodemos was taken," said Folcaut. "One of three such mortals."

"And Caine alone knows what the Red Brothers will learn from them…" muttered Bardas. "Very well, Zoë. You say you've done nothing to provoke the monks for five years. If anyone here can definitely refute that, now's the time to speak up."

Silence.

"Then that's that until anyone learns different. Am I clear? Now let's stop soul-searching. The night wastes away, and most of our survivors now lack shelter for the coming day, our Zoë included. We've got to patch up the lodge and at least four or five of the huts."

As they all filed out, Zoë came to a sudden realization. She could see none of Anatole's other followers here except Gerasimos. True, there might be a few Cainite stragglers drifting around elsewhere in the camp. Iskender had only counted eight dead so far. But Komana, she'd been one of Anatole's first adherents. And Nosferatu, clanless—all that sort of "rabble" made up most of the madman's disciples. Folcaut claimed his own lot had been away at Mass. Maybe they were. Still, just supposing the Paris Heretics *had* taken it upon themselves to study the monks who'd attacked them so furiously five years ago, to find some means of luring them just as Anatole had—

Iskender was already drawing Bardas aside to lambaste him. Zoë grabbed Gerasimos' elbow and pulled him along to follow.

"Bardas," the Turk was hissing urgently, "you *know* the timing's too good. You know that scheming Toreador must have…"

"Iskender, I see that Folcaut's followers all survived and many of the rest of us didn't. Now you can call that the providence of Caine if you want, or you can call it something else—"

"What are you saying? The one who can call down the plague must be God? Of all the people I never expected to buy into this kind of—holy blackmail—"

"Iskender! Leave him alone, it's useless." Zoë shook the bandit-chief's shoulder. "Let's go. Quickly!"

"Quickly…?" Gerasimos repeated blearily. But Iskender quickly gleaned Zoë's thoughts, and turned in the same direction she did, to the north. The three of them ran, leaving the stammering Bardas behind.

"Dear God," said Zoë when she saw the churned-up soil marking the passage of several horses northwards out of the camp. She gritted her teeth to stifle a despairing cry.

"Save it till we get there," Iskender told her grimly. They followed the tracks.

***

The little crevice was unblocked, the rocks and mud that had been used to seal it up dislodged, the moss, the bush, and the little tufts of weeds that had grown up to cover it over the years torn out by the roots.

Zoë stood and sobbed against Iskender's chest. Gerasimos did not even seem to have it within him to sob.

"Nikodemos drew the monks away from my shelter," he murmured. "If I'd known, I would have told him to be here instead… or perhaps I would have just told him to save himself, since he at least could flee in the daylight…"

"I—I should see if anything's left," said Zoë at last.

"I'll do it," Iskender broke in.

"No. I must." She wormed herself partway in.

"Is there anything?" called the bandit-chief.

"I don't see anything."

"Not even his ashes?"

Zoë wiped her hand on the rock. There was ash, or whitish dust anyway, but not enough to gather together. She closed her fist to feel it in her hand, thinking: There is no relation. Then she put the tip of her finger in her mouth, tasting it. It seemed to have just the barest taste of blood. There was still no relation.

"Not really," she called back.

"It's just as well," Gerasimos said. "To be honest, I'd rather there weren't relics to start a cult by."

"How can you speak of a *cult*?" Zoë emerged, started to brush off her skirts, then stopped herself. "Who's left, brother? How many disciples are there? You, me…"

"Stephanos and Albertus," he whispered.

"And that's it, isn't it?"

"I believe so."

Zoë glanced at Iskender, who looked genuinely lost. He'd never been a believer, but Anatole had been a fixture at the camp for a long time; even asleep, the prophet's name was still mentioned almost nightly.

"Are you still willing to help?" she asked Iskender.

"Help?" he echoed. Then he realized. "You mean with Isidro? Of course, I told you I would. But what about Folcaut?"

"What about him? He's won," she said tersely.

"You could say the same of the Red Brothers. You know as well as I do that Folcaut has some kind of part in this, and he's the nearer enemy—"

She turned to face him. Suddenly it was all back, all the steel that had bent for so long springing back into shape just as though it had only awaited the right moment to do so. She'd met this crossroads before. She'd heard it from Andreas, from Mascaro, even from Anatole in his own way. What made all these people think that simply pointing out the folly of it would make her turn back? It was folly that made it perfect. She would have no more truck with the notion of some empty, sorry, half-hearted, *convenient* vengeance.

A girl alone cannot take two militant brothers in the heart of their fortress. I think it would be wise—

Two is not enough! Not for such a man! My God, can't you see that?

"Yes, I know. I also know that Isidro was *here*, slaughtering my people yet again, this afternoon," she said. Her voice sounded guttural in her own ears, almost rasping. "Tomorrow if you want we'll go around to all the mortals and ask, but—"

"No, I'm sure he was among them. That I don't argue."

"And *he* is the one who started it all, not Folcaut. It all leads back to him."

"I know…"

"But the prophecy," Gerasimos said, hollowly, as if he knew the answer quite well.

She bent her burning gaze on the monk now. "There is no prophecy. There is no prophet. There is no mission, Gerasimos. Bid those all goodbye yet again. But as God is my witness, whether He approves or not—there will be *justice*. Just this once."

Gerasimos fell to his knees in desperate prayer before the shattered tomb mouth.

"We can come back to get him later," Iskender said softly. "Let him be. You have what you need to go on now. Let him find his."

She nodded and let him take her by the hand as they turned back toward camp.

Chapter Twenty-Four

The Theodosian Abbey at St.-Denis
Feast of St. Raphael, 1219

Gervèse paced outside the door. Every so often he stopped and tried to listen, but in vain. On his own orders and with money from the small bequest Marzone had laid upon them at his parting, certain of the doors to the abbey's more specialized chambers were now good heavy oak reinforced with iron bands and fitted with both locks and bars. He could hear Isidro's voice, and he could hear the prisoner's words as well—first coming in brief moaning waves, then more freely. But neither side of the converse was intelligible.

Gervèse had been hard in the initial interrogation, not sparing the rope. Isidro had merely stood by and transcribed with a slight frown on his face, occasionally breaking in to mildly counsel Gervèse to patience. Afterward, when Gervèse had asked him what in blazes he was about, giving the prisoner the idea that mercy might be had, Isidro had explained that that was exactly his purpose. He played the carrot to Gervèse's stick; now that they'd led the man to think one captor was cruel and the other kind, the "kind one" could now go in and coax even more out of the prisoner with the implicit promise that the "cruel one" would be placated thereby. Gervèse had to admit it was a clever theory.

At last Isidro emerged, wordlessly, carrying his tablet. Gervèse followed him all the way to his cell, but finally he couldn't stand the waiting anymore and blurted out his question.

"Well? Did it make a difference?"

"It seemed to, *Abba*," Isidro nodded. "He still says he's a Christian, of course, not a heretic…"

"It's quite possible the deluded creature actually believes that."

"I think he does. He told me that as a young man he was taught to revere the Cainites as keepers of inner divinity, but that other Cainites have since taught him to reject that belief." Isidro opened one of his chests and began to go through it.

"Other Cainites?" Gervèse repeated, mystified.

"Yes. He makes it almost sound as though there are… schisms in the anti-church. I—I took it down, it's all very interesting, you can look at it if you like." He took a bundle of cloth from deep within the chest and sat down on the bed to unwrap it. Gervèse looked: a little brass bird-head with an enameled beak, brass bird-legs banded with onyx, tiny diamond-cut bronze feathers allowed to verdigris to a blue-green shade, and an unassembled heap of many little tabs, rings and tidbits spilling out of what would once have been the sculpture's belly.

"That's that—thing, one of those bizarre oddments from the demons we brought to Bergamo," Gervèse exclaimed. "Prior Ugo smashed it, when it seemed to move of its own volition…"

"It did move of its own volition."

"And then you swept it up, I thought to throw it away. I should have known better."

"I haven't been able to put it back together. I don't know if that would even restore it to… to whatever it had before," Isidro finished lamely. He toyed with one of the fragments, a round ring with a toothed edge. "Some of the pieces, I can see how they must have gone together, but I'd have to have tools sized for a mouse to move them into place in that tiny body. And then there are others whose workings remain a complete mystery. But you see, for instance, this must have gone against this, so. And when this piece was turned, it caused this little rod to throw in and out, so."

"Stop that, Isidro!" Gervèse yelped. Then he regained himself. "But what turned the wheel in the first place?"

"This wheel, I think."

"And then what turned that? What drove the whole thing?"

"I don't know. I'm sure it was some kind of sorcery."

"Then why keep fooling with it?"

Isidro shook his head and looked away, heaving a frustrated sigh. "Don't you ever wonder what it was *for*, Gervèse? Why a demon would go to so much trouble for something so apparently useless?"

"Out of envy for the true Creator, I suppose. How should I know? You could always ask that wretch in there."

"That's what I just did."

"What!"

"I asked him. I asked him if he knew anything about the—one who made this, Gregory."

Gervèse stiffened. "The one that attacked you in the garden. And?"

"He knew of him. He said that in Constantinople the other Cainites called him Gregory the Wonder-Maker. And that he was indeed known for making beautiful and clever things, many of which he did put into a garden beside his house."

"Did he tell you what the beautiful and clever things were for?"

"Yes." But Isidro didn't finish the sentence at first, nor did he turn to Gervèse. "To make people happy, he said."

"And thus ensnare them to the Devil…"

Isidro closed his fist. Gervèse heard the snap of metal breaking.

"Isidro?" He approached his friend's hunched back.

"Is it demonic to make someone happy?" Isidro's voice, too, was strained taut.

"It is when a demon does it," Gervèse answered quizzically. "Isidro, I don't understand. What's the matter?"

"What is the matter? What was the matter at Bergamo?" The Spaniard stood, all energy and no outlet. "You were there, Gervèse. You watched and listened. Gregory asked for confession. He asked for unction. He wanted the sacraments of *our Church* before we destroyed him."

"What good could it have done to give the sacraments to a demon?"

"Yes, that's what Prior Ugo said, isn't it? But let me ask you this, Gervèse. What *harm* could it have done?"

All at once Gervèse's thoughts turned inexplicably thick, sluggish. He opened his mouth to answer but nothing came out.

"By what reasoning did Ugo refuse him? By what conceivable right did I stand by and let it happen? When a dying man, no matter how stained his soul, asks for reconciliation with the Father, we don't dare deny it to him. We say our blessings and leave judgment to God. That is the way of the priest, it always has been."

"But, Isidro," Gervèse stammered. "This was not a *man*..."

"Are you so sure he was what we thought he was?" Isidro cried out. "Gervèse, there's so much we still don't know about these creatures. So many questions we haven't even thought to ask yet. Did we really refuse him unction because we suspected a trick—or was it because we were *afraid*? Afraid he might say something in contrition that would give the lie to everything we'd built up in our minds?"

"Afraid he might say something that would weaken our resolve." Gervèse stepped carefully toward him and just as carefully laid a hand on the tensed shoulder. "Yes. And with good reason, I see. Isidro, I hope this hasn't been eating at you since Bergamo. You shouldn't bear such terrible doubts in silence for so long. They bloom poisonously in the imagination and become a thousand times more frightful. I am your friend, sometimes even your confessor... please."

Isidro shuddered and moved back. He stood there shamefaced for a moment; then, to have something to do, he began wrapping up the brass bird to put it away.

"And he does have a daughter," he said at last.

"You talked to the prisoner about that as well," Gervèse half-asked, half-accused.

"A little girl named Zoë, an orphan girl that he took under his wing, and several years later 'brought into the Blood,' as the man puts it."

"If she is 'brought into the Blood,' then there is no little girl anymore. If she was the creature that leaped onto you four-footed in Bergamo, there certainly was no little girl left in that. Set your conscience at ease, Isidro. It does you credit, but in this case it overreacts."

"How fiercely would you attack the demon that killed me, or—or any of the brothers or sisters in our Order? Once, at least, there must have been a little girl." Every mark of weariness that years of seeing Hell's reach upon earth could make fell into Isidro's face, and suddenly he seemed more than middle-aged. "And once she must have loved the one who took her in, regardless of what he was."

"Let me in at that miserable villain," Gervèse said, heading for the door. "I'll get the truth out of him…"

"No!" Isidro stopped him with a hand on the elbow. "Don't act out of anger, please. Certainly don't take your anger at me out on him. That accomplishes nothing."

"I'm not angry at you!" Gervèse protested.

"Oh? Then who are you angry at?"

"I don't know!" The truth was out before he could stop it. "At him, I suppose, at the blasted Cainites. At whoever is trying to do this to us, to you."

Isidro stared at him, dark eyes hollow. "And what if no one is trying to do it, Gervèse?" he asked quietly. "What if my doubts are my own?"

The question shook him down to his foundations. Yet somehow they stood.

"That's not how it works, Isidro," he said at last. "*Someone* always stands to benefit. Someone always stands to lose. And there are only two sides to the game."

Isidro went back over to the bed and sat down on it again. He picked up the little cloth bundle, delicately, as though the bird within were not destroyed but merely wounded.

"I know," he answered. And something in the way he said "I know" overtook every ounce of Gervèse's compassion and drove him out of the room, out into the hallway, out into a maze of corridors where no turn was the correct one anymore.

***

"You're telling me that no one else yet knows?" Veronique of Orléans paced back and forth in her Parisian quarters. It was late at night on the Feast of St. Gregory the Wonderworker.

"Not yet, Mademoiselle," said her visitor.

"Well. I must confess myself honored, then—and intrigued. Why should I be the first?"

"Because I'm told you have something that I need."

"Really? I wonder what that could be."

"A letter."

"I'm afraid I have many letters."

"This letter is neither addressed to you nor sent by you. You watch all the cat's-paws of the Knowing Lady—"

"*La Savante*... ah, alliteration. Do you always nickname people?"

"And then one cat's-paw acquired a cat's-paw of his own, and you fear the red plague as much as any sane vampire, so you finally took the risk necessary to find out. The good father and his master know their courier disappeared, but they don't know you're the reason why—and in any case it was too late by then to put out the fire they'd started."

"I see. But if you're already aware of the letter's contents, then why do you want it?"

"It's not I who needs convincing."

"Interesting. A new hour tolls, perhaps. Yes. I observed a pattern. More converse than usual between the bishop and Saviarre *La Savante*, always followed closely by couriers riding out to the southern woods and back. And all year I've marked the same priest visiting both the bishop's house and St.-Denis. The juxtaposition made me uneasy."

Sarah Roark   247

"Of course it did. It should. The game they play is one we all could lose, mademoiselle. I'm told that's why you'll help me now."

"Your sources presume a lot."

"My sources also tell me that rather than appointing Tiberius, Augustus seems bent on becoming him."

"I'd say Caesar has long since bypassed Tiberius and launched headlong into Caligula, or perhaps Nero."

"And how long are you willing to wait for Nero's suicide?"

"Now *you're* presuming a lot."

"The time's past for shadow-sparring, mademoiselle. I do much better in the arena. I only need the gates opened to me. And if I succeed, then you too are in a better position to do—well, whatever you wish with it."

"You're a persuasive man. But words won't suffice in the arena you speak of. You must have power as well. A gladiator needs his sword."

"That's why I must have the letter."

"And you think you'll use it to better effect than I could?"

"Consider it my proving ground, if you like. Consider what I might accomplish if you only give me the chance; and what might happen should *La Savante* and the shadow-shepherd gain their way instead."

"Hmm. Very well. *If* you come to the arena with sword in hand, then I will indeed open the gates." She turned to her oathbound aide. "Thierry, fetch the letter for my guest."

Chapter Twenty-Five

The Bière Forest
The Feast of the Circumcision, 1220

Tomorrow night. Tomorrow night.

This thought was the evening's *ostinato*. It circled round every other thought, ensnaring it, dragging it down into uselessness. It snaked up under every attempt at rationality. She found herself muttering it at odd moments, muttering it repeatedly like a penitential prayer. The moon was waxed not quite halfway. She didn't care. She had to get this vampiric thought out of her head. If she didn't, it would kill its own prophecy. She couldn't think past it.

She dragged the blade across the skin. She hadn't sharpened it recently enough, and it snagged as it went. She gasped and her eyes welled up. But then relief surged inside her that more than matched the pain. Of course. All existence was just so. God dealt out His blows unexpectedly, cruelly.

She added another three long hatches in a row, exactly parallel, taking great satisfaction in the order she could impose upon her own suffering.

Once the blood began to flow, she at last became aware of things outside the fever realm of her own mind. It was a quiet night. The stream rolled musically on behind her, behind Anatole's meditation rock against which she leaned for support. All around her the ancient wood breathed. This place had been here long before Anatole; it would remain long after tomorrow's issue was decided. It, unlike her, had been born to immortality. She allowed its solemn calm to invade her as she crouched, her head resting back against the cool stone, and watched the little lines of red bead down the skin of her thigh.

Do you ever think to ask why he fed you the blood, and you so young? Now that you know what it does to the living, the slowing of mortal age?

—It was what it was, Meribah.

Could it be that part of him didn't really want you to grow up at all?

—I think he cringed at the thought of my growing up, and yet at the same time wanted nothing more badly than to watch it happen. Just like he wanted me to hate the curse as he did, and yet to love it, since if I could love the curse then I could love him. It was a lot of things, Meribah, none of them easy. With time we might have solved the puzzle. Now I can only bleed for us both.

The wounds had dried already. She reopened one with her fingers to see if that would be enough, but a moment later she was reaching for the knife again. She made a single streaking gash across the top of the vertical slashes. The difference between the sensation in the uninjured and the injured flesh fascinated her. The tiny flap of skin that came loose at one of the intersections was like a bloody affront. A frazzled edge, vulnerable, lingering in some despicable half-state between purity and oblivion. She could smooth it back down and it would soon graft itself back into place, painfully, gracelessly; or she could take hold of it now and *tear*—

"Zoë!"

Every limb of her body jerked rigid. She scrambled to her feet, dropping the knife. In the next moment Iskender was on her, pinning her against the rock, his powerful hands seizing hold of her shoulders.

"Zoë, what are you *doing*—"

"Get off me!" She writhed in his grip. "Off!" Finally she took her feet, planted them against his midsection, and shoved with all her might. He let go and reeled back. Spotting the knife on the ground, he dove to grab it up. He stared at its reddened edge. Then he shook himself and splayed out his free hand to ward her away.

"I'm off, I'm off!"

She snarled at him, starting up from where she'd fallen.

"Zoë, stop it! What in hell is going on?"

"Give me back my knife."

"No. Not if you're going to keep doing *that* with it," he grimaced.

"It's not your business and it's not your knife. Give it back."

"No!" But he hardly seemed to know what he did want to do with it. "Zoë—I don't understand."

"No one's *asked* you to understand." The lovely sweltering peace of just a moment before was gone. The blood on her leg felt like a slime now. He'd ruined it all. "What in hell are *you* doing, following me out into the woods, sneaking up on me like a, a thief?"

He looked stung. "I—came out to tell you Gerasimos changed his mind about helping, with the disguise—"

"Well, couldn't it have waited?"

"Waited?" Now his voice hardened to match hers. "*You're* the one who's insisting that none of it can wait anymore! How was I to know you were out here doing… whatever in Caine's name it is you're doing…"

A long, painfully awkward silence passed between them.

Then he stepped toward her. "Zoë, *sevgilim*. I've been thinking. I said I'd help. I keep my word. And I know this might be the only chance we'll have at him for months. But before we go, you must answer me one question. I think I deserve that much."

"And what is that?" she returned, eyeing the knife.

He hesitated, then stuck the blade in his belt. He moved to lean beside her on the rock. She considered whether to move away and decided against it. He stroked her cheek with his thumb.

"Is it really Isidro you want to kill?" he asked at last.

"What—what do you mean?" she stammered.

"You know what I mean." He glanced down toward her skirt, toward the patch of red that had soaked through. His eyes burned with Cainite hunger, with the lust to take her as she had taken him, but he spoke gently. "I know what it is to want revenge, to want it so badly that even your own existence seems cheap. I will defy the odds with you. But I won't help you destroy yourself. If it turns out that all you really want is to suffer and die…"

"No. No, Iskender, that's where you don't understand." Slowly, she reached over and took her knife back. She wiped the blood off the blade with a bit of her skirt. "I suffer so that I can *live*. Don't ask me why it must be so, but it must."

"Zoë. My Zoë… I swear, if I had any power to dispel nightmares and not just to create them…"

"Well, you don't. And neither do I." She circled her arms tight around him. He returned the embrace. "Somehow we must manage regardless."

***

Early the next morning at the St. Denis Abbey, before Lauds, Brother Isidro was praying with a sinner. "*Confiteor unum baptisma in remissionem peccatorum,*" he murmured.

"*Con—confiteor unum baptisma, in remissionem peccatorum,*" Nikodemos repeated through parched lips. Isidro gave him another sip of water from the ladle. The man craned his head up from the table-surface of the rack to swallow.

"*Et expecto resurrectionem mortuorum, et vitam venturi saeculi,*" the Spanish monk finished. "*Amen.*"

The Greek monk echoed the words, stumbling over a few. "Your pronunciation's improving," Isidro remarked.

Nikodemos gave the very slightest of smiles. "I always did want to learn Latin…"

"Not under these circumstances, I'm sure."

"No. But you are a fine teacher, nonetheless."

"Would that were so. I'm due at the university by noon and I still have to finish my notes…"

Isidro stood and made the sign of the cross over Nikodemos, then placed a hand on his head. "Yet you still won't ask for the sacrament," he mused. "If it weren't so terrible, I would find irony in it—that it's not your servitude to a Cainite, but your claimed loyalty to the Eastern Church, that leads you to refuse our absolution."

252   Ravnos

Nikodemos said nothing for a moment. Then he whispered, "More water, please, brother. My thirst, it's worse every day."

"I know." Isidro gazed down at the man. Torture wore at the body and soul quickly, but usually not quite this quickly; hair that had been jet-black and curly was now salted through with gray, and skin once supple as any youth's now sagged just a bit under the eyes. Isidro gave him another mouthful. He felt at the Greek's tight-drawn elbow joints. He hesitated. Then he relaxed the bottom wheel by a small fraction of a turn. Nikodemos gave a sharp exclamation of renewed pain, but sighed immediately afterward. Isidro picked up the bucket and left the room.

Nikodemos let his head lower again as he listened to the now-familiar noises. The door opening. The door shutting. The key turning in the lock. Leather-clad footsteps retreating. Then silence.

Silence.

No sound of the bar sliding into place.

He forgot to bar the door?

Inconceivable. He continued listening, but all was absolutely still.

He forgot to bar the door!

Nikodemos' heart pounded. *Patience*, he told himself. He must wait just a bit for the bells, and then almost all the monks and lay brethren would be at morning prayers. They wouldn't hear the lock break or see him pelting across the field…

He stared at his weltered left hand, willing the thick pad of flesh at the base of his thumb to soften, melt, stretch. As it changed shape, the rope began to slide over it.

There were still some things he had *not* confessed; there were some things even clever, kind Isidro had never asked about. And thank God, even a thousand Latin prayers said over his wracked body could not destroy the last few precious drops of his master's power lying dormant in his veins. A monk of the Obertus Order had blessings no Roman priest could ever understand.

Agnes cried as she struggled, tears streaming down her face. Her nose began to run. She couldn't wipe it. Joie simply would not lie still, and bleated in distress whenever Agnes tried to work her hand around further. She called out again; still no one came. It was after sunset, she was all alone and freezing, and no one would come from the farm to help. Ewe and lamb would both die and it would be her fault.

A silhouette filled the barn door, features indistinct in the dim light. She looked up. "Father?" she asked unsteadily, but she knew it wasn't Father. The man who came in had the look of a distant foreigner. He wore an odd dark little cowl over a brown robe. His eyes were soft, hurt, and more than a bit wild, like Joie's. His face was dirty and his dark hair prickled with straw, as though he'd slept in a cowshed. He limped heavily toward her.

"Please—do not fear," he said in thick French. "I am only lost… I need to know which way is Melun, or even Paris… "

"Go away!" she shouted at him. "Can't you see I'm having trouble!"

He stared at Joie and then back at her. Then he came and knelt down beside them. She considered whether to scream or run, but he looked so sad that she found herself transfixed instead. Gently he took hold of her arm and slid it out. Then he faced the drizzling opening and put his own left hand in.

"There's two," she babbled, caught between unease about what Father would say if he saw her letting a stranger at their finest ewe, and vast relief at having someone grownup take charge. "This one's leg is bent the wrong way, and I felt a leg in there but I don't know if it's the right one."

The man frowned as he felt around for what seemed eternity. Then all at once his frown vanished and his face slackened into something like a smile. After a few moments' close-leaning work, he sat back again. The tiny nose and both front hooves protruded now; with his left hand he took a hoof, pulling gently, and with his right he slipped two fingers inside atop the head to make sure it came along. Joie heaved and strained. At long last the shoulders finally came free and the rest slipped out as easily as a sigh. Agnes began to cry again.

"Oh, you're kind, you're kind…" But the man just sat there with the newborn lamb in his hands. The umbilical cord had torn against something and was bleeding. The blood covered the thin membrane veiling the little creature. It had gotten on the man's hands. He stared at it as though he thought it were his own.

"Sire, the lamb, it must breathe," she reminded him, putting a hand on his elbow. That was when she finally saw *why* his left hand had so easily moved within the womb: it was deformed, oddly thin and long, stretched out like softened beeswax. She recoiled with a gasp. He lifted the monstrous appendage. It shook. He brought the red-slicked fingertips toward his shuddering mouth and opened his lips.

This was no tender-hearted pilgrim! Agnes shrieked and stood up. He stood hastily too, depositing the lamb on the straw.

"No," the man whispered urgently. "No!" But she wouldn't be quieted and ran out of the barn still shrieking. He started to rush out after her, then thought far better of it, turned and started across the fields instead.

He limped all the way to the church and fell down to his knees on the cold ground of the churchyard, addressing the building as though the statues and paintings could hear him through the walls.

"God, my God, oh Father forgive…" Gerasimos had warned him once that it might be so if he ever had to go without, that the Cainite thirst itself would come upon him. To taste even a portion of eternity was to taste a portion of the curse. But he'd never thought how it must really be for his poor master, to behold the most innocent flesh and wish only to tear into it and draw out the living salt.

A cold hand came to rest on his shoulder.

"Ah, suffering son." The voice was low, almost a purr. "I think I know what troubles you. It's been far too long, hasn't it?"

He only sobbed in response. A bare white arm entered his field of view, a tendril of cherry-dark blood twining around it like ivy. He was past all questioning, all caution. The sight of it was like a gasp of air to a drowning man. He literally had no choice. He fastened his mouth to the gleaming fountain.

The hand that had been on his shoulder moved up to his head, lying atop it a moment and then beginning, almost maternally, to pick out the straw.

"Yes, I know. That's better. Mend your distended bones. Now, my son… tell me everything."

Chapter Twenty-Six

"But *magister*—"

A mass sigh moved through the room. The *disputatio* was dragging on far longer than was either usual or (by most reckonings) warranted. Of the handful of senior scholars who'd decided to cross lances with their guest lecturer only one now remained, but that one seemed determined to argue it down to the last jot and tittle whether anyone else present cared or not.

"*Magister*, what about the passage in the dialogue where the Student says that Lucifer can't have wanted to be 'as God,' since God is by definition unique and unassailable, thus for any being to become 'as God' is an utter impossibility; and surely Lucifer must already have known this, therefore how could he have wanted what he knew to be impossible? By your own argument you've apparently just made the Teacher's answer null. So how then do *you* reply?"

Isidro pursed his lips a bit in thought before answering. "Come, Aimery. Couldn't you and your fellows entertain, at this very moment, the wish that night were not dark so that you could see your notes better, or that men need not eat so that you could save your coin for classes? Wanting the impossible is by no means foreign to humanity. I see no particular reason why it should be foreign to angels either, fallen or otherwise."

One good effect of the prolonged sparring was that the crowd dispersed all the quicker once it was finally done. Darkness had fallen a good hour hence; most students fairly ran out, eager to see if perhaps a warm cabbage-pie or eel-tart could still be had on the cheap from one of the vendors trudging home. A few die-hards did knot round the red-clad monk, nevertheless; he briefly but affably answered their questions, promised to show one of the quarrelsome seniors the precise wording of the passage in the *Etymologiae* he'd mentioned sometime tomorrow, and then gathered up his little *vademecum* notebook, his papers and his lantern.

Now, Zoë urged herself. *Go now.*

"*Magister.*" She tried to pitch the word low, but instead it came out husky, half-present. Well, that should be all right. The slight down of hair Gerasimos had planted on her chin and upper lip, her slight build, all spoke to a lad of fifteen or sixteen, freshman age. Hopefully the awkwardness in her stance, the slight stiffness she felt in her limbs would be read as boyish nerves. Hopefully he saw only what he was supposed to.

Isidro glanced up. "Yes?"

She bobbed respectfully.

"*Magister,* forgive my impertinence, but I'd been hoping to ask you a question about a—a few books that I have. I don't know whether I should keep them, or perhaps sell or burn them…"

"Oh?" Instantly there was less hurry in his movements. "What kind of books?"

"Well, they speak of some subjects of which it seems the venerable Saint Isidore disapproves. Here… this is one of them, see for yourself."

He took the little leather-bound volume from her and paged through a bit of it, murmuring.

"*Geomantia.* Yes, I see…" He frowned, studying a diagram. "Fascinating. I've heard of this work, but never actually seen it. What about the other books?"

"I left them back in my room, *magister.*"

"Mm."

"I… I could show them to you, and you could tell me."

"Yes." He flipped another page. "Yes, that would be fine. What about tomorrow?"

"Oh, tomorrow—tomorrow I have classes and reviews all day."

He glanced up at her. His black eyes traversed her as though she too were a page to be read. For a moment she was absolutely sure her disguise was pierced.

"Then I suppose it had better be tonight," he said at last.

She nodded fervently. They walked together out of the churchyard and started down the Rue des Ecoliers. She wrapped her cloak close and dipped her mouth below the rim of the face-opening in her hood—remembering that it was lack of visible breath in the winter air that had given away that Cainite in Arles so many years before.

The monk was silent, but not peacefully so; he seemed just on the verge of saying something. She felt the same way, but that was a ridiculous notion. What was there to say, except the truth that would have to wait just a little longer?

Still, the void unnerved her. She tried to think of Anatole. Anatole never froze like this in the presence of his godly enemy, never stood meekly accused.

"*Magister*," she began. "I... I'm thinking of what the other boy said, about Peter Lombard on the fallen angels. That they're changeable by nature but not by grace. That even though they were created with free will to turn to either good or evil, the good angels are so confirmed in grace that now they *can't* sin; and the bad angels are so hardened in their vice that they can no longer choose to do well. Yet how can that be known to be so?"

The Red Brother ruminated on that a moment. "Peter Lombard is the standard scholar's text for a good reason," he answered at last, "and you'll do better in your studies here not to question him."

Zoë nodded numbly.

"...But," he finished, "I do think it a bit presumptuous of both him and Isidore to so qualify Saint Jerome, who clearly stated that it is only God upon whom sin cannot fall, that other things are of free will and can turn that will in either direction; and that Christ Himself redeemed the robber at Calvary to show that repentance is never too late."

These words sent a thrill of shock through her. They walked a little way further before she could bring herself to reply.

With difficulty she found herself again. "But... but then... why would such venerable men just presume, without reason?"

He shrugged. "Perhaps they think backwards from their desired conclusion. After all, if demons could repent and angels fall at any given moment, that makes things confusing for everyone, doesn't it? Men like to be certain about whom they can believe."

"That would be wrong of them, though, wouldn't it, to think backwards?"

"Yes. Yes, it would be wrong. If that is what they're doing. What do you think, lad?"

A bit desperately, she searched her memory of the *disputatio* again. She'd missed most of the *lectio* on account of the sun, of course. "The other boy," she remembered suddenly, "he also quoted the Damascene. 'Death is to men what the fall is to angels,' he said. Doesn't that imply that just as men cannot repent after their deaths, angels cannot repent once they have fallen?"

"And yet we have masses for the dead," Isidro pointed out.

He was arguing her own side for her. She'd heard that in the university it was so; that professors would play devil to see if students could be led astray. But if he insisted on playing devil, what else could she play but God?

"But... that doesn't apply." She'd run out of borrowed quotes to parrot. She was no Paris scholar. She fumbled on regardless. "I mean, surely the demons sinned gravely when they fell, and no mass or prayer can save those who died in grave sin, or unrepentant..."

"*Did* you die unrepentant?" he asked quietly.

She stopped. He stopped alongside her. For a long, horrible moment she literally could not force her body to turn toward him—as though he himself were some terrifying illusion of blood-art that would disappear if she refused to believe it.

And then, somehow, she managed to unstick her bones. She stared at him. His gaze bent fixedly down on her, but his breath seemed to be coming shallowly. The hand with the stack of books in it hefted them for a moment, then dropped again.

"Your geomancy book, I looked at the colophon," he said. "*Frater Martinus Bergamensis scripsit.* I did meet a Brother Martin in Bergamo once, at our order's house there. Then just a few days after I left, he disappeared, somewhere along the same road I left by. I wish I could say I was shocked when I heard about it…" His voice wobbled a bit. "Honestly, I was only shocked that I'd escaped his fate. Certain things had been done at Bergamo recently, for which retribution had already been sought once… but you know all this, don't you?"

Incredibly, she found herself nodding.

He nodded with her, no less mesmerized.

"Why—" he began, then stopped himself. Then he spoke again, the words coming out hastily, crowdedly, as though he already regretted them even as he said them. "Look here, the Fathers say a demon can sometimes tell truth, though always in an ill cause, and so it's better not to listen even then, but—I'm not a saint or a Solomon, I can't compel you to speak plainly, but I *ask* you, just this once, if you can, put aside the charade and say *what it is* that you want of me—"

"Isidro?"

They both recoiled. Zoë saw a crack of light widen and narrow at the front door of one of the scholars' houses. The sound of laughter swelled out from within and then subsided. A stout, cloaked figure had emerged, its hand cupped alongside its mouth to call out. When the figure lifted its lantern Zoë saw a flash of red.

"Isidro, there you are!"

Zoë's gaze lit again on Isidro, whose head snapped back and forth as he looked from the figure to Zoë.

"Run," he hissed. "Run!"

She ran.

***

"Isidro!" Gervèse ran up. "What the—" He turned to his friend, who stood there pale and wide-eyed. "What is it, Isidro?"

The Spaniard's mouth opened but nothing came out. The answer broke upon Gervèse then.

"One of them!" he cried, and started up the street after the fleeing figure. Isidro ran after him and caught his shoulder.

"No, Gervèse, don't!"

Gervèse rounded on him. "Why not?"

"It was leading me into a trap," Isidro said desperately. "It said it wanted to show me books—"

"Books! And you went?"

"Gervèse, I think it's to do with Bergamo—"

"Bergamo? You mean it's *that* one again!" Gervèse roared. "This will be the last time, so help me God!"

And with that he burst into a pounding run.

***

Zoë cursed herself as she turned down the crabbed little street. On top of everything else a gusting breeze had picked up. If only she'd moved faster, Iskender could have had a clearer shot of it, and one target instead of two; but she'd simply have to trust to the famed skills of the Turks. She stopped halfway down the length of the street. Then she reached beneath her cloak and brought out her knife. Glancing up hurriedly, she could, only because she knew where to look, spy the gleam of an arrowhead and the whites of keen eyes within a lampblacked face on one side of the street—Iskender—and on the other side the same evidence of Tomasz and Roric, the two of his band who'd agreed to come along. For an instant she considered calling up to warn them about their doubled enemy, but decided against it. That second Red Brother ran damned quickly for someone no longer in his youth and a bit thick in the middle besides. He could be nearly close enough to hear.

Indeed, it was only the space of the briefest prayer before the two monks came tearing around the corner, Isidro lagging behind. The stout one had in his outthrust fist a chain from which several metal charms dangled: pilgrims' medals and crosses, perhaps. He bore down on her, chanting in Latin, and to her eyes he seemed to grow ever taller and grimmer as he neared.

"For Father and Anatole," she muttered, standing firm. She couldn't run. She had to provide the clear target and the clear path. She could by God prick that belly open with her knife if he reached her, though.

Suddenly Isidro shouted "Gervèse!" and fairly leapt forward to overtake the other monk, knocking him aside. An arrow plunged through Isidro's flesh where shoulder and neck met. He gurgled and collapsed. His books and papers fell askew into the gutter-mud.

"No!" cried Gervèse. He bent down to lift up his fallen companion. Two more arrows whizzed past his head from either side of the street and narrowly missed Isidro. For an instant Gervèse vainly looked up; then he turned away and barreled headlong into Zoë instead. Zoë dodged and tried to stab at him. He seized her arm and gave it a vicious twist. She heard the joint pop and a jolt of searing pain ran through her, but the knife somehow remained in her grip. She growled, baring her teeth; his eyes widened but he didn't back away. She yanked back on the arm he held, pulling him off balance. He was a quick thinker, all right—he knew they wouldn't waste arrows on the one who was already down and his own best chance of avoiding their fire lay in entangling himself with Zoë.

Tomasz and Roric jumped down out of their hiding-places with swords drawn. Zoë got loose and ran clear of their charge. An odd light kindled in the monk's eyes as he saw them coming, and he grinned. He closed in on Roric just as the latter's sword drew back for a swing, then dashed the baubles on his chain into the Cainite's eyes. They struck sparks from the undead skin like steel from flint. Roric howled and cowered away. Tomasz launched into Gervèse then, but the monk seized him by the cloak and whirled him around backwards. That very moment an arrow thudded into the bandit's back. He stiffened and fell to the pavestones. Without blinking an eye Gervèse wrenched the sword out of his clenched hand. Then he turned back to Roric, who hissed and lashed out blindly, and buried the edge of his blade in the middle of the Cainite's skull.

Zoë, stunned at first by the brutal suddenness of this transformation from soft cleric to savage warrior, came unfrozen and rushed in, taking the knife in her other hand now. Gervèse parried her strike, then followed up with a swing that arced out in a flash of reflected moonlight and caught her neck at its edge. She tumbled back to the ground, scrabbling at the open lip of the streaming wound as if to close it with her fingers. When she tried to lift her head it would only come up lopsided—a sinew was cut.

Another arrow flew at Gervèse and speared his cloak. A howl of frustration echoed down from the gable above them.

Wrath, she thought suddenly. *No!*

But it was too late. The Turk leapt down from the rooftop and all at once was no longer Iskender at all, but a terrible being wreathed in a ring of dark violet flame, a giant with multiple arms each holding a weapon, its hair streaking out from its head in wild rivulets, snakes and skulls draped around its neck and arms, its feet invisible amongst a mass of wriggling cobras that seemed to propel it forward.

Gervèse stood awestruck as the monstrosity reached and enveloped him. An instant later it dissolved like mist back into the bandit-chief, who knocked the monk flat and made a wild snarling swing with his saber which should have cut him in two and instead only opened a diagonal slash across the very surface of his chest. Zoë struggled to her feet, willing her wound to heal.

"Iskender," she tried to call through the blood flooding her throat.

Not enough for such a man! My God, can't you—

Gervèse seized hold of Iskender's leg, which was planted atop his belly. In that hand he still held the chain of holy trinkets.

"*Adjuro te,*" the monk muttered, "*serpens antique, per judicem vivorum et mortuorum…*"

Iskender's body went rigid and began to tremble violently. The saber dropped from his nerveless fingers. Still muttering Gervèse sat up, toppling the Turk over, and laid the chain across his chest. Iskender was like a man in the throes of falling sickness, except that no froth of foam coated his lips.

The red monk raised his sword.

Iskender's head turned, painfully, jerkily, to look at Zoë. His eyes opened onto the gentle darkness of the womb.

Zoë screamed and lunged forward as the blade came down. A curtain of red descended on her and for the next few moments, everything was tinged in the colors of blood and fire. She saw her enemy lift his sword again, lambent now with white heat. She still heard the terrible Latin words, only now they seemed to be coming from within her very bones as much as anywhere else. She screamed again in defiance.

And then, as if in answer to her scream, the curtain dropped away. The monk crumpled, his knees buckling. Zoë lay there beside him for what seemed a small eternity, blinking stupidly; then she sat up.

Anatole stood there with one of Isidro's books clutched in both hands, top edge out.

Somewhere on the periphery of her hearing mortals were opening and shutting windows and doors, but in the immediate circle there was only utter silence.

She found that she was sprawled across Iskender's prone body. His head lay just nearby, already beginning to wither, the skin tightening and shrinking. The sweet smell of Cainite blood seemed a nauseating sacrilege, like dancing a *saltarello* round a funeral bier. She gathered the head toward her lap. A humming filled her ears and through it she could hear the sound of tearing sobs.

"*Enfante.*" Anatole started out with the old French endearment but then immediately switched to his clumsy Greek. His arms circled around her from behind. "Childe,

childe. Come. We must hurry. We will bring him, I promise. But you must get up… Zoë, say 'yes' if you can hear me."

Someone with her voice said "yes." Her legs would not straighten up by themselves but when Anatole lifted her and set her on her feet they held. She had Iskender's head in her hands still. The silken hair began to feel dry, brittle, dusty under her fingers.

"All right, childe. You hold him if you want." The Malkavian looked around, then put his fingers to his lips and whistled. "Nikodemos!" he called. He yanked the arrow out of Tomasz' back; the bandit coughed back to a semblance of life and struggled up to sitting.

Then Anatole went to Isidro and looked the fallen Red Brother over. He clucked softly and bit into his wrist. Tipping the monk's head back, he dribbled a little of the blood into the open mouth.

"No. Not just yet, *mi cordero*…" He broke the arrow shaft and pulled it back through the wound. Then he tore a length from Isidro's cloak and stuffed it under the monk's habit for a makeshift dressing.

Nikodemos emerged from the alleyway. His habit was torn and stained and he seemed literally to have aged twenty years, but he spoke alertly enough.

"Anatole—Zoë—"

"Come take this one, carefully, and press your hand here," Anatole ordered him, gesturing toward Isidro. "Tomasz. Tomasz. Where are the horses?"

"A—around back, with two of our breathing brothers," Tomasz answered, dazed.

"Bring them, quickly. Nikodemos, there's a ball of leather twine in the satchel, let's use that to bind their hands and ankles…"

"There's rope in the saddlebags," Tomasz interjected.

"Good. We'll want to blindfold and gag them too." Then he got up again and went to Zoë, touching her shoulder. "Zoë, look at me."

"Nikodemos," murmured Zoë as the man's presence at last registered on her stumbling mind.

"Yes," said Anatole. "Do you see? *The prisoner is set free.* Now is the hour. Now we must *move.*"

"But…" *How could he have been* set free? A dozen questions crowded onto her tongue. She felt too numb to voice them, but one did tumble out on its own. "Anatole. I thought you—"

"Shh, childe." He bundled her into his arms. "I wasn't there when they came. The many hands of the Lord converge. He guides each of us to the place of judgment. And so He brought me up from the earth at the appointed time. Just as He brings me back to you now, at the appointed time…"

She didn't sob anymore, but her whole frame shook. Anatole gazed down at the moldering limbs of the bandit-chief, so strong and fleet just a little while before, now so swiftly reduced as the grave's long debt came due.

"Not a moment too late," he finished quietly, "nor a moment too early."

***

Just before dawn, as they finished making camp, Anatole checked on their prisoners. He wiped away the trickle of dried blood from Gervèse's nose. The monk moaned.

"Don't let him sleep too deeply," Anatole told Nikodemos. "Rouse him every so often."

Nikodemos nodded impassively. "And—the other one?"

"Isidro," said Anatole wryly.

"Isidro, yes." The Greek looked away for a moment.

"Just tend him as best you can. They must both live."

Anatole hunkered down beside Zoë, who sat squeezing her yellow tiger tooth in her fist till the point of it dug into her palm.

"I don't understand," she said tightly.

"I know." Kind, but unyielding. He waited while her thoughts and feelings silently wound and unwound. She could fairly *feel* him reading them, like a gloss on the conversation.

After a long time he spoke again.

"I'm afraid there's something I still need from you, *enfante*." He glanced at the dangling leather thong. She jerked it away.

"No, not that. But something else you've worn around your neck for far longer. The scarab."

She looked up, blinking her sand-dry eyes.

"Why…?"

"Because wonder has not touched that camp for a long time, and not all Cainite hungers are for blood. Zoë, this is the first of two questions. Perhaps even the more fateful, in its way. You must decide for now, for ever, whether you believe that I am what I pray God that I am."

She buried her face in the top of her knees. It was one thing to *believe* and another to *like*. But somewhere, in her deepest heart, she understood that her liking had never been the question. She sat up again, reached under her tunic and drew out the little jewel. It twirled on its chain, almost excitedly, as she passed it over. He cupped it in his hands.

"Thank you, Zoë."

"What's the other question?" she asked through her exhaustion.

"Tomorrow," was his only answer.

Chapter Twenty-Seven

The Bière Forest
The Following Night

They stumbled in like a defeated army, despite the human booty slung over their saddles. Anatole had told them to return to the camp without him; he would enter under the cloak of his blood-art and join them a few hours later. Isidro and Gervèse, too, were not to be revealed yet, but well-swaddled in their cloaks to hide their red habits and tonsures. Both monks were wide awake now, though they no longer struggled. Zoë and Anatole had quickly learned that the quickest way to stop mischief from either one was to lift up the blindfold just enough to show him the knife against his brother's neck, and then inform him that only one of them would be needed alive to make the proper demonstration.

Tomasz presented Iskender's saber, bow and horn thumb-ring, as well as the bundled cloak full of his ashes, to his new chief Yosef, who took them gravely. Yosef turned to Zoë.

"I should spit at your feet," he said. "After ten years of successful marauding, our chief dies following the madman's daughter into Paris." Then he shook his head. "But if I do that, I'm sure his very ghost will come back and hound me to my own grave." He handed her the saber. She took it, unsheathed it and gazed at it. With a dull ache she recalled Iskender's talk of life after life on earth, dream after dream.

Then she began to hand it back. "I already have a gift from him," she said. "I'm not a warrior or a bandit."

But Yosef refused to take it. "Aren't you?" he returned. "He would want you to have it. It's that simple."

Gerasimos sidled up to Zoë and murmured in her ear. "It's time," he said. Zoë offered the assembled bandits the finest, most solemn curtsey she knew how to make. Then she hurried to follow, rubbing a bit at her upper lip as she went; Gerasimos had removed the facial hair just an hour before and for some reason the skin still itched and tingled a bit.

A crowd was already gathering by the pallet as Anatole stepped up onto it and held up his hands. Behind him, his two Cainite acolytes Stephanos and Albertus, their pale faces alight with exhilaration, carried the captives up onto the platform and set them down on their knees, then stripped away the enveloping cloaks. A collective cry of astonishment and fury arose at the sight of the russet cloth.

"Behold!" Anatole cried. "The authors of your torment! Wait! Stay your hands! I tell you this red tide is only dammed, like the sea of the same color, bound back, but not destroyed! Stray but a little and it will flood over you again. The Father does not deliver His gifts all in a piece. Before any of you dare to raise a hand to these holy men…"

Boos and shouts. Some of the crowd surged forward. The mortals on stage shrank, and moved their heads as though to try to peer through some gap in the blindfolds; but the two other Cainites held their shoulders fast. Anatole forged on over the objections, raising his voice another notch.

"Yes, I say before a single one of you *dares* raise his hand in judgment, you must also dare ask yourselves whether you are worthy to do so. Think! Have we here done the will of God with greater faithfulness than they? Have we been the children of Caine that we ought? Our Dark Father even now wanders the outer night, weeping and repenting in his hard-earned wisdom. If even mighty Caine does thus, how is it that *we* turn our faces proudly up to the moon and say: There is power in my veins and by it I claim kingship over man and beast, and by my own black blood I justify my sins?"

Zoë neared the pallet. He didn't even seem to see her. That in itself was nothing new, but something *was* different about the Frenchman tonight. His voice seemed tuned to a strangely resonant pitch.

Folcaut, who had drifted over along with the rest, pushed in closer as well. Cainites and mortals alike parted for the Heretic priest. Some bowed as he went past. "What is this new spectacle? Anatole back from the dead, like a mystery-play Christ—or perhaps better, a mystery-play Lazarus? What are you conniving at now?" He stopped and surveyed the platform. "Very well, lunatic. You have your Red Brothers at long last. Why do you wait? Deliver us from this evil just as you've long promised to do."

Gerasimos stepped forward as though to fend him off, then suddenly stopped.

Anatole simply gazed at the priest as though he were a stranger. "You speak of it as such a light thing," he chided.

"I'd think that if you were the true servant of God that you claim to be, it should be a light thing." The beginning of a smile tugged at a corner of the Folcaut's lips.

"And what about you, Father?" retorted the prophet. "Has the Heretic church not suffered from the cruelties of the Red Order and those who ally with them? Shall the marvelous, precious shining blood that was spilled not be avenged?"

The smile vanished then. "You, blasphemer, cannot goad me. The shining blood is beyond the reach of your vile tongue…"

"Ah, now we see the color of your faith. Will you not even face them?" Anatole strode over and tore off the monks' blindfolds, then, after a moment's hesitation, removed Isidro's gag as well. The throng recoiled, rippling away like water into which a pebble is thrown. Zoë thought to herself that Isidro hardly looked in a state to subdue anyone, especially not with his parched, cracked lips or his dazed eyes which cast desperately around and finally settled on the tall, white-skinned, cassocked creature standing alone before him.

Folcaut reached for the little silver vial that hung from his cincture and took it in his hand.

"I am confirmed in the true baptism," he said quietly. "I fear nothing of Pilate's church."

He walked slowly toward Isidro. For all her dislike of the priest, Zoë could not help thinking how oddly noble, how imposingly forthright he looked as he stepped up onto the platform. The crowd was affected too. An expectant hush fell over them. Isidro watched him approach. Wariness pierced the mortal man's fatigue.

With a glance, Folcaut caused Stephanos to step away from Isidro. Folcaut laid a hand on the Red Brother's shoulder. For a moment Isidro seemed transfixed by Folcaut's tourmaline eyes; then he shuddered.

Folcaut opened his mouth, revealing slender ivory fangs. He bent his head toward Isidro. Gervèse tried to cry out through his gag but all that emerged was a strangled sound.

"Iao, Sabaoth, Michael," Isidro shouted hoarsely. At these words a corona of blue-white flame ran up and down the monk's body, lighting every inch of his skin and clothes yet not igniting them. But Folcaut's hand charred black at the edges; he screamed and seemed almost to fly backwards, landing on his feet again a good pace distant. The crowd milled in on itself, some trying to turn and flee, all shouting in various languages to whatever powers they revered. Isidro remained where he knelt. He kept on muttering prayers through his gritted teeth.

Folcaut cradled his singed arm to his chest, gulping for control. His eyes were completely bloodshot. No trace of the otherworldly dignity that had so captivated everyone a moment before remained. Albertus kept his post at Gervèse's shoulder, but even he had shifted away as far as he could from the cold radiance.

"You see?" Anatole called. "Even the ordained of Caine Himself must beware." Folcaut snarled. Anatole ignored him. "But it is written that 'God hath chosen the foolish things of the world to confound the wise; and God hath chosen the weak things of the world to confound the things which are mighty. And base things of the world, and things which are despised, hath God chosen, yea, and things which are not, to bring to naught things that are.'"

With that he turned to Zoë, who'd stood till then unnoticed in the crowd, clutching the saber in both hands as though expecting it to be stolen. He reached out his hand to her.

"Come, childe," he said.

She obeyed. No need to push anyone aside. The area before the two monks was well cleared. When Isidro saw her, he stopped praying and fell silent.

Anatole took the saber, removed the scabbard and returned the naked blade to her. Something convulsed at the very bottom of her awareness then, the Leviathan of unknown passions. Last night she'd tried to force her sluggard mind to reconcile with the idea that Anatole, not she, would be the one to decide Isidro's fate. Clearly he'd had some plan in mind. He'd been so resolute and set. Now all at once he was handing over the power? Turn and turn about.

The Frenchman leaned down and whispered in her ear. "I know you'd never forgive me if I didn't leave you the choice. And you would be right." With a dirty finger he slid a stray lock off her cheek and behind her ear. "Just remember one thing, Zoë. Whatever you do, everything past will be as it was and everything now will be as it is."

He straightened.

Zoë stared at the pale, blotched face of the man whose death had been her sustaining thought for eleven years and tried to remember why.

Gregory. This man had murdered Gregory, had tortured him, had filled his last nights with misery and terror. Gregory, who'd once been the very earth she orbited. Where was that atrocity now that she needed it? The same place as all her bad dreams afterward, the day-visions where she'd rescued him, failed to rescue him, spoke to him, failed to speak to him, told him she loved him, been unable to find a word.

The same place as Iskender, who'd loved her also. Her grasp on the saber's hilt became a stranglehold. It, at least, was real and solid under her fingers; and that pain was far nearer. The monk beside Isidro was the one who'd actually put an end to the ready smile, the quick wit. But they were of an ilk. The arrogant men with their crosses upraised, the ones who could debate in their universities about whether a tenth, ninth or third of the host fell with Lucifer and whether the war in heaven raged for one, two or three instants and yet never think to ask who this God of theirs was that demanded that children in Constantinople burn. There were many crimes to bring to account. Too many.

Too many…

With a little cry she brought the edge of the blade up to the base of Isidro's throat. He flinched but did not look away. Her hands tingled, then ached. The white flame licked along the blade, and something of its power seemed to carry even through the metal and horn. God's rage enveloped him, but she could see none of it in his expression. He merely looked tired and hurt. There, that finally touched off a spark of hate in her.

And he looked older than when she'd first seen him burst through the doorway at Bergamo. He *was* older.

For the first time ever it occurred to her that she could have simply waited for him to die.

Andreas had said it at the time, more or less. She just hadn't understood. Proserpine had said it: *Let their eyes be dimmed and their ears be stopped. Let their limbs wither and their teeth rot.* Time would take every enemy for her, just as it would take every friend, every beloved, until one night it took her as well. She walked forward from here a ghost among ghosts.

Slowly, deliberately, she let the sword down until its tip dragged in the mud at her feet.

"You're right," she said. With those words her heart unlocked at last. She began to cry. Cold blood-tears spilled unheeded down her cheeks. "He *is* dead. He was my father, the only one I can remember. He saved me, he loved me and then he killed me. And I hurt him too, though I never wanted to… that is the truth, and I will never be able to change it. I can't go back now and love him the way I should have loved him, or say what I really meant to say. Every mistake we made is made. That's all."

Isidro's gaze was helplessly locked with hers. Tears streamed from his eyes as well. As she spoke they came ever faster and thicker, and his face twisted in silent agony. She was free now; he was bound.

The white flame sunk away, cooled and died. "*Alleluia*," murmured Anatole. He stepped behind Isidro, bent down and sank his fangs into the Red Brother's throat.

A low susurration of awe moved through the crowd. Anatole stood then, lifting Isidro into his arms as easily as if the monk were a small child. He stepped down from the platform and offered the bleeding throat to Zoë.

"Drink," he said. Zoë met the Spaniard's eyes one last time.

"Forgive me, Zoë," whispered Isidro, still weeping. "I did not *know*..."

"I forgive you," she answered. The words cost nothing. A miracle. She dipped her mouth to the wound Anatole's teeth had made and drank a single sip. She did not wipe the blood from her lips.

"You are forgiven, my son," Anatole echoed gently. He carried Isidro out to the crowd, who drew in like filings toward a lodestone.

"Take, drink," he called to them, "this blood that is shed for you."

One by one they drank. Zoë stood aside. Her attention was drawn for a moment to Gervèse; the monk's face had drained to Cainite white, his eyes wide. He screamed again and again through the choking fabric and didn't stop. She was able to wonder quietly at the brush of pity that touched her heart. She knew all too well how hard God's will could be to endure. Then she moved to help Gerasimos, who'd begun to order the Cainite communicants into a line. Even Bardas and Urbien fell obediently into place as she directed them, not even elbowing their way to the front.

After a while, some of the Heretics who had stood uneasily on the periphery began to move in as well, heads bowed. That was when Folcaut seemed to rouse as though from slumber. He leapt down from the platform.

"No!" he bellowed, seizing one of his erstwhile follow-ers by the arm. "Apostate!" But only Gallasyn and two others of his cult came forward to help him pull the rest away.

Folcaut then tried to push up towards Isidro and was thrust away by those in line. "Stop! The blood of Pilate's Church is no basis for a sacrament! You must cast away this sacrilege and deny this madman. You betray the Father—you betray your mission here in Paris—most of all, you betray yourselves!"

"I wouldn't speak so carelessly of betrayals, if I were you, Folcaut." Gerasimos broke away from the growing throng of those finished partaking, who now embraced joy-ously, giving each other the Kiss of Peace on either cheek. He walked up to Folcaut. "After all, who was it that be-trayed this whole camp just a few months ago?"

Folcaut's lip actually curled. "I have no idea what you're talking about, lapdog. Unless you simply mean to revive old empty slanders."

Zoë glanced toward Anatole. Anatole paid no heed to the argument. His entire focus was on delivering the last few drops of blood from the monk's stilled heart to his last few congregants.

Gerasimos withdrew a folded parchment from his purse. Folcaut stiffened.

"Old slanders; new evidence. Your master enticed the Red Brothers to us."

"That's ridiculous," exclaimed Gallasyn scornfully. "His Grace is this camp's shepherd and always has been!"

Bardas and Urbien crowded over. "Let me see that," Bardas snapped, snatching the parchment away. "Hell. This is in Latin, Gerasimos. What's it say?"

"It says—"

Folcaut cut Gerasimos off. "He has no idea what it says because he doesn't read Latin. Do you, brother?"

"I only know a little," Gerasimos admitted, "but Anatole told me."

"There, you see? Anatole told him!"

"Well, who else in the camp reads Latin? It's Anatole or nothing. Half a moment. *You* read it, Gallasyn, don't you?" Bardas thrust the letter into his fellow-councilor's hands. "Here. You take a look."

As though Gallasyn would tell the first drop of truth about it with no one here but Anatole to contradict him, Zoë thought disgustedly.

Gallasyn's eyes tracked back and forth over the letter. "It does look like the Father's hand," he said. All at once he sounded worried.

"What does it say, Gallasyn?" Bardas prompted him evenly. "Read it."

"'To my resplendent father in His Name,'" Gallasyn read. "'I…'" He stopped and started again. "'I acknowledge receipt and will faithfully attend the signal you describe, so that like Noah I may populate my ark before the northern flood descends. I also pray God may smile upon our endeavors and tear up not only the branches but the very root of the evil we have endured for too long. Yours in reverent devotion, given by my hand this vii Id. Oct. MCCXIX.' I— I don't understand…."

"A week before the attack," Gerasimos pointed out triumphantly.

"What's this?" Bardas' shoulders visibly drew taut. "Exactly what evil did you think needed 'rooting out,' Folcaut?"

Folcaut tried to break himself away from staring bewilderedly at his clansman Gallasyn. "That's all about a different matter entirely," he protested. "A Parisian matter. It has nothing to do with the camp."

"How could it have nothing to do with it?" Gerasimos retorted.

"And a week before the raid," Urbien seemed still to be putting things together, but his frame too began to coil with suppressed anger.

"I knew nothing about it," the priest argued helplessly— and vainly. The crowd now circled him instead of Isidro, faces contorted with fury.

"You must have known." Gallasyn brandished the letter at him. "Noah and the Ark, Father? Didn't you lead your followers to high ground just before the flood from the north—from *St.-Denis*—descended? If the letter wasn't about that, then what *was* it about? And that time in late September when you sneaked off into the woods and the next night wanted me to say that you'd passed the day in my haven? Whom did you meet?"

"Gallasyn!" Folcaut blurted, horrified. He looked around at all the Cainites closing in on him and decided, belatedly, to change tacks. "You don't understand. Try to understand. Everything I have ever done was for the ultimate benefit of the settlement. It is this madman who truly leads you towards doom—"

"You *have* deceived me," Gallasyn cried out. "You've deceived all of us. Convert or be murdered in your sleep; that is the only salvation you deliver. You've been proven for what you are—a sham from beginning to end."

At that moment Zoë caught the blue glint of her scarab on the councilor's finger.

"*Traitor*," shouted Bardas, teeth out now. "*False prophet!*"

And then all was blood.

Zoë touched Anatole's elbow anxiously. His face was still, grave as they watched the slaughter, just as it was in his deepest trances.

"And he that shall blaspheme against the Holy Spirit hath never forgiveness," he said.

She nodded.

***

Nikodemos dragged Gervèse behind the hut in a panic. Fumblingly, hastily, he cut the Red Brother's bonds and tore out his gag.

"Stand up. Stand up!" When Gervèse could not or would not, he rubbed at the man's shins and ankles in a desperate bid to bring the circulation back. Then he hoisted him again. "In the name of God, stand!"

Gervèse seemed to stir a bit at that, though his eyes were still vague, doelike. His legs held, but they wobbled and verged on collapsing again.

"You—" he croaked.

"I don't know whether he just forgot to bar the door or left it undone," Nikodemos blurted, his voice wavering with terror. "And I don't care. Just go. Go now! Now, before…"

He bodily turned Gervèse around. "There, do you see? That way. North. Keep the moon on your left until the sun comes up. Don't sleep. Just run. They will come after you."

"Do you see her?" Gervèse stumbled forward a step, then fell to his knees again. Nikodemos pulled him up.

"Who?"

"The Virgin… she beckons, just there in the trees."

"No, I don't see her," Nikodemos hissed, "but if she's pointing north then for her own sweet sake follow her."

"*Salve regina, mater misericordie,*" Gervèse muttered, staggering hollowly toward the shifting radiance.

He looked back only once, just before the charnel scene behind him receded behind a tall hut and out of his sight forever. He thought he saw the blond one's head turn in his direction. He thought perhaps he saw a smile.

But he couldn't think about that. He turned away again and followed the light as best he could.

Epilogue

Paris, 1220

Paris, the St.-Jacques Gate
The night before the Nones of January, 1220

The lantern hanging just outside the gatehouse window creaked slightly in the wind. One of the pair of guards looked up, uneasily, from their game of tables.

"Are you cold, sister?" he asked the woman who sat on a stool by the window, straight-backed and unmoving, gazing out into the night.

"No," she said. "Thank you." He saw from the shape of her mouth that she wasn't angry at the question, but could tell little else. Her face was shadowed beneath the hood.

He made his roll. If not for the lady in the room he would have leaped out of his chair crowing, perhaps with a shout of thanks to Saint Martin. As it was, he simply nodded at his partner, who likewise contented himself with frowning back. They cleared and reset the pieces.

"Would you like some watered wine, sister?" he asked after another several minutes of silence.

A bit of a smile touched her lips then. "I promise I won't trouble you kind *serjanz* much longer."

He emptied the contents of the bit of tied-up rag she'd given them onto the table. He counted out the coins, splitting them evenly, then took a couple from his share to add to the new pot.

"That's all right. If you don't mind my asking, though — just what *are* you waiting for?"

She stood, leaning her head out, peering down into the darkness just outside the gate. Below, a bedraggled figure emerged from a nearby stand of trees and collapsed, face down, on the dirt road.

"That," she said, and dashed for the stairs.

***

Gervèse woke to the light of a tiny, sputtering tallow candle. He stirred fitfully. Every part of his body that he moved was answered by mirror-opposite sensations: the protest of bruised and lacerated flesh and the cool tingling of some sweet-smelling unguent. He was clad only in his *braies*, although the bed's mulberry-colored coverlet had been pulled up over his chest.

A noise came from somewhere else in the room. "Hello?" he called fearfully.

A black shadow separated from the dim perimeter of the candlelight and settled itself on the bed. He tensed and recoiled, but then he saw the face.

"Cecilia —!"

She lifted her hands. "Shh. You're safe, Gervèse...Abbé."

"We're not at the convent..." He tried to sit up and look around. She restrained him with a hand on the shoulder.

"No, of course not. It's just a room. Your legs gave out, and I couldn't carry you." She turned his face and looked behind his ear with a little moue of dismay. "You've got battle-sign. You must have taken a blow to the head..." She touched the skin there. It felt slightly mushy, and ached when she pressed a bit on it.

"Ow. I did. I think I dreamed strangely. For some reason I woke with a song in my mind, that I haven't heard since I was a boy."

"That's probably my fault," she said quietly.

"You were singing while I slept."

"It seemed to soothe you."

"What's in this poultice?"

"Attar of roses," she told him, "among other things. Mère Teresa said the recipe came from her grandmother."

He allowed his head to sink back into the bolster. It was much like the one he had at the abbey, a simple sack of old chaff. He couldn't believe how soft it felt. "How…how did you find me, sister?" he asked at last.

She was examining his wrist, turning it this way and that, and didn't answer at first.

"Sister?"

"I…" She stopped, and then began again. Something in the shape of her face looked wrong; he couldn't tell what. "I went to bed last evening and I couldn't begin to sleep. I got up, and everything I looked at seemed to turn into a tree or rock or stone. I'd put my hand out on a chair to steady myself and vines grew around my arm…And then a little later I fainted in the middle of Nocturns. It was indescribable. All the strength drained out of me from head to foot, and I went cold…"

She shuddered and placed her hand upon her neck then, and turned and looked at him. It all rose in his throat like sour bile. The words fractured, crumbled even as he tried to speak them.

"They — I tried to — he's —"

She slid up to him, gathering his head in her hands and bending hers to touch his forehead. "I know," she moaned.

He burst into racking sobs. She clung to him and rocked him. His hands spasmed up to cup his face, pressing into it as though to crush it, but the grief would not be contained. It hemorrhaged, swelled, clamored; and she sobbed too. For longer than either of them would have cared to say the only real word uttered between them was Isidro's name.

At last they ran out of tears for the moment. A silence almost more terrible than the grief welled up between them. Gervèse's fingertips reached out to touch her cheek and her arms uncircled, sought out his chest. He glanced up into her swollen eyes to see if the same thing was in hers as in his. It was.

Her hair was the color of old walnut, lovingly polished for many years.

***

"I suppose you'll make confession tomorrow," he said later. The sensation of her legs next to his, that was for some reason the thing his body found most pleasurable of all. Whenever she stirred in her drowsing and moved them against him, he felt another pulling in his loins. She laid her head on his unbruised shoulder and her hand on his thigh. Thank God there'd been no pain for her, or there hadn't seemed to be, though she'd cried a little with his first stroke. Poultices had been disturbed and would need reapplying.

She made a sleepy sound of negation. "It will have to wait, I'm afraid."

"Will it?"

"Faustina and I leave tomorrow."

He allowed his heart its necessary moment to register that pain. Teresa's order had moved quarters from Tyre to Madrid during Cecilia's sojourn. It was only half a world away, not a whole world; but there would be little real difference. Then he kissed her head, her hair that carried a faint scent of sweat and the lavender the sisters washed their veils in. She kissed him on the lips.

"Yes," he said. "I suppose you do."

They lay there, simply listening to each other's breath. He waited in vain for the sense of trespass. It should not feel like a *sacrament* to Isidro, to lie beside her like this.

"Do you think…that sometimes God's purpose can be served by a sin?" he mused at last. "Not just a mistake, but a deliberate sin?"

"I think," she answered after a slight hesitation, "that Mère Teresa knew what she was doing."

He nodded. "What will you do now?"

"Go on." No hesitation that time, just quiet strength.

"Yes. That blond one, that Anatole, he was dangerous enough before…but…" His voice cracked slightly. "It seems he's won the obedience of a number of his kind now."

"I don't doubt," she said, "that St.-Denis and its abbot will persevere against him."

"For *his* sake," he returned grimly. A thousand demons would never be enough. He knew that even now. But they'd make a passable start.

"Yes. And far from his alone." She looked out the window. It was lightening to purple outside. She sat up and picked up her shift to put it on.

He closed his hand over hers.

"You will still write me, won't you?" he asked. He did not dare put hope into his voice. But she smiled ruefully.

"I suppose we must not let ourselves approach the danger of too much purity," she murmured. "Pride is Lucifer's sin."

He watched her dress as dawn slowly filled the room.

About the Author

Sarah Roark is a professional writer, violinist, teacher and (as should be obvious from the foregoing) masochist. She has worked on a number of White Wolf's roleplaying products, including various supplements for **Vampire: The Masquerade, Dark Ages: Vampire, Dark Ages: Inquisitor,** and **Mummy: The Resurrection**. She has also authored two short stories: "The Prodigal Son" for **Penance by Firelight**, companion volume to the **Dark Ages: Vampire** core book, and "What Shelters Them" for the **Demon: Lucifer's Shadow** fiction anthology. This is her first novel. Some of her personal projects can be viewed at the *World Lit Only by Fire* website (http://www.wyrdsisters.org/), which she coauthors with fellow White Wolf freelancers Myranda Kalis and Janet Trautvetter.

She lives in Sammamish, Washington—beautiful lakeside community and former hunting grounds of Ted Bundy—along with her husband Brett and the world's two coolest cats.

Acknowledgements

The author would like to thank her esteemed fellow authors and coconspirators, Janet Trautvetter and Myranda Kalis, for their unflagging support and aid throughout this and every other project; her husband Brett for his love, faith and tolerance of the prolonged writer's hermitage; her editor, Philippe Boulle, for his valuable suggestions, patience and encouragement; and the nice folks over at the Medieval-Religion mailing list for answering the occasional absurdly picky historical question.

The Clan Brujah Trilogy

by Tim Dedopulos

An enforcer and executioner among the undead, Theo Bell is the strong arm of the Camarilla. He is quick on the draw, potent in the blood, and those vampires who'd challenge the sect have reason to fear him.

Theo has his own problems, though. In the Midwest, he discovers evidence of a new breed of slavery. Bound by his own sense of honor, Theo begins a hunt that will ultimately shake the foundations of the Camarilla itself—and may cost him his own freedom.

BOOK ONE:
THE SLAVE RING™
WW11120; ISBN 1-58846-814-3
On Sale in May

BOOK TWO:
THE OVERSEER™
WW11121; ISBN 1-58846-815-1
On Sale in September

BOOK THREE:
THE PUPPET MASTERS™
WW11122; ISBN 1-58846-816-X
On Sale in December

VAMPIRE
THE MASQUERADE